MW00489745

Melanie Clegg is a pink haired art history graduate, casual historian, gin taster, lapsed goth, failed Parisienne, Versailles obsessive, proud Ripperologist, Georgette Heyer fanatic and Victorian Prostitute re-enactor who lives in deepest darkest Bristol with her family but would rather be in either Whitechapel or Paris. *Blood Sisters* is her second novel.

She blogs as Madame Guillotine at

www.madameguillotine.org.uk

Also by Melanie Clegg

The Secret Diary of a Princess

Before the Storm

Blood Sisters

Melanie Clegg

Burning Eye

Copyright © 2013 Melanie Clegg

The author asserts the moral right under the Copyright, Designs and Patents Act 1988 to be identified as the author of this work

All rights reserved. No part of this publication may be reproduced, stored in a retrieval system, or transmitted, in any form or by any means without the prior written consent of the author, nor be otherwise circulated in any form of binding or cover other than that in which it is published and without a similar condition being imposed on the subsequent purchaser.

This edition published by Burning Eye Books 2013

www.burningeye.co.uk

@burningeye

Burning Eye Books
15 West Hill, Portishead, BS20 6LG

ISBN 978 1 90913 615 1

Printed by Grosvenor Group, London

For Dave and all the boys with all my love.

1773

SIDONIE

Paris, October 1773

They came for me while I was still asleep. I always knew that one day my luck would run out. But I'd hoped it would be when I was wide awake and the very picture of innocence in my prettiest white silk gown, armed with clever little lies and excuses which would fall artlessly from my rouged lips. Instead, I was dressed only in a thin cotton chemise, and was momentarily bewildered when the men burst into my bedroom in the middle of the night and shouted at me to wake up. My eyes blinked in the fierce amber light of the lanterns they held above me.

I knew, of course. I knew what they had come for and who had sent them.

Rolling from the lily-scented warmth of my bed, I stood before them, trembling with fear and clutching the embroidered pink silk counterpane to my breasts.

They knew why they were there too, and I flinched as their lustful eyes roamed freely over my body.

Usually such men would glance at me from the corners of their eyes and then look away, terrified of a horsewhipping if I chanced to notice. Now there was a contempt mixed in with the lust that made me take a step back from them.

'You are to come with us, madame,' said a tall pockmarked man that I had never seen before

He stood a little apart from the others, his dirty, straggling hair hanging down the back of a threadbare coat that had clearly seen better days. Like the other men, he stank of sweat, grease and smoke, all odours that were entirely alien to my lovely pink and white bedroom, deliciously fragranced by the lavender that the maids placed in between the folds of my clothes, the freshly cut roses that I insisted be arranged in a blue and white Sèvres vase by my bed every night, the violet-scented powder that was used to dust my hair and the delicate jasmine and lily scent that I had worn every day since my father had first introduced me to it on my fourteenth birthday.

I hid my disgust and forced myself to smile at the pockmarked man, who was clearly the leader.

'Can I not at least get dressed first?' I asked, allowing the counterpane to drop a little.

Now that I had woken up, my mind was racing. If I could only be alone, just for a few minutes, then I could slip out through the secret little wainscoted door next to my bed. Then it was just a question of running down the servants' stairs and out on to the Rue des Francs-Bourgeois. I did not know where I would go, but I was sure that someone would take me in.

The pockmarked man's eyes did not leave my face. 'That is up to you, madame,' he replied. 'You are at liberty to get dressed. But as Monsieur le Comte has ordered that you are not to be left alone, not even for one second, you must dress with my men in the room.'

I stared at him and pulled the counterpane back up again. 'Then I will remain as I am,' I replied, trying to sound light-hearted. 'And pray that I do not catch a cold.' Damn.

'As you wish, madame,' he replied, utterly indifferent. 'You must come with us now.' He went to my door and held it open. 'Your carriage awaits, madame.'

'Wait!' My voice broke a little as I struggled not to show fear in front of this slovenly mob. 'Can I not at least say goodbye to my children?'

I thought of my children as I had last seen them: tousle-haired Lucien asleep in his little bed in the airy lavender-scented, yellow painted nursery upstairs, his favourite cloth doll, his Nou-Nou, clutched close to his warm, sleep-flushed cheek; the beautiful auburn-haired twins, Cassandre and Lucrèce, who started the night in separate beds yet somehow always ended up in each other's arms; and little Adélaïde, only nine months old, gently snoring in her green muslin-hung crib on the other side of the room with her chubby, dimpled hands curled up like pink petals on either side of her head. 'Will you not even allow me this?' I pleaded.

The pockmarked man shook his head. 'Monsieur le Comte has expressly ordered that you are not to see his children before you go.'

I felt my heart collapse within me. So this was how it was to be from now on. I had ruined everything and now I must pay the price. No wonder the men in my room all stared at me with mingled lust and hatred. I was worse than nothing in their eyes now: a faithless wife and a failed mother. A whore.

To my shame, I began to cry.

Angrily, I wiped away my tears with the back of my hand, determined to show no sign of weakness.

'I could scream.' I wrapped the counterpane around myself, slipped my feet into the embroidered slippers beside my bed and walked, my head held high, to the door. 'I could smash the window and scream into the street.'

'Do as you wish, madame.' He shrugged. 'This is Paris and you could scream the house down without anyone giving it the slightest consideration.'

He was right, of course. I heard screams on the street all the time and did not so much as bother to look up from my cards, nor ask what had happened the next morning when I gathered up my silk and taffeta skirts to step lightly in my high-heeled shoes over the bloodstains on the pavement. When I was a young bride, just fifteen years old and newly come to Paris from my father's pink stone château in Normandy, I would have been shocked and terrified by screams in the night and blood on the pavement. But that was six years ago and I was a very different person now.

I allowed myself a final look back at the room that had been mine throughout those years. I had unwillingly lost my virginity in the pink and gold lit à la polonaise that stood so snugly in its alcove, had conceived my children there in the velvet darkness of night, and given birth to them, my agonised screams floating out through the open windows and soaring up into the grey Parisian sky.

We made our way down the wide marble staircase down to the entrance hall. I paused in front of the portrait that Greuze had painted of me in happier days, when I was just sixteen, had recently given birth to Lucien and was still flushed and ecstatic with the joy of new motherhood. My husband had wanted me to be depicted as Hebe or Diana, draped in silks and brocades like all the other ladies of the court. But clever Monsieur Greuze had ignored him and painted me as a simple girl, resplendent with youth and beauty, dressed in white silk with my thick corn-coloured hair hanging loose about my shoulders and my eyes turned lovingly upon my infant son, who dozed plumply and rosily in my arms. I couldn't help but imagine what Greuze would have made of me now, tear-stained and frantic, turned out of my home in the middle of the night in a thin chemise and a pair of slippers. I needed only a broken plate or a dead canary and I could have passed for any of his paintings of fallen young girls.

'Take your last look,' my husband's sardonic voice called up from the hall below. 'Like you, it will be gone by morning.'

I turned to face him, noting how pale he looked in the flickering candlelight. Claude was twenty years my senior, but you would have to look closely to notice the wrinkles about his eyes and the grey strands in the red hair.

'And what will you hang in my place?' I asked in a light, conversational tone as I walked down the remaining steps towards him, determined to show no fear whatsoever. 'One of your whores maybe? Mademoiselle Rosalie from the Opéra?

Mademoiselle Minette from the Comédie Française? Or some other unfortunate young girl too dim or venal to see you for what you really are?'

I was pleased to see that Claude looked a little discomforted, while the men behind me shifted a little, no longer sure who was the villain of the tragedy unfolding in front of them.

'That is none of your concern.' My cheeks flamed as I recoiled from the disgust in his face. 'I rather thought that I might hang a portrait of my mother there so the children could always have before them an example of how a lady should behave.'

I recovered myself. 'How nice.' His mother, of course, being an infamous, over-rouged old bitch who treated both her son and grandchildren with contempt and couldn't visit for more than ten minutes without reducing Lucien and the twins to tears with her pinches of their plump arms and her barbed comments. 'Your dear mother must be so thrilled by all of this.'

He smiled then. 'She is beside herself.'

I could well believe it. Athénaïs, the old Comtesse, had never troubled to hide her envious dislike of me, despite coveting the huge fortune I had brought to her family upon my marriage. I remembered her pursing her lips in disapproval as her tiny blue eyes flicked over the exquisite taffeta gown I had worn at my wedding, then turning away and remarking to one of her cronies that 'She is not one of our sort and would never have done for my boy in the old days, but oh la la, the terrible debts, mon cher, so what can one do?'

'She has never liked me,' I agreed, rather pleased that I would never have to see his mother again nor suffer her mean-spirited remarks. Even the darkest cloud has the potential for a silver lining and this was mine. 'Please do try and keep her greedy fingers out of my jewellery as I would like my girls to have it one day.'

It was hard to remain calm as I thought of my beautiful, adorable girls growing up without me. One day they too would be brides and mothers, would fall in love and be disappointed, would suffer losses and joys, and all without me there to support

13

them. Lucien needed me too, of course, but in only a few more years he would be sent to Versailles to be a page just as his father, grandfather and great-grandfather had done before him. From then on, he would enter a world of men and would have little need for a mother's caresses. My girls though would always need me.

'The girls will be well cared for,' he said curtly. 'You need have no concerns about them.'

I heard my baby wail in her crib at the top of the house and the sharp clip-clop of her nurse's shoes against the floorboards as she went to tend to her.

'Adélaïde...' I began, before tears overwhelmed me and I had to stop, not trusting myself to speak without sobbing.

'She will be treated in the same way as her sisters,' Claude said coldly. 'No one who bears my name will ever suffer unjustly.'

I reached out and grasped his wrist, clinging on as he twisted his arm and tried to shake me off. 'Please let me take her with me. She is only a baby.' I didn't bother trying to hide my distress now. I had no pride left when it came to my children. 'I will go quietly if you only allow me to take my baby with me.'

I felt desperate and slightly unhinged. If there had been a knife in my hand, I would have stabbed him without a moment's hesitation and without a shred of remorse if it meant I could take my children with me.

The Comte looked me for a long moment. 'You ask too much, madame,' he replied at last. 'The children have nothing to fear and will remain here with me. Only think what damage it would do to your ... our daughters if they were to remain with you.' He pulled his arm away and rubbed absentmindedly at his blue velvet sleeve where it had been crushed by my fingers. 'They would be forever tainted by your infamy. It would be impossible to marry them well, to get them positions at court. Is that what you want for them?'

'I can change,' I whispered. 'If you let me stay with them, I would be anything that you wanted me to be.' I meant every single word. 'I know that I have been a disappointment to you but that can change. I can change.'

He was turning away and again I gripped his sleeve, desperate to be heard. 'Just tell me what you want me to do, Claude.' I fell to my knees, almost pulling him on top of me. 'Please, I am begging you. Let me stay. Don't send me away from my babies, Claude. Please, please don't send me away.' I was sobbing now, my tears splashing on the chill black and white marble floor. 'I can change, I promise. I won't see him again.'

My husband pulled away then and straightened up. I had gone too far. 'Do not mention him in this house.' He looked down at me as I remained kneeling, crumpled on the cold floor at his feet, my chemise dishevelled, my hair tumbling loosely down my back. 'You are a disgrace, madame.'

Fastidiously, he wiped at his sleeve with a white handkerchief and stepped away, distancing himself from me and the mess that was my life. 'This conversation is at an end, madame. You are overwrought and should compose yourself.' He crooked a finger at the men who lurked in readiness on the staircase, and they moved forward. 'It is time that you left.'

'No!' I ran forward, my arm upraised. 'You can't do this, Claude! You can't!'

The men grabbed hold of me and dragged me back before I could strike him. I sobbed and struggled, then went limp in their grip. My husband turned then and looked at me for a moment, his face inscrutable before he briskly jerked his chin towards the door.

'Take her away.'

'Maman!' I heard Lucien call for me as I was dragged away and the great door swung shut behind me for the last time.

For a second I managed to break free and claw at the wood with my fingernails, hammering on the door with my fists and screaming until I was hoarse. But the men soon had me in their clutches again. A small crowd of curious onlookers had gathered on the street, their faces shocked and concerned as they peered through the darkness. 'Please help me!' I implored them as I struggled and kicked. 'Please! They are taking me away from my

15

babies! You have to help me!' They looked at each other and a couple of the women stepped forward as though about to intervene. 'Please!'

Without a word, the pockmarked man slapped me across the face. Then he flung me inside the coach. 'Be silent,' he spat as he slammed the door shut. 'No one cares.'

No one cares. I wrapped my arms around myself and curled up into a ball on the floor as the carriage shuddered to life, then slowly began to rumble down the Rue des Francs-Bourgeois.

1789

ADÉLAÏDE

Paris, February 1789

I woke with a start, clawing at the damp bed sheets and twisting my head from side to side, just as I always did when I had The Dream.

'Adélaïde?' Hortense hissed from the next bed.

I turned my head to look at her, unable to see much more than her round face, white cotton nightdress and long blonde plaits in the gloom.

'Did you have the dream again? The one about your mother?' Her soft, still faintly provincial voice was concerned.

We had slept in neighbouring beds for seven years, ever since Hortense had first arrived at our school, Penthémont on Faubourg St Germain. She had been woken by The Dream at least twice a week since then. I was amazed and grateful that Hortense still cared enough to ask and didn't just kick me hard and leave me to it as most of the other girls would have done. I wasn't exactly popular at school, thanks to a combination of being unbecomingly bookish and disappointingly unlike my two beautiful elder sisters.

'She was running through the woods,' I whispered, sitting up in the bed and hugging my knees. I rubbed my hot

19

cheeks against the scratchy cotton of my nightdress. 'She was running so fast that I couldn't catch her.' I waved my hands in front of me just as I had done in the dream, flexing my fingers as I desperately tried to catch hold of my mother. 'And then, just like that, she was gone.'

'How do you know that it's your mother, Adélaïde?' Hortense asked, reaching across the gap between our beds to take my hand. 'It could be anyone.'

She had a point. My mother had left when I was a baby and I had never even seen a portrait of her. Either none had ever existed or Papa had removed them all. I strongly suspected the latter. Lucrèce had once told me that our mother was tall and slim and fair, with pretty eyes and soft hands. But in my mind she looked exactly like the sad-faced plaster Virgin in the school chapel, and so it was her that I desperately chased night after night, her blue cloak floating and whirling in the wind, her sandalled feet making no noise as she ran ahead of me through the crisp, golden leaves.

'Maybe she will come back one day,' Hortense whispered now, just as she always did.

I nodded. 'Maybe.'

Neither of us really believed it. My mother had been away for so many years. I didn't even know if she was alive or dead. No one had ever told me and I was too afraid to ask. All I knew was that she had gone and that she had not taken me with her.

'Do you want me to get in with you?' Hortense asked shyly.

I hesitated for a moment, thinking that one day I would have to cope with this on my own but as usual I nodded, giving in helplessly to the need to not be alone. 'Yes, please.'

I shifted across the narrow bed in order to make some room for her, and shivered as my toes stretched out into the cold patch at the end of the mattress. Every evening the convent maids ran about busily shoving hot bricks into our beds, heating them up in readiness for bedtime. It was bliss at first to climb into a

20

lovely warm bed but it didn't take long for the heat to vanish and the ever-present fingers of icy cold to pry beneath the covers.

Hortense giggled softly as she hopped into my bed and put her warm arms around me. 'It is too cold to sleep alone anyway,' she whispered, her breath smelling sweetly of the cinnamon pastilles that she was addicted to and hid in a tin underneath her pillow. 'I heard Soeur Agnès say that they found another beggar sitting dead against the convent gates this morning. He was only a young boy apparently and was frozen stiff.' She shuddered a little with cold or horror, it was impossible to tell which. 'Everyone says it's the worst winter since the old King's time. Imagine being so poor that you have to live on the streets in this weather.'

'Neither of us can imagine what it is like, Hortense. How could we?' I thought about the time my sister Lucrèce and I had seen a frozen beggar woman lying dead in the doorway of our house on the Rue des Francs-Bourgeois. The swarm of maids and footmen that surrounded us at all times had not been quite quick enough to shield us from the terrible sight. I still remembered how the dead woman's dark eyes had stared sightlessly into the distance, her blue lips slightly parted as though trying to speak. 'It is terrible that such poverty exists in a city like Paris. It is almost the nineteenth century and we should be moving forward, not allowing some of our fellow men to dwell in misery as though it is still the dark ages.'

Hortense sighed. 'My father says it is their own fault and that if they only worked harder, then they wouldn't be so poor.' I loved Hortense dearly but she was a little too fond of beginning statements with 'My father says'. Her dear Papa, the Duc de Chevereux, was a self-centred idiot, devoid of all empathy and tolerance. He was one of the 'old' nobility who had hovered for over a hundred years at the silken elbow of the King at Versailles and remained in wilful ignorance of what life was like in the real world.

'Hortense, your father is wrong,' I said very gently. 'People are poor because they have no choice. Men like your father and mine should be helping them, not telling them to work harder.' I thought of the ragged, pinched-faced peasants who worked on Papa's estate near Fontainebleau, and how they would down their tools in the fields and stare at us as we drove past in our gilded carriage.

There was a long silence. I looked down to see that Hortense had fallen asleep, which was a blessing as I didn't want to argue with her and we had fallen out before about 'My father says'.

I lay for a long time, watching the first grey slivers of sunlight appear beneath the curtains at our window. I had lived in this room for seven years ever since I had first arrived at Penthémont. Up until that time we had lived on our father's country estate under the care of one of his unmarried sisters, Mademoiselle Aglaé, until she had died and it had been decided that we should be sent to school.

Upon arrival, my elder sisters had been whisked away to the rooms reserved for older girls while a young nun, Soeur Jeanne, clad in the white habit of the Cistercians, took my hand and escorted me briskly through corridors that smelt of boiled cabbage and soap to the tiny blue-painted room that I would share with two other girls.

'A maid, Lucette, will look after your needs,' Soeur Jeanne explained as we hurried along. 'She will help to do your hair and dress you in the morning, then undress you in the evening before you go to bed.' She looked at me out of the corner of her eye, taking in my pale, set little face and trembling hands and cleared her throat. 'It must seem very strange but all the girls get used to it eventually. No one will be angry if you cry a little at first.'

I shook my head so that my long dark plaits, tied at the ends with red silk ribbons, rattled around my ears. 'I never cry.'

Soeur Jeanne came to a standstill and turned to look at me. 'Never?' She put her long fingers beneath my chin and tilted my head upwards so that she could look down into my eyes. 'Not even once?'

I wriggled away from her. 'No, never.' I stared at the

wooden rosary that hung from her waist. 'I don't like crying.'

I didn't want to add that I left that sort of thing to my sister Lucrèce, who could often be found sobbing over what seemed to me to be the most trivial things.

I was still thinking about Soeur Jeanne and those long ago days when the chapel bell started to peal in the distance, calling us to Mass and shortly afterwards our maid, Lucie bustled cheerfully into the room, clattering her enamelled water jugs together and ripping open the curtains. 'Another cold day, mesdemoiselles,' she announced with a grin that revealed several gaps in her teeth. 'Wrap up warmly before you go to chapel.'

Hortense opened her eyes and struggled up onto her elbows. 'Oh, Lucie, why are you always so happy when it is cold?' she asked with a loud yawn. 'I do not know how you bear it!'

Lucie grinned and shrugged her plump shoulders. 'I am happy whatever the weather, mademoiselle. Surely you must have realised that by now?' She winked at me. 'And how are you this morning, Mademoiselle de Saint-Valèry?' Lucie knew all about The Dream. 'Today is art day, isn't it?'

I nodded with a smile, my heart beginning to lift at the thought of my art lessons, which were definitely the high point of my week.

It was more usual for the young ladies of Penthémont to be taught the rudiments of drawing and painting by the effete, prancing little drawing master who came in every day and seemed to spend more time flirting with his pupils than actually teaching. But I had insisted that I wanted to be taught by a real artist. After much tedious wrangling and bargaining with Papa and Madame Abbesse, it was arranged that I should go once a week to be taught by the great Monsieur David himself. Having given way about the lessons, Papa would have preferred that I be taught by someone fashionable and refined like Madame Vigée-Lebrun or Madame Vallayer-Coster, both of whom were favourites of the Queen. But I was adamant that only Monsieur David would do.

'When I go to the Royal Academy salon, it is David's

paintings that inspire and inflame me,' I had told my father, almost shouting in my desire to make him share my enthusiasm. 'Did you not admire his painting of the death of Socrates?'

'I do not admire paintings,' my father replied with a look of distaste, 'and I have never pretended to understand art. You may have your lessons with Monsieur David, but please do not imagine that it will ever be anything more than a pastime.' He began to fiddle with a huge gold ink pot that stood on his desk. 'A Saint-Valèry cannot be a professional artist. Such a thing is unheard of.'

I stared at him as the exquisite porcelain clock on his marble mantelpiece chimed the hour. 'I don't understand.'

My father pressed his fingers together and frowned as though something pained him. 'As my daughter, as a Saint-Valèry, you have certain obligations,' he explained. 'Like your sisters, you will marry well and then take up a position at court, just as the women of my family have always done. If you harbour dreams of doing anything else with your life then I would advise you to save yourself almost certain pain and abandon them now.'

'I don't want to get married,' I replied, lifting up my chin defiantly but hiding my shaking hands behind my back, 'and I don't want to live at court. I don't know if I want to be an artist either. I just know that I want to be something and to have an existence that isn't entirely tied up with getting married or being decorative or having children.'

My father looked at me from behind his desk as though he had never seen me before. 'When you speak like that you remind me of someone else,' he remarked. He stood abruptly and walked to the window, which looked out over the busy street where vendors wandered to and fro proclaiming their wares and shouting rude comments at the passersby. I couldn't see his face but could tell by the set of his shoulders beneath his russet velvet coat that my father was frowning.

'Sidonie,' I replied, my heart thumping in my breast as I said her name, horribly conscious of the fact that I had never dared to mention my mother to him before. Her name felt odd on

24

my lips, and I repeated it under my breath, enjoying the sinuous sound that it made. Sidonie.

'You have her eyes,' he said in a toneless voice. 'Grey. She was very proud of them.'

Now was the moment. I had so many questions to ask. 'Is there a portrait?' It was all that I could think of to start with. Surely there could be no harm in wanting to know what she looked like?

'No.' My father turned away from the window, his face closed and expressionless. 'As I said, I do not like paintings.'

I knew that he was lying. I was sure of it. There was nothing I could do though but thank him for agreeing to the lessons and then leave. He acknowledged my thanks with a curt nod and had returned to his books before the door had even whispered shut behind me.

Outside, I paused for a moment and leaned my back against the door, wiping sweaty palms against the embroidered muslin of my skirt. My sisters always said that I was the 'clever' one of the family, Mademoiselle Prunes and Prisms, who always knew an answer to everything and was more likely to be found at a boring science lecture than a ball. How come then, if I was so very clever, did I find it so hard to talk to my father, to twist him around my fingers the way that Lucrèce, Cassandre and even Lucien did?

That morning we drove from Penthémont on the Rue de Grenelle to Monsieur David's studio in the Louvre. Madame Abbesse had insisted that I be accompanied at all times when outside the school and so I was joined in the school carriage by a young nun, fresh from the provinces, called Soeur Clotilde, who looked forward to our weekly trip with as much relish as I did. She sat beside me now, almost bouncing in her seat with excitement and gazing joyously out of the windows, chattering while I smiled and nodded.

Paris should have been beautiful that day. There was a sharp nip of frost in the air and snow had fallen all night long. But the pristine whiteness had long since vanished and now the streets were filled with grey, ugly slush that churned beneath the wheels of our carriage and splattered against the already grimy windows.

As Soeur Clotilde chattered on beside me, I gazed out at the streets which, despite the freezing cold, teemed with life as usual. It seemed as though it would take more than a terrible chill to make Parisians want to stay indoors. I saw fashionably dressed ladies with enormous fur muffs rubbbing shoulders with market women and beggars as our carriage rumbled over the Pont Royale, over the frozen Seine where skaters ventured out onto the ice and twirled in intricate patterns, grinning and hugging themselves against the cold.

The carriage drove around the vast, gold, stone edifice of the Louvre, then pulled up in one of the huge courtyards. The palace had been abandoned when the royal family moved to Versailles in the last century and was now filled with ramshackle apartments, mostly inhabited by artists and their families while the once great galleries were used as studios for their work.

I looked up at the tall, stately windows as I jumped down from the carriage, smiling to see gaily coloured curtains hanging there and jugs of milk on all of the sills. When the weather was warm, laundry was hung from the windows to dry, giving the courtyard a festive appearance. The smell was the same though, the rich, delicious scent of meat stews and soups cutting through the frosty air.

'You wouldn't think this was once the home of royalty,' I remarked to Soeur Clotilde as we crossed the icy courtyard to the entrance to David's studio. It was quiet that day with only a few pupils bravely enduring the cold as they smoked their pipes on the steps and put the world to rights.

I glanced at them enviously as I went past, wishing I could be like them and live free from my family and all the social constraints that they imposed upon me. I wondered what their lives were like and imagined myself in their place, living in an apartment in the streets around the Palais Royal, going out every morning for my own bread and staying up late over a bottle of wine discussing art and politics.

They stared at us too as we walked to the door, their eyes curious and a little mocking as they obviously wondered what a nun and a little Penthémont girl were doing here. Soeur Clotilde's white habit and my prim red woollen uniform marked us out as conspicuous amongst the art students, who were both sombrely clad and bohemian.

'Who is that girl?' I heard one of them ask, not troubling to lower his voice. 'Not one of the models surely?' They all laughed and I blushed crimson.

'Ssh, it is the youngest daughter of the Comte de Saint-Valèry,' someone else replied, a handsome boy with keen blue eyes and a mop of blond hair that fell about his shoulders. 'You know ...'

My ears strained to catch the rest but the big door swung shut behind us and muffled his voice.

I noticed Soeur Clotilde giving me a curious look and realised that I was frowning and biting my lower lip, beset by the familiar feeling that there was some big secret people weren't telling me. I wasn't an idiot. I had seen the looks and the way that people broke off conversations when I approached. I had heard the whispers. I guessed that it was something to do with my mother, with Sidonie but what? What did everyone else know?

I forced myself to smile as we stepped into the vast, white gallery that served as David's studio. The air was filled with the sharp, acrid odour of oil paints and turpentine and all of the walls were covered with canvasses: some finished, others waiting for their final touches. Leaning against the wall by the door, in pride of place, was his recently completed portrait of the great chemist Antoine Lavoisier and his young wife, Marie-Anne, who worked as his assistant. I paused for a second to admire the masterly way that David had painted the soft folds of her muslin dress and to gaze up at her pretty face, filled with envy for this other girl who had had the good fortune to marry a great man and then be treated by him as an equal. It was exactly what I wanted for myself but had no hope of achieving.

27

'Mademoiselle de Saint-Valèry,' David himself greeted me from the front of the class. That day's model, a young blonde girl, was sitting in a chair beside him, draped with sheets in a classical fashion. Her eyes rolled up dramatically towards the ceiling in a pose that I was sure was very difficult to hold. 'I am glad that you were able to get here.'

I smiled and nodded. 'It would take more than snow to keep me away, monsieur.'

I handed my cloak to Soeur Clotilde. A few of the other pupils had looked up curiously as we walked in but most now bent their heads to their work again with only one or two continuing to stare at me. I was not the only girl in the class, but I was the only one in a school uniform.

I looked at the model for a moment. Then I set to work, outlining her figure on the paper, and softly adding some shading to round out her contours.

David came and stood behind me. 'Very good, very good indeed, mademoiselle but...' He leaned forward. 'May I?' He took my charcoal and then went over my careful lines with bolder, darker strokes that made the drawing somehow come to life. 'It is always the same, mademoiselle, you start off so carefully, so precisely and we have to tease the art out of you all over again.'

'I wish that I could devote more time to drawing,' I said with regret. 'I always feel so rusty when I come here. Perhaps I should ask Madame Abbesse to let me have some time to spend on my art?'

He smiled. 'Perhaps.' There was a pause and I stifled a giggle, knowing what was coming as he cleared his throat. 'Is Madame la Marquise in Paris this Winter?'

He meant my sister, Cassandre, who had married the Marquis de Vautière two years earlier amidst great fuss and pomp. Monsieur David had the most terrible crush on her and never failed to drop her into our conversations. He was desperate to paint her and I didn't have the heart to tell him that my sister had only two requirements from portrait painters – that they be fashionable and that they be flattering. Poor Monsieur David was

28

neither sufficiently fashionable nor flattering to please Cassandre.

'He is far too insightful,' my sister had said with a laugh when I last broached the subject with her. 'If I allow him to paint me then everyone will know just how awful I really am, and I won't have any friends left.'

'Alas, no,' I told David now, gently. 'My sister is at Versailles at the moment and I do not know when she is coming back to Paris.'

The lesson went quickly, just as they always did. At the end, the other students went together to the Palais Royal, while I gathered my things and went back with Soeur Clotilde to our carriage. I watched enviously as the other students filed out, slapping each other on the back and laughing. I longed to go with them to the Palais Royal, which sounded like a hotbed of excitement and novelty. But they had never once invited me along with them, and who could blame them?

'One day,' I promised myself, as I pulled up the hood of my grey woollen cloak. One day I too would walk around the famous arcades of the Palais and linger over a coffee in one of the dozens of cafés there. It seemed so strange that life was buzzing so close to my convent walls and yet, except for my art lessons, I was excluded from all of it.

As we left the studio, Soeur Clotilde clattering in her wooden-heeled shoes at my side, we walked into a great fuss and hubbub in the outer vestibule. A tall, very handsome middle-aged man in a splendid purple silk coat had just arrived, surrounded by a coterie of admiring minions and highly rouged ladies. The tall man looked about himself with disinterest and contempt as he brushed snow from his wide shoulders, his dark eyes scanning the adoring, upturned faces that surrounded him.

'Monsieur Bertrand!' David bustled past me, his paint and charcoal stained hands held out in welcome.

Ah, of course. The great Bertrand, one of the most famous actors in Paris, in all of France even. I smiled to myself, imagining the envious reaction of the other girls at school when I told them about this unexpected treat.

At that moment his eyes fell on me and suddenly, as though someone had slapped him, all of the disinterest drained away and in its place was confusion and something akin to fear.

Bertrand took a step forward then checked himself, his eyes still boring into mine.

'Come now,' Soeur Clotilde took hold of my elbow and hurried me past. 'I do not like the way Monsieur Bertrand is staring at you. These actors are all the same. It's absolutely shocking! Come away please, Adélaïde!'

'Who is that girl?' I heard Bertrand ask David, his voice rich and deep. An actor's voice designed to recite Shakespeare, Racine and Moliere. I could have closed my eyes and listened him speak forever, letting the beautiful tones of his voice roll over me.

'The school girl?' David replied. He sounded nervous. 'That is Mademoiselle Adélaïde. The youngest daughter of the Comte de Saint-Valèry.'

'Saint-Valèry!'

I turned my head, astonished by the raw anguish in his voice, and for a moment our eyes met before the door swung shut behind me.

LUCRÈCE

Paris, July 1789

I sat in front of my dressing table mirror, my stomach rumbling with hunger as I waited for someone to come and fetch me. Every so often I turned my head self-consciously from side to side, patting my frizzed and powdered red hair, stiff with rose-scented pomade, and admired the way my diamond earrings flashed in the sunlight.

Grandmère had ordered my gown for the occasion from Mademoiselle Bertin: a heavy lemon yellow silk, trimmed with fine lace and spangled with diamonds. I had taken one look, then cast it aside, choosing instead a plain white taffeta dress with a simple muslin fichu over my shoulders and a red silk sash at my waist. I regarded myself with a great deal of satisfaction in my mirror, tweaking my long tight sleeves and thinking that my outfit struck exactly the right balance between simplicity and elegance.

'Madame la Comtesse will not be happy,' my maid, Aglaé, said . 'She expressly ordered that you wear the pink silk when you meet Monsieur le Duc.' She held the gown up wistfully to her rosy cheek, testing its luscious softness against her olive skin. 'Are you quite sure that you don't want to wear it, madame? Can I wear it instead?'

I shook my head, laughing. 'Oh, Madame la Comtesse is never happy. It is time that we stopped caring about that, don't you think?'

Our eyes met in the tarnished mirror and we shared a smile. Aglaé had only been with me for a year, ever since I left Penthémont in fact, and in that time we had become allies of sorts against Grandmère, her whims and the countless pointless edicts with which she attempted to run our lives.

I gave a shrug. 'After today it won't matter any more anyway.'

'That's true enough.' Aglaé gave a sigh and regretfully put the dress back down again, with one last stroke of the shimmering silk. 'After today everything will be different.' She did not look at all pleased.

Soft summer rain began to fall against the windows, pattering at the glass. I remembered how it had rained on my wedding day as well, three long years ago. The heavy drops had thundered on the roof of the carriage as we drove to the church of Saint-Louis on the bustling, noisy Rue Saint-Antoine, where the blackened stone Bastille rose like a monster, looming ominously over the surrounding houses. Shrieking and laughing, we had all gathered up our heavy, flounced skirts and sprinted into the church, our carefully arranged hair falling about our ears in clumps of sodden ringlets, the powder running in thick white rivulets down our faces.

I was still laughing, all nervousness forgotten, as I stepped lightly up the black and white chequered aisle, my hand resting on my father's sleeve. As we grew closer, I could see the Duc's expression change from well-bred boredom to amusement as he took in my disordered state, my rain-splattered cream silk dress and my hair, which despite Cassandre's best efforts now hung in damp ringlets about my shoulders. We had met only once before, six months earlier when he had come with my father to Penthémont, and I could barely remember him, recalling only his great height and the way he had not smiled. His blue grey eyes had looked down into my blushing face, scrutinising me for defects. 'She is very small for fifteen,' he had remarked carelessly to my father, in the manner of one who feels that they have been presented with a poor bargain. 'I do not like how thin she is and you did not tell me she has red hair.'

But there had been no trace of disappointment in the Duc de Saliex's pale eyes as he took my hand in front of the altar and slipped a heavy, ancient gold ring set with rubies and sapphires on to my finger before bending his handsome head and kissing me chastely on the mouth. I still dreamed of that moment, tracing the contours of my lips with my finger as I tried to remember what it had felt like, the memory fading with each passing year.

We had returned in bright, spring sunshine to the house on the Rue des Francs-Bourgeois and sat awkwardly side by side during a lengthy and elaborate wedding breakfast that had taken up most of the day. Each magnificent course had been brought out on borrowed silver and gold platters by sweating, liveried footmen while in the next room hired musicians played the harpsichord and harp and sang popular airs. I had sat, fascinated and terrified, as my husband crumpled his white linen napkin in his lap and sipped at his glass of champagne, pausing every so often to glance curiously at me.

Unable to think of a single intelligent thing to say to him, I took a bite from a strawberry tart and closed my eyes, breathing in his very masculine scent of lavender, neroli and sweat. It mingled with the heady scent of the flowers that had been arranged in dozens of Sèvres vases around the room: roses, lilies, carnations, jasmine and lilacs. I listened to the music from the next room, the sharp chink of heavy silverware against fine porcelain, and the laughter and whisperings of the guests as they stared at us, their voices muffled by the fans in front of their red-painted mouths. The tall windows that led down to the gardens had been flung wide open and the chandeliers that hung overhead tinkled softly in the breeze, casting bright prisms of light on the yellow walls.

'What a lovely bride little Lucrèce makes,' I heard one of

the female guests murmur. 'How pretty she looks.'

'All Duchesses are pretty,' her neighbour said with a laugh. 'Even the ugly ones. Did you not know that?' There was a tinkle of crystal as they giggled and touched their glasses together.

After the final course, the Duc had stood up and offered me his hand, bending his head to chastely kiss my lips as everyone laughed and applauded. 'May I present my wife?' he said with a smile, still tightly holding my hand as though he feared I would take flight and run away. 'Madame la Duchesse de Saliex!'

He lifted his glass, which a footman hastened forward to refill with champagne. 'A toast!' He held the glass aloft, the golden liquid sloshing over us both. 'Madame la Duchesse!'

'Madame la Duchesse!'

I blushed as they all toasted me. I did not like the way they all stared at me: the men openly ogling, their bloodshot eyes flickering over my face and small breasts, while the women with their enormous hair and glittering diamonds smirked and looked me up and down in the brittle, contemptuous manner typical of Parisian women.

Still holding hands, we led the guests out down the stone steps and into the gardens. The musicians continued playing and their beautiful music floated out over the lawns, statues and shrubs. We were lucky to have such a big garden in the Marais, an oasis of fragrant, colourful peace in the middle of the city. Sometimes I would take my books outside and sit alone for hours, reading in the shade of one of the ancient, spreading trees, imagining myself in the countryside, not the centre of Paris.

'You look charming,' the Duc murmured to me as we strolled arm in arm past the stone fountain in the centre of the lawn. 'I had forgotten how pretty you are.' He looked up at the statue of Flora festooned with gilt garlands of flowers. 'Quite beautiful in fact.'

I gazed up at him, utterly tongue tied and uncertain as to whether he was complimenting me or the statue. He must have thought me such a silly little idiot with my round-eyed staring, my blushes and awkward silences. I am only fifteen, I longed to say to him. Is it really fair that you all expect me to think, speak and act like a grown woman when I am actually just a child?

'Ah, I do believe you are about to be rescued from my unworthy clutches,' he said with an ironic smile.

I turned to see my twin, Cassandre, and two schoolmates from Penthémont advancing with great determination and much giggling upon us both. I watched the trio of girls enviously as they sauntered across the lawn, their arms around each other, their heads thrown back in laughter, seemingly unconcerned that every eye was now upon them. They were dressed in matching gowns of frothy muslin over pink silk with wide blue satin sashes tied around their waists. Their unpowdered hair hung in artfully teased ringlets over their shoulders and down their backs. Cassandre had gone further and wound a length of white muslin around her head, giving herself an ethereal appearance at odds with her merry, dimpled countenance.

'You would not think that you are twins,' the Duc remarked, observing my sister as she came closer. 'And yet at the same time ...' He looked confused, seemingly unable to pinpoint where the resemblance between us stemmed from. 'She seems much older than you.'

'Cassandre smiles more than I do,' I said quietly, repeating what I had always heard Grandmère say to her friends when discussing us both. 'She never looks serious.'

The Duc looked at me in surprise, perhaps remembering my laughter as I had walked up the aisle towards him. 'Yes, that that must be it.' He bowed to Cassandre as she came closer, giving her a long look that I couldn't quite decipher. 'I hope that you will forgive me if I leave you alone?'

He bowed one last time and then was gone.

Cassandre swooped on me, forcing me to sit beside her on the fountain's stone rim. 'You have to tell me everything!' The other girls giggled and leaned forward, their long ringlets swinging around their faces. In an attempt to appear more grown up they had liberally applied as much rouge as possible to their cheeks and lips, and smothered themselves with violet and jasmine scents pilfered from their mothers' dressing tables. The combined smell was overpowering and I recoiled a little as they came closer.

'Come on, Lucrèce! What is it like? We are all dying to know!' They fluttered around me, their soft muslin skirts billowing prettily in the breeze.

I stared at them all, frowning a little. 'What do you mean? Nothing has happened.'

I knew that one day something interesting would happen between the Duc and I, as Madame Abbesse had called me into her parlour the day before and told me all about it. But that would not be for many years to come, as after today I would be returning to Penthémont until I was considered old enough to be a proper wife.

'Silly!' Cassandre looked at me rather contemptuously and rolled her eyes. 'We mean what does it feel like to be married?'

'And to be kissed!' One of the girls, Cécile leaned in and whispered, her blue eyes alight with curiosity and excitement. 'Oh, I can't believe it, Lucrèce! You have been kissed before any of us! He is so handsome too!'

'Cécile practises on her pillow every night,' Cassandre interrupted with a sigh. 'It would not be fair to deny her your knowledge of the real thing.' She nudged me sharply with her thin elbow. 'So come on, tell us what it is like? Do you feel different?'

'Do you love him?' Cécile demanded, her eyes round with awe as she looked at me.

Cassandre laughed. 'Of course she doesn't love him,' she said. 'Honestly, Cécile! They barely know each other!' She rolled her huge hazel eyes and turned back to me. 'Ignore her, she doesn't know what she is talking about. I blame all the dreary romance novels she reads when she is supposed to be learning Italian.' She grinned and leaned forward. 'So, tell us everything about the kissing.'

'Oh. Well.' I tried to think of the right words, well aware

that they would be satisfied with nothing less than swooning and fluttering hearts and passion. 'It was very nice.'

'Nice? Oh dear, Lucrèce, even you can do better than that!' my sister said with a laugh. 'Did it make you tingle all over?'

I blushed. 'No.' I looked around, praying that the Duc was not within earshot but he was nowhere to be seen. 'It just felt nice.'

Cassandre rippled her long pale fingers through the lukewarm water of the fountain. 'Is that all there is to it?'

'Maybe not for you,' I conceded. 'Maybe you will be lucky and marry someone whose kisses make you tingle all over.'

She sighed, shaking her wet hands over the grass. 'Maybe, but how likely is that?'

'Oh, I would say that it was very likely,' I replied before standing up and brushing down my crumpled silk skirt. There was a strawberry stain on the bodice that I tried my best to remove with a wetted finger. 'Have you seen Adélaïde anywhere?' I asked, shading my eyes with my hand and looking around the wandering groups of guests. 'I haven't seen her since we came outside. Do you know where she is?'

'Tiens, how would I know?' Cassandre said with a shrug of her thin shoulders. 'She is probably sitting inside with her nose stuck in a book as usual. What a bore she is.' She turned to the others. 'Now there, ladies, we have an example of a girl who is destined never to be kissed.'

I frowned. 'Don't be unkind, Cassandre. It isn't fair.'

I felt rather than saw Cassandre stick her tongue out at my back as I walked away, looking around the garden and trying to imagine where Adélaïde was most likely to be. Cassandre was probably right, of course, and she had hidden herself away indoors. But there was always a chance that she was sitting in one of the white Chinese pavilions, tucked between the huge, blossoming rhodedendrons that edged the garden. I made my way to what I knew was her favourite spot, stopping every few moments to smile and nod pleasantly whenever someone congratulated me.

As I ducked behind a lush, red-flowering rhododendron bush I could see Grandmère advancing purposely upon me. Her diamonds flashed in the sunlight and her heavy blue satin skirts streamed behind her as she strode across the lawn. I offered a silent prayer that she be distracted from her course, then tiptoed down the narrow path to the pavilion, the sound of voices having alerted me that someone was indeed there.

'Don't be absurd, Honorine,' it was a man's voice, deep and melodic that I recognised at once to be that of my new husband. 'This won't change anything.' I tiptoed around the edge of the pavilion until I could see his back. The Duc was dressed in only his fine linen shirt and cream silk breeches and had taken his powdered wig off, casting it aside on to a nearby marble bench. He ran his hands through his short dark hair so that it spiked up.

I could see the woman with him clearly though. She was small, blonde and very pretty with a slut's red, full-lipped mouth and huge, melting blue eyes which were currently fixed seductively on my husband's face. She was dressed in bright pink watered silk with enormous diamonds hanging from her ears and in her curled hair. 'Oh come now, Armand, do you really expect me to believe that?' Her voice was shrill and peevish and at odds with her luscious appearance. 'You go off and marry some little schoolgirl and don't expect me to be even the slightest bit upset?' She narrowed her eyes. 'What if she turns out to be like her mother?'

'Honorine, she is just a child. An innocent, pretty, rather boring child,' the Duc replied with a sigh, reaching out to caress her white, bare shoulder. 'Can't we just forget about her for now?' He put his arm around her narrow waist and pulled her close, his fingers crushing the delicate pink taffeta of her gown. 'She goes back to her convent school tomorrow and I don't expect to see her again for many years to come.'

He bent his head to her throat and she closed her eyes with a sigh and threw her head back, her diamond ring covered fingers digging into his shoulders. 'Lucrèce has nothing to do with us and our pleasures,' he murmured huskily, his lips moving over her breasts.

She groaned, twisting her hands in his cropped hair. 'Oh, Armand.'

The Duc lifted her up in his strong arms and carried her to the wall, her long white-stockinged legs wrapped around his waist.

'Oh, Armand,' she panted, bending to kiss him as he fumbled at his silk breeches. 'My love, my only love. Only you can make me feel like this.'

'You drive me mad, Honorine,' he whispered as he pushed against her. She flung her head back with a sharp cry, her fingers gripping his white shirt, pulling it up so that his muscular back was exposed. 'This is sheer madness and yet I want no one but you.'

He moved against her and I watched in fascinated horror, my cheeks crimson with shame as the woman arched her back and moaned with pleasure, rubbing herself against my new husband, shameless as a cat.

A knock on the door brought me back to the present and I realised that I was still sitting at my dressing table, twisting my silk skirts angrily between my hands and almost crying with shame and chagrin.

'Who is it?'

Please God let it be someone come to get me at last. Hurriedly, I checked my reflection in the mirror, then added a dusting of powder to my flushed cheeks. Why had I thought about that day again? I hadn't understood what I was watching at the time but I understood now and the thought of it sickened me.

How could I ever respect or love a man who had behaved so appallingly?

'Are you ready, Duchesse?' It was my brother, Lucien, at the door, handsome as ever with his wavy auburn hair tied back with a black silk ribbon. 'They are all downstairs waiting for you.'

He advanced into the room with a flirtatious smile and a kiss of his fingers for Aglaé, who tried to look primly disapproving but failed utterly. Was that a blush I saw? No one could resist my brother when he set out to charm them.

'Now then, let me have a look at you.' He blew a low whistle as I obligingly twirled around. 'You look perfect, Duchesse.'

'Doesn't she just?' Aglaé agreed with a nod, the yellow silk now completely forgotten. 'She looks just as a bride ought.'

I blushed. If only they knew.

'You can't be a bride without some flowers,' my brother pointed out with a laugh, pulling some purple lilacs from the blue and white vase that stood on my dressing table and tucking them into my bosom. 'And some roses as well, I think.'

He selected the loveliest from the vase and placed it carefully into my hair, mimicking the mincing antics of a fashionable hairdresser as he did so.

'There, you look wonderful. The Duc will fall at your feet in adoration and you will live happily ever after like something from a fairy tale.'

'That would be nice.' I suddenly realised that the screams and shouts from the street below had not stopped, even though the rain was long gone. 'What is happening out there?' I asked Aglaé, who immediately went to the window, pushing it open further and looking down.

'I can't tell, madame,' she said, screwing up her face and slamming the window shut. 'There is a big crowd gathered in the street but nothing much seems to be happening. Perhaps your father will know?'

'Perhaps.' I brushed imaginary fluff from my sleeve. It was time to face them all. 'Shall we go downstairs?'

'Yes, let's.' Lucien grinned and offered me his blue velvet arm. 'Between us, Lucrèce, I think someone is going to slap Grandmère if she mentions "My granddaughter, the Duchess" one more time.'

He winked and led me from the room, not giving me enough time for more than one last look over my shoulder.

'It is nice that Grandmère is so proud of me,' I said with a smile. We walked together down the worn white marble stairs that led to the hallway below. 'She is so difficult to please.'

I glanced quickly up at her portrait by Nattier, where she stood thin-lipped and severe in pale blue silk. It had hung on the staircase wall for as long as I could remember.

Lucien noticed me looking and gave me a gentle nudge. 'Do you remember the painting that hung there before?' he asked. 'It was of our mother holding a baby. Do you remember, Lucrèce?'

I turned to him in surprise, suddenly ashamed for having forgotten, even though I was just a little girl when our mother had gone away. 'Did it? I don't remember that, Lucien.' I looked up again at Grandmère's stern portrait, trying to imagine another, softer one there in its place and failing. 'Do you know where it is now?'

Lucien sighed and shook his head. 'No, I don't.' He gave me a quick, sad smile. 'I wish that I did.'

Holding hands, we walked through the hall. 'Are you ready?' Lucien whispered in my ear as we came to the salon door where one of my father's footmen was waiting to admit us. 'Take a deep breath, my beauty.'

The door swung open and we stepped into the room, still tightly holding hands. For a second, I looked around the room, hung with portraits of my ancestresses, their heavy lidded eyes watching me with lazy mischief. The windows which led down to the garden had been pushed open so that the air was tinged with the scent of honeysuckle. There was Papa, standing rather self-consciously by the red marble fireplace, one hand tucked into his silk waistcoat, while the other idly played with a small porcelain snuff box. Beside him sat Grandmère, dressed in black taffeta with a white lace cap arranged on her neatly powdered grey coiffure and the magnificent Saint-Valèry diamonds that had once belonged to my mother glittering in her ears and around her throat. Papa had promised that they should be divided between Cassandre, Adélaïde and myself as soon as we were married. But it looked like Grandmère was determined to cling on to them for as long as possible.

Cassandre was sitting beside a window, her head turned

away as she stared at something just out of sight in the garden. Her unpowdered hair was arranged in elaborate curls and ringlets, with two sleek red ringlets hanging down to the small of her back. Her young husband, the Marquis de Vautière, was standing beside her, one hand pressed possessively to her shoulder while his pale eyes stared down at the top of her head. At his side stood my younger sister, Adélaïde, dressed simply in white muslin tied at the waist with a carnation pink silk sash and with her thick dark hair tumbling about her shoulders. She was looking across the room at Grandmère with a puzzled expression on her pale face as though concentrating hard on some complicated mathematical conundrum.

I could barely bring myself to look at the two men who stood on the other side of the fireplace to my father: the eldest of the two was just as tall and lean as I remembered, and just as handsome. The younger was a stranger to me, with smiling grey eyes and long chestnut hair tied back with a velvet ribbon.

Cassandre jumped up from her seat and ran, her silk skirts rustling to take my hands. 'Here you are at last!' she cried with a grin, kissing me noisily on both cheeks. 'I thought you were never going to come downstairs!' She gave me a quizzical look. 'How serious you are!'

'Cassandre...' I flushed, embarrassed, and quickly looked to the Duc, who had not moved from his position beside the fireplace. 'This is a serious occasion.'

My sister smelled deliciously and overpoweringly of violets, and I noticed now that there were lilacs and violets arranged in her frizzed and curled hair. 'Oh well, yes, I suppose so,' she agreed. She took my hand and led me, smiling to the Duc, who stepped forward and bowed as we approached.

'May I present my cousin,' the Duc said, 'Monsieur le Comte de Chaulnes?' He gestured towards the other man, who smiled shyly as he bowed over my hand, barely touching it with his long fingers. I shivered as a tendril of his thick hair escaped its ribbon and fell forward, whispering across the back of my hand. 'Cousin Sébastien and I were raised together from boyhood. He is

42

like a brother to me.'

The two men grinned at each other and I imagined them together as little boys, running across a corn field with fishing rods on their backs.

I curtsied to Cousin Sébastien, liking the way that his smile reached his eyes. I began to feel suddenly light-headed and breathless. 'I am pleased to meet you.'

'It seems like such a long time since I last saw you,' my husband remarked, looking me over with a look of approval mingled with surprise. 'You were just a little girl then.'

I turned and curtsied to the Duc, too shy to meet his grey eyes. 'Yes, I was.' I lifted my eyes to his face and saw that he was smiling, the tanned skin around his eyes crinkling just a little. 'You look just the same though.'

The Duc took my hand and led me to my grandmother, who nodded her head to me in a frosty manner, making it clear that I had let her down at this important moment by not wearing the splendid dress that she had chosen for me. 'Do I really look the same?' he asked. He lifted my hand to his warm lips. 'I think that you must be flattering me, my dear.'

'Oh no, not at all.' I blushed, fully aware that everyone in the room was watching us with interest, wondering how we would get along. I could hear Cassandre and Lucien sniggering. 'I have never forgotten you.' I glanced up at him quickly from beneath my lashes. 'I thought about you every day after you left.'

'Truly?' The Duc looked astounded and a little ashamed. 'You were so young ...'

'I know.' I forced a smile. 'It is different now.'

We walked together in the gardens, enjoying the sunshine while Adélaïde played her harpsichord in the salon with the windows flung open so that the beautiful music floated through the air. The others watched from a discreet distance, straining their ears to hear our conversation and smiling behind their fans as the Duc picked a beautiful, blooming white rose and tucked it into my red silk sash.

'I am sorry that I left you here for so long,' he remarked

43

as we paused by the fountain. 'I should have claimed you as soon as you were old enough to leave Penthémont but then I was sent to Rome on a diplomatic mission.' He looked up at the figure of Flora, just as he had done all those years ago. 'I came for you as soon as I returned. I expected to find a child but you have blossomed in my absence.' He took my hand and pulled me closer towards him. 'Ah, now you are blushing. It is quite charming. They did not tell me how shy you are or how pretty.'

My husband put his fingers beneath my chin and pushed my rosily blushing face upwards. 'You are too silent though.' He kissed my eyes, the tip of my nose and then, gently, my lips. 'I wish that you would speak more.'

'I do not know what to say,' I replied in a low voice. 'I am not very interesting.' I looked past him to where Cassandre strolled slowly in between Lucien, her husband and Cousin Sébastien, all of them laughing and talking over each other without seeming to pause for breath. 'I am not like my sister.'

The Duc smiled. 'Nonsense. Talk to me, Lucrèce.' He smiled down at me. 'Tell me about yourself. I want to know all about you.'

'Where should I begin?' I felt breathless as he gazed into my eyes. 'What do you want to know?' I could hear Cousin Sébastien excitedly telling Cassandre about an ancient statue that he had seen being unearthed in Rome while she nodded politely and yawned behind her painted fan. 'I am still very young, monsieur. I have seen nothing, done nothing and been nowhere. What could I possibly say that would be of interest to a man like you?'

'What indeed?' My husband lifted his eyes to the blue skies overhead. 'I do believe it is beginning to rain again. Shall we go in?' He smiled. 'I remember the rain on our wedding day.'

'Do you?' I looked straight at him then. 'I saw you,' I said, unable to remain silent for a moment longer. 'I saw you with that girl, Honorine.' I was shaking with anger and upset now. 'How could you do that?'

I couldn't believe what I had just said and put my hands

across my mouth in shock, trying my best to prevent any more words slipping out to betray me.

My husband stared at me, aghast. 'I had no idea,' he said. 'I don't know what to say, Lucrèce. You were such a child, a little girl. I didn't think it mattered.' He took my hand and lifted it to his lips. 'I am truly sorry if I hurt you.'

'I am not angry with you,' I said, surprised to find that this was true. 'You did not know me, nor I you. I should have known that you would have other interests. I was hurt but what option do I have but to forgive you if we are to live together harmoniously?'

'You are too good for me,' he replied. 'We should go inside.' He gave me a sidelong look from the corner of his eye. 'Are you sure, Lucrèce? Forgive me, but I hope you are not doing that womanly thing of saying all is well while on the inside you wish me to the very devil?'

I took a deep breath. 'No, it isn't like that.' I would have said more but my attention was caught by more shouts from the street as we walked up the stone steps into the house. 'What is happening out there?' I asked, suddenly afraid.

The Duc put his arm around my waist as we went inside. 'There have been riots in Paris today. It is nothing to worry about and will soon be over.'

He seemed so confident that I instantly relaxed, no longer afraid of the strange shouts and screams from the streets of the Marais.

We left my father's house in the pouring rain after an elaborate and lengthy dinner. Cousin Sébastien went in his carriage to his own house on the Place Dauphine on the Ile de la Cité while the Duc, Adélaïde and I were to travel together to the Rue de Grenelle, dropping Adélaïde off at Penthémont on our way to the Hôtel de Saliex.

I shivered, thinking about the enormous, beautiful mansion that was now to be my home. It was just a short walk from Penthémont and I had often found excuses to stroll slowly past the huge stone gate and peer wistfully past the gilt railings at the exquisite sandstone house beyond, hardly able to believe that it was now mine, even though I had never once set foot inside. The elderly, sour expressioned concierge who sat by the gate always looked at me so suspiciously when I stopped. I wondered what he would have said if I had ever identified myself to him. He probably wouldn't have believed me.

Adélaïde came downstairs in her plain red linen uniform, her pretty muslin dress regretfully left behind. 'Is it true that there are riots all over the city?' she asked the Duc, her voice trembling with excitement.

He smiled at me reassuringly before replying. 'Yes, it is true, Mademoiselle de Saint-Valèry. I do not believe we are in any danger however.'

'Oh.' She looked so absurdly disappointed that I could not prevent myself from laughing. 'How dull.'

'Come now, Adélaïde,' I said, drawing on my white gloves and adjusting my hat in front of the huge mirror that dominated the entrance hall. 'You do not really mean that.'

Since when had my quiet little sister become so bloodthirsty? What radical ideas were infiltrating the sunny, tranquil cloisters of Penthémont?

'Yes, I do!' She laughed then and shook her head so that her hair escaped from its pins and began to fall in heavy tendrils around her shoulders. 'Oh, Lucrèce, can't you remember how boring it is to be cooped up in Penthémont all day long? Did you never long for excitement and adventure as I do?' She turned to the Duc, who was observing her with a look of amusement. 'I think that it would have been better if I had been born a boy. You men seem to have all of the fun.'

'She is just like her mother,' my husband whispered to me as he took my hand. 'The same mutinous look and engaging ways.'

'Really?' I looked up at him in surprise. 'You knew my mother?'

The Duc smiled down at me. 'But of course.'

There was no time for more as everyone came into the hall to say good bye. Each member of my family stepped forward to kiss me on both cheeks and whisper their congratulations, good wishes and final snippets of advice.

'You need to learn to dress like a Duchesse so that you do not disgrace us all. I shall send Mademoiselle Bertin to you in the morning,' Grandmère murmured.

'If you drink some wine at bedtime, it won't be so bad,' Cassandre whispered into my ear. 'Remember what I told you: the more frightened you are, the more it will hurt.' She stepped back, her high-heeled shoes tapping on the marble floor and smiled, with a sidelong look at her handsome husband who stared sulkily into the distance. 'It is worth it though. Oh yes, indeed.'

I laughed and kissed her rouged cheeks. 'I am delighted that you are happy but please, spare me the details!'

Cassandre winked. 'Oh, just you wait. All you new brides are the same: simpering one minute and boasting the next.'

Darkness was beginning to fall as we left the courtyard of the Hôtel de Saint-Valèry, lit by flickering torches held aloft by my father's liveried footmen. I had to lift my white silk skirt above my ankles in order to avoid the muddy puddles. Despite the gathering gloom, the Rue des Francs-Bourgeois still teemed with people, both well dressed and ragged. Some marched arm in arm, swigging from bottles of wine and singing drunkenly as they swarmed towards the Place Royale. Others were more threatening, waving swords and sticks above their heads, and shouting at us as we climbed into our carriage.

'You don't have to go now,' my father said anxiously, hopping over the puddles so he could come to the carriage window and take my hand. 'You could stay another night.'

I looked anxiously to my husband, already keen to defer to his judgement. 'It is quite safe,' he said with a short nod to my father. 'The rabble of Paris are always looking for an excuse to cause trouble. I don't anticipate any problems getting home.'

My father did not look as though he agreed. He hesitated for a moment, looking from me to the Duc, then gave a shrug. 'As you wish, monsieur,' he said, with one last look of concern at me. 'I am sure it is as you say.' He brought my hand up to his lips, then quickly relinquished it. 'Be good, Adélaïde,' he said with a nod at my sister, who sighed and rolled her dark eyes.

'How furious the mob look,' I remarked to the Duc when my father had returned to the house. I tucked my long warm cloak in around me and pulled up the window, which my breath immediately began to mist up.

The Duc smiled, thumping the roof of the carriage with his ebony walking stick to let the coachman know that we were ready to leave. 'I have seen much worse than this, and it has never amounted to anything.' He grinned confidently at my sister and as the carriage rolled out of the courtyard and onto the cobbled street. 'The bark of the Parisian rabble is infinitely worse than their bite. I can assure you that we have nothing to fear from them.'

'How exciting it is!' Adélaïde was sitting on the edge of her seat, staring out of the window at the mob as we rumbled past, their faces an eerie, flickering yellow in the light of the torches that they held aloft. 'How I wish that I could march with them.'

'You don't even know what they are marching for!' I scoffed, with an impatient look. 'It could be anything!'

Our carriage rolled slowly through the narrow, cobbled streets of the Marais, past the beautiful carved stone archways that led to the hôtels particulaires and the shops with their wonderful, exotic window displays.

'My family used to have a house here,' the Duc observed, peering out into the darkness. 'We moved across to the Rue de Grenelle when it became fashionable to do so. My grandfather built our house there.'

Adélaïde looked at him with amusement. 'It is usual in your family to do things just because they are fashionable?' she enquired. 'How very odd. You must think us all very strange for remaining on the unfashionable side of Paris.' She gave a little shrug. 'The Rue de Grenelle is very nice and orderly, if you like that sort of thing. For my part, I prefer the Marais.'

'Oh it is not so very odd,' I interjected with a grin before the Duc could reply. 'Haven't you heard Cassandre say that she would rather be dead than outmoded?'

'Oh, Cassandre. We are so different. I often wonder how we came to be related,' Adélaïde observed with a shrug before she returned to staring out of the window at the immense crowd. The people stared back but their mood was still good natured and other than a few thumps against our windows, we were left unmolested and allowed to continue on our way.

The carriage picked up speed past the looming Louvre and Tuileries, and along the slippery, cobbled Quais alongside the Seine. I gazed across the dark water at the familiar sight of Notre Dame, towering over the low buildings that surrounded it and further along, the turreted façade of the Conciergerie. It looked more like a castle from a fairy tale than a prison, the feeble candlelight from its arched, barred windows reflected on to the river below.

I gave a scream as our carriage juddered to a sudden halt, throwing me forward from my seat. 'What happened?' I gasped as Adélaïde helped me back up. 'Have we lost a wheel?'

I peered out at the filthy, dishevelled mob surrounding our carriage, their lanterns held aloft as they stared in at us with hostile expressions and scrutinised the coat of arms on the side of our vehicle. I could just about make out a rudimentary blockade of carts piled high with barrels and straw that had been lined up across the bridge, blocking the path of anyone that tried to cross. In front of us were two other carriages with their well-dressed occupants standing confused and bewildered beside them, shrinking away from a jeering crowd who waved their grimy fists in their faces and tried to force them to drink from bottles of vinegary red wine.

'This carriage belongs to the Duc de Saliex,' I heard one unkempt man remark; he took a drag on his pipe, then spat noisily on the ground by the rear wheels. 'He is friends with the slut Antoinette.' He strode forward, roughly pulled open the carriage door and jabbed one filthy finger at my husband. 'Get out.'

I turned to stare in horror at the Duc, who merely raised an eyebrow. 'What on earth for?' he asked, making no move to leave his seat. 'We have done nothing wrong.'

The man glowered, then gave a shrug and pulled out an ancient pistol, which he pointed at my head. 'Get out or you can kiss goodbye to your pretty little whore.' He gripped my arm, his blackened fingers sinking into my flesh and marking my white silk dress as he pulled me closer. 'I don't have all day.' He sniffed my hair as I closed my eyes and prayed for him to release me. 'She smells good. Where did you get her? The Palais Royal? You aristocrats really do get the best of everything, don't you? Even your whores smell like princesses.' He gave a nasty laugh when he spotted Adélaïde sitting beside me, fresh faced and wearing her distinctive red school uniform. 'What's this? A schoolgirl? She looks just like the real thing. What tricks does she do?'

'Be silent.' The Duc's tone was sharp. To my surprise, he reached out to take Adélaïde's hand in his. She was looking less excited now, and was pale and shaking. 'Insult me as much as you please but leave the ladies alone.' He released Adélaïde's hand and climbed out of the carriage. 'Kindly release my wife now. You have what you wanted.'

'Wife, eh?'

For a moment the man's grip tightened. Then he released me and the gun was no longer pointing at my head.

I crept along the seat towards Adélaïde and we put our arms around each other as the Duc closed the door and walked away, surrounded on all sides by a baying mob who chanted his name over and over again: 'Saliex! Saliex! We've got the Duc de Saliex!'

'What are they going to do?' Adélaïde whispered. 'They won't hurt him, will they?'

I shushed her and stroked her dark, tumbled hair. 'I don't know, Adélaïde. I just don't know.'

I stared out of the window and listened intently to what was happening outside, bracing myself for the inevitable moment when they came back for us as well. It came sooner than I had expected. A dirty, ugly woman with greasy black hair appeared outside the window, then wrenched open the door, almost pulling it from its hinges.

She pointed her pistol at us both. 'Come with me,' she ordered us gruffly, waving her gun around in an alarming manner. A dozen other women had gathered behind her, all of them staring at us and muttering amongst themselves.

'Not so fine now, are you?' one of them called nastily as I stumbled down from the carriage.

I put my arm around Adélaïde, who had jumped down after me and now looked like she was going to cry. 'Be brave and put up your chin, little one,' I said to her. 'They would not dare to hurt us.'

We walked past the women, ignoring their foul-mouthed taunts, their sickly stench of sour wine, sweat and cheap cologne, and went straight to the Duc. He was surrounded by a group of armed men who unwillingly moved aside so that we could get to him.

'Did they hurt you?' my husband asked immediately, his eyes full of concern. He removed his powdered wig and thrust it into a coat pocket before running his fingers through his dark hair and loosening it so that it fell about his shoulders, lifting slightly in the breeze.

I shook my head. 'Not at all. What are they planning to do to us?'

The Duc shrugged. 'I have not the faintest idea and I don't think they know either.' He gave a sad smile. 'This is not at all the evening that I had planned for you, Lucrèce,' he said, taking my hand. 'I will make it up to you one day, I promise.'

I tried to return his smile. 'It doesn't matter.' I turned my head and looked across the Seine, the view blurred and obscured by the rain that was beginning to fall heavily now, catching in my husband's dark hair and eyelashes. 'With any luck they will get bored soon and let us go home.'

'I certainly hope so.' He looked past me to the other

captives, some of whom were beginning to make a fuss and loudly demand to be allowed to go.

'I insist that you let us leave immediately,' an overweight man in a straining pink silk coat was shouting. 'Don't you know who I am? I am the Marquis de Durfoy! I know the King and I could have you all horsewhipped for this impudence!'

'What a stupid, ridiculous fool,' the Duc murmured beneath his breath as the man tried to charge past his captors to his carriage only to be pushed back against the wall of the bridge and punched several times in the face. Adélaïde and I both cried out in shock and fear as he sank heavily to the ground, blood dripping thickly onto the pink silk of his coat.

'Let that be a lesson to all of you!' one of the crowd shouted, shaking his fist. 'We are the masters here now.' He jerked his head to the others. 'Round them all up. I do not think we have seen our last aristo blood this night! By morning the Bastille will be ours and we will be the masters of Paris!'

There was a scattered cheer at his words. To my horror, the mob began to advance upon us, waving their pistols and rusty sabres.

'Please, monsieurs, do not hurt me,' begged an older woman. 'We have done nothing wrong.' The men turned on her and she backed away until she was standing against the wet stone of the bridge. 'I am the Comtesse d'Almont,' she protested fumbling for coins in the velvet purse that hung from her waist. 'I have done nothing to you. I have always been kind to the poor.'

I stared in horror as the shouting, laughing crowd surrounded the Comtesse and dragged her away from the bridge wall. 'Don't watch,' I whispered to Adélaïde, pulling her close so that she could hide her face against my shoulder. 'Close your eyes.'

'Wait! Stop what you are doing!' We all turned our heads to see who had shouted out. A neatly-dressed young man with auburn hair came striding across the bridge towards us. 'Let that woman go! I order you!' He swept past us and advanced upon the crowd of men. They instantly released the bedraggled Comtesse,

who sagged to the ground, exhausted by her ordeal.

A dark, short man reeking of brandy stepped forward with a belligerent swagger. 'On whose authority?' He stood directly in front of the young man so that their chests were almost touching, and spat the tobacco that he was chewing on to the ground.

The newcomer did not so much as flinch, and the other men began to look at him with a new respect as they backed away.

'On the authority of Monsieur le Duc d'Orléans,' he replied, naming the one man in Paris that the mob had any respect for. 'He personally requested that I come here to ensure that the bridges are being manned in the proper manner. He will not be pleased to learn of what is happening here.' I let out my breath with relief, knowing that the Duc d'Orléans, who had placed himself directly against the royal family and on the side of the common Parisians, had more authority here than anyone. 'Now, are you going to let these people go or am I going to have to go straight to the Palais Royal and let him know that you disobeyed his orders?'

A moment passed and we all held our breath, waiting for the short dark man to reply.

'Well?' the young man prompted with the ghost of a smile, knowing that he had won.

'And who might you be?' The dark man was not giving up so easily.

'I am Xavier de Saint-Benoît,' the auburn haired one replied, smiling properly now. 'I am one of Monsieur le Duc's lawyers You can ask him yourself if you care to step across to the Palais Royal.'

'You don't look old enough to be a lawyer,' the man spat, looking doubtful now.

Xavier sighed and shrugged his shoulders. 'What can I say, monsieur? I am very clever and graduated early.' He began to turn away, impatiently shaking the rain out of his auburn hair. 'Monsieur le Duc would be more than happy to vouch for me should you have any doubts.'

The dark man looked furious but grudgingly nodded his head. 'As you wish, monsieur.' He jerked his head at the other men. 'Stand back and let the prisoners go.'

'Oh, thank God,' Adélaïde breathed.

We walked briskly back to our carriage, fearing the mob would change their minds and demand that we come back. Adélaïde climbed up first and I was about to follow when I realised that Xavier de Saint-Benoît was standing at my elbow, holding out his hand to help me up.

'I do not think that I could ever thank you enough, Monsieur de Saint-Benoît,' I said, turning to him with a grateful smile. 'You came just in time to save us from who knows what awful fate.'

He returned my smile. 'It was nothing, madame.' He looked past me to the Duc and gave a slight bow. 'I trust your journey will be without incident from now on, Monsieur le Duc.'

'Thank you,' my husband said with a grin. 'Now, tell me the truth, Monsieur de Saint-Benoît. Are you really a lawyer?'

Xavier laughed and shook his head. 'No, he was right. I am indeed far too young.' He helped me up into the carriage. 'I have no qualms using the Duc d'Orléans' name though, as he is my godfather and well used to getting me out of trouble by now.'

The Duc laughed and held out his hand. 'Then I am doubly grateful to you, monsieur, for asserting an authority you did not really possess in order to assist us.' The two men shook hands and smiled at each other, clearly liking what they saw. 'I hope to see you again one day, monsieur.'

'It would be an honour,' Xavier replied before closing the carriage door and stepping back with a final bow to myself and Adélaïde.

'How handsome Monsieur de Saint-Benoît is,' Adélaïde said with a little sigh as we pulled slowly away. 'I wish that all young men were as resourceful and courageous!' She rested her head against the carriage window to catch a last glimpse of him.

The Duc and I exchanged a smile. 'Yes, indeed,' I replied. 'Perhaps we should invite him to dinner at the Hôtel de Saliex and

get to know him a bit better?' I said idly, teasing her a little. Shyly, I used my husband's first name. 'What do you think, Armand?'

The Duc laughed. 'I think that it would be rude not to invite him, under the circumstances.'

After dropping Adélaïde at Penthémont, it did not take us long to get to the Hôtel de Saliex, the wheels of our carriage jolting noisily over the damp cobbles. The Duc and I sat in silence, gazing listlessly out into the street. Somehow I managed a smile, enjoying the unusual spectacle of so many people wandering past with their arms linked and faces upturned to the sky as they sang snatches of popular tunes.

The carriage pulled through a stone archway and rolled into the courtyard that lay before the colonnaded main entrance of the Hôtel. 'Home at last,' the Duc said as a swarm of liveried footmen ran forward and opened the doors before letting down the steps for us.

The Duc offered me his arm and we strolled slowly up the marble steps into the entrance hall. A group of blushing young maids in starched white aprons ran forward to take my cloak, hat and gloves.

I smiled at them and they giggled, bobbing low curtseys.

'This house hasn't had a mistress for many years now,' my husband remarked. 'This is new to all of us.'

After a subdued supper, I went upstairs to find the little gaggle of maids waiting for me in my enormous bedroom with its vast canopied bed and tall windows overlooking the beautiful gardens at the back of the Hôtel. I looked around me in delight, pausing below a portrait of a very indecently dressed lady with long blonde ringlets that barely covered her exposed breasts.

'That was your husband's grandmère,' one of the maids said with a giggle. 'The first Duchesse de Saliex.' Another maid pulled a face and nudged her but she shrugged them off. 'She was mistress to the old King Louis.'

'Really?' I picked up a delicate crystal bottle of scent and removed the stopper. The room filled with the delicious and heady smell of violets and lilies.

'The Duc had the room decorated just for you,' the same girl offered with a smile as I continued to look around. 'He asked your sister to help him design it, as a surprise.'

'Cassandre?' I might have known. The room was more to her taste than mine but I would love it all the more for that. It would be like she was with me every morning and night.

The girls clustered around me as they brushed out my long hair, unclipped my pearl earrings, slipped off my silk shoes and stockings, then wiped my face clean with lavender water. I sat all the while before the dressing table mirror and pressed my fingers against my anxiously beating heart.

They were dabbing rose oil on my temples when the bells began to ring out across the city. At first I thought it was just the bell of a church nearby, perhaps that of austere Saint Sulpice. Then I quickly realised the sound was too loud to be simply one bell and that it was in fact the work of many.

The girls looked at each other as I sprang up from the dressing table and ran to the window, pulling the heavy curtains aside and peering out into the darkness. 'What is happening out there?' I asked of no one in particular, not really expecting an answer. 'Why are all the bells ringing?'

'It's the Bastille, madame,' one of the girls explained. 'The people of Paris are planning to seize it for themselves. The bells are a call to arms.' She looked at me almost defiantly.

'The Bastille,' I whispered. 'It can't be.' I thought of the enormous black edifice that had towered over the Rue de Saint Antoine for as long as I could remember. 'No, that simply isn't possible.'

CASSANDRE

Versailles, October 1789

I had known from the very first moment that he would be mine, striding confident and vital into the midst of the throng in the Hall of Mirrors. He saw me at once, and stared at me for a long moment before turning away to greet the rustling, giggling huddle of ladies who rushed up to him, their pastel silk and muslin skirts clustered together like blooms in a garden.

'Who is that?' I whispered to Lucien, pointing my mother of pearl handled fan at the newcomer just in case he was in any doubt who I meant. 'I have never seen him before.'

Lucien laughed. 'That is Monsieur le Vicomte de Barthèlmy. He has been lurking on his estates in Brittany for the last three years.' He shrugged. Like every other man in the room he regarded the Vicomte with a mixture of admiration, envy and vexation. 'His mother was an English adventuress who happened to marry into the Breton nobility. I believe that he chose to retire there when Paris became too, shall we say, hot for him.'

I turned to my brother and grinned behind my peacock feather fan. 'Oh? Tell me more.'

Covertly, I watched as the Vicomte walked down the gallery, greeting old friends and kissing the hands of all the ladies.

To my chagrin, he did not glance again in my direction but I had been at Versailles for long enough to realise that this was all part of the game, annoying though it might be. I have always preferred a more direct approach in my flirtations but if that is how he wanted things to be, then so be it.

I saw my husband, Eugène, leaning against one of the huge mirrors that lined one side of the gallery, ostensibly listening to the simpering of the over-rouged woman in bright pink standing next to him, but with his eyes fixed as usual on me.

I had fancied myself in love with Eugène when we were first betrothed, and he came to Penthémont with Papa and Grandmère one balmy, lemon-scented afternoon to pay his respects and present me with a diamond ring to mark our engagement. My friends and I had hung over the banisters, giggling and shamelessly ogling him as he walked down the corridor with a swift wink and smile up at us.

Only Lucrèce stood a little apart, pale and tight lipped as she watched the young Marquis swagger past.

A year had passed since her wedding to the wickedly handsome Duc de Saliex. After her one day of glory as a bride, she had been sent back to Penthémont in her virgin state and with very little to show for her new status. Her new husband had hurried back to his diplomatic duties in Rome with Honorine, Comtesse d'Evrémond, in hot pursuit. It was understandable that Lucrèce had no reason to be excited by the prospect of a wedding.

'Your Marquis is handsome,' my friend Cécile had whispered. 'You are so lucky, Cassandre.'

'That's quite enough of that, Mademoiselle de Pons,' Soeur Thérèse ordered as she clumped heavily up the stone stairs in the muddy boots that she wore in the garden, knocking clods of earth all over the floor and scattering all of the girls except myself, Lucrèce and Cécile in her wake so that they ran, laughing and shrieking down the corridor.

'Mademoiselle de Saint-Valèry,' she said, fixing me with a stern look from beneath her bushy, greying eyebrows, 'are you ready to come with me? Monsieur le Comte has someone that he would like to introduce to you.'

I had felt quite sick with dread as Soeur Thérèse knocked briskly on the door, then led me without ceremony into the room. I was horribly self-conscious about my school uniform, plaits and plain black leather shoes that squeaked slightly as I walked.

What would he think of me? It would have been so much better if I could have worn one of my own pretty dresses and put my auburn hair up so that I could at least look like myself rather than just a schoolgirl. But the nuns would never have agreed to such a thing.

I need not have worried, for his eyes lit up as soon as I walked into the room. Eugène took both my hands and raised them to his lips while Soeur Thérèse clucked her tongue disapprovingly. 'You are far more beautiful than I had expected,' he murmured with a touching mixture of approval and relief. 'They said that you were pretty but I was not expecting you to be so lovely in every way.'

I raised my eyes to his face, drinking in his chiselled good looks, his elegant build and the way his long blond hair was pulled back in a simple pony tail. There was a spray of apple blossom tucked into the brim of the black hat he had thrown onto a nearby chair; its fresh scent filled the room as we looked at each other and smiled.

We were married shortly afterwards in the beautiful but austere church of Saint Sulpice in Paris. With the royal family and most of the court watching, I walked slowly up the aisle in a gown of white taffeta with a gold-fringed scarf and fragrant peach roses in my powdered hair. I would never forget the look on Eugène's face as I sailed towards him. It made me feel beautiful, grown up and above all, desirable. His fingers were warm as he took my hand and we stiffly knelt down together before the altar. I remember glancing across at him from beneath my eyelashes, and thinking how lucky I was to have such a handsome husband.

I floated through that day, unwilling to stray too far from my husband's side as I gazed up at him in lustful adoration and thrilled every time someone told me what a lovely couple we made. Which was often. Even the Queen, who had come wearing a blue silk gown with white roses and diamonds at her bosom, kissed both my cheeks and whispered how lucky I was. You can say what you like about Marie Antoinette, and people frequently do, but you can't deny that she has an eye for a handsome young man.

I was still excited when all of the guests had melted away and we found ourselves alone in the vast blue and silver bedroom that we were to share in the Hôtel de Vautière on the Rue de l'Université. My maids undressed me quickly, giggling as they unlaced my exquisite wedding dress, now sadly stained with wine and cake crumbs ,then let down and brushed out my long red hair. 'This will inflame his desire for you,' they whispered as I sat pale faced and nervous in front of the tarnished dressing table mirror, which I noticed was decorated with dimpled, rose bedecked gilt cupids. 'I have never seen a man so hot for a woman,' they said as they pulled a fine lawn chemise over my head, then dabbed me with lily and rose scent.

They drifted away with muted laughter and sly, sidelong looks as soon as my new husband came into the room. He was dressed in a crimson velvet robe and with his thick blond hair hanging loose about his shoulders. He stood for a moment staring at me as I rose slowly from my chair and then walked towards him, my heart hammering nervously in my breast.

'You are so beautiful,' he whispered, reaching out to touch my long hair. 'You cannot know how much I have longed for this.'

'Oh, I do know,' I murmured. 'I have longed for it too.'

He reached out and pulled me towards him, crushing me to his bare chest as his hot mouth sought mine. I clung to him, my fingernails digging into his shoulders as he lifted me up and clumsily carried me to the enormous wooden four poster bed, which was hung with beautiful blue and silver brocade hangings edged with silver fringing.

'I had the room redecorated just for you,' he murmured. 'I hope it makes you happy.' He kissed my neck, his lips moving lower and lower as the chemise dropped from my shoulders.

'I am so happy, so happy,' I agreed as he kissed my breasts, his warm tongue flickering over my hardening nipples.

I stretched my arms up above my head, then dug my hands in his hair, pulling him closer as he reared up and kissed me. His tongue intertwined with mine, his fingers touching every melting part of me.

'Are you afraid?' he whispered in my ear, his hot breath making me sigh and wriggle beneath his hands. 'I will try not to hurt you, Cassandre. I want you so much.'

I smiled and bit his shoulder. 'I don't mind if you hurt me,' I whispered back, pulling the robe from his shoulders and kissing his chest. 'I just want you to do it.' I felt him hard against me and moaned. 'I know what I want, Eugène.'

My husband grinned and kissed me. 'What did they teach you at that school of yours?' he panted as he thrust hard into me, stifling my cries of mingled pain and desire with his mouth.

I closed my eyes and dug my hands into his shoulders, holding on tight until suddenly he cried out and slumped heavily against me. It was pleasant enough, if a bit sore but not quite the explosion of sheer blissful pleasure that I had been anticipating all day long thanks to my furtive readings of certain novels.

I looked fondly at my new husband as he lay prone beside me, his chest rising and falling. I was ready with a happy, satisfied smile when he finally opened his eyes, brushed his fair hair impatiently out of his face and looked directly at me.

'Are you sure that you are a virgin?' he asked, his sulky voice falling heavily into the cosy silence that had fallen between us. Or rather, I had thought it cosy. Yet while I was happily smiling to myself and thinking about how much I wanted him to kiss me again, he had been brooding upon my imagined iniquity and, already, my failings as a wife. 'You seemed more enthusiastic than I had expected and it didn't even seem to hurt you.'

'I ride horses a lot,' I replied quickly, moving away from him to the other side of the bed, shocked by how quickly his amorous mood had changed to jealousy and suspicion. 'I go every other day to the Bois de Boulogne to put my horse, Reinette through her paces. I have heard that riding can make the loss of virginity much less painful.' I wrapped the sheet around me and looked directly at him with my head to one side. 'I thought you enjoyed it.' I reached out and tried to take his hand but he pulled roughly away.

'Were you a virgin?' he demanded again petulantly. 'They all said that I should be careful because of your mother but I decided to marry you anyway. Now I am not so sure.'

I caught my breath at the mention of my mother. Surely she had no place here, in my marriage bed? And who were "they" anyway? Did I already have enemies about me in my new life? I thought about my new mother-in-law, a fussy woman with a breathless little voice and silly, affected manners. Did she hate me? What about his trio of mousy-haired, pop-eyed, shuffling little sisters? Did they hate me too? I wouldn't have thought they had enough spirit to hate anyone, let alone me.

'Of course I was a virgin,' I replied soothingly, hiding my agitation behind a smile. 'I have had no dealings with any other men. How could I when I was so closely watched at the convent and in my father's home?' I sighed and moved towards him, letting my chemise fall from my shoulders again. 'How can you doubt that you were my first? I have been saving myself for this moment. If I was too enthusiastic, it is only because your touch inflamed me so much.'

'Is that true?' he asked, closing his eyes as I nuzzled against him, kissing his neck and taking his ear lobe between my teeth.

'Of course it is true.' I put my arms around his shoulders and kissed his lips until finally he relaxed and kissed me back. 'Don't ruin our first night together, Eugène,' I whispered against his mouth as his hands began to move towards my breasts. 'We have both wanted this so much, let's not allow anything to come between us.'

I smiled invitingly as he pushed me on to my back and pulled my legs apart, but it was all pretence. I sighed, moaned and gasped whenever he touched me. But all the while, my mind was elsewhere. I was thinking about what I was going to do now that my great romance, my wonderful marriage, was ruined.

Or perhaps not? The next morning he smiled at me shyly across the breakfast table and rubbed his foot against mine while the liveried footmen rolled their eyes and pretended not to notice. I watched nervously as he poured himself a cup of hot chocolate from the silver pot at his elbow, then added sugar and milk.

'I thought that today we might go to my château near Neuilly,' he said brightly, looking up at last. 'Would you like that, Cassandre?'

I forced a smile and nodded. 'Of course.' I crumpled my white linen napkin and dropped it on to my plate, then looked slowly around the exquisite dining room with its cream and gold mirrored walls. I had barely had enough time to become acquainted with his enormous Parisian house and now he wanted to carry me off somewhere else? Why could we not stay in Paris and get to know each other instead?

He noticed my hesitation. The charming smile was swiftly replaced by the sulky look I was learning to dread. 'Or we could always stay here?' he said, petulantly throwing his napkin aside. 'It is up to you, of course, and it is all the same to me.'

I saw the footmen begin to shift nervously, glancing at each other and raising their eyebrows. They had seen it all before. One or two of them might even have pitied me a little.

I lifted my chin and smiled as though I had not noticed anything amiss. 'How silly you are, mon cher,' I said with a laugh, pouring more thick hot chocolate into my delicate Sèvres cup. 'I can think of nothing nicer on such a lovely day than a trip to the countryside.'

And it was lovely. The house at Neuilly had powdery pink walls and tall, white-shuttered windows overlooking an enormous garden that ran all the way down to the river bank. We ate strawberries and cream, and toasted each other with champagne while sitting on the lichen-covered marble steps to the terrace. We then went upstairs to a bedroom with billowing muslin curtains, where he made me temporarily forget everything that had happened the night before. And then later on, frantically in the little Grecian pavilion that overlooked the Seine, where I wrapped my legs around his waist and finally realised what all the fuss was about.

Of course, I hoped that his odd moods and sulks would disappear as we became more used to each other. But this proved not to be the case. If anything he got worse, especially once the honeymoon period was over and I returned to Versailles to begin my new duties as one of the Queen's ladies-in-waiting. If my handsome new husband was suspicious and petulant when we were alone, then he was doubly so once I was surrounded by the charming young men that Marie Antoinette loved at her court, men with sly eyes, painted and powdered faces, and a tantalising hint of muscle beneath their rose-scented silk coats.

There were sulks, jealous scenes, and even threats to have me removed from court and sent to a convent. Finally, he strode across the polished parquet floor at one of Madame de Polignac's intimate little parties, and slapped me across the face for daring to laugh too loudly at one of the Duc de Lauzun's admittedly improper jokes. The sound of his slap resounded through the cramped, hot little room. The music drifted away as everyone turned to stare at me, their crimson painted mouths slack with shock. I stumbled slowly away from him, holding one hand up to my red, stinging cheek and the other out before me, preventing him from coming near me again.

'My dear Marquis,' Lauzun began to say, laughing a little nervously as he placed his hand on Eugène's grey silk arm. 'I think you must have forgotten yourself.'

Lauzun was an old friend of mine and had known me since I was an impudent little mademoiselle in white muslin sitting at my Grandmère's elbow in her red and gold salon in Paris. Despite his shocking reputation, he had always been a favourite with the old ladies of the court and had flirted innocently with me whenever her back was turned, pinching my cheeks, showering me with practised but nonetheless charming compliments and making me blush. It shamed me that he should witness this awful scene.

'I am not the one who has forgotten himself,' Eugène retorted with one last contemptuous look at me before he turned on his high red heels and walked from the room, leaving a fluttering of fans and a whisper of rumour in his wake.

'My dear, you should sit down.' Lauzun took me by the elbow and gently steered me through the staring, murmuring crowd to one of the pale blue upholstered chairs that stood against the wall. 'You have had a terrible shock.'

He shook his head at Madame de Polignac who looked as though she was about to come after us, With a tight-lipped smile and a shrug of her thin shoulders, she turned away.

'Thank you.' I sat down, blinking away my tears and doing my best to keep my head held high despite all the stares in my direction. 'They are saying that I am just like my mother aren't they?'

It was not really a question. People had been comparing me to Sidonie for as long as I could remember. How unfair. As far as I could tell, the poor girl had taken just a couple of lovers, whereas the women at court who stared at me and whispered about my mother must have had dozens in their time.

Lauzun was silent for a long, uncomfortable moment, then inclined his head slightly. 'They are fools,' he said, stretching his long legs out in front of him. 'Your mother was one of the most charming women that Paris has ever seen and was more sinned against than sinner.' He looked at me then as I stared back at him, unused to hearing my mother defended. 'I hope you know that, Cassandre, and do not judge her too harshly.'

I must have looked ashamed because he sighed and put his hand over mine, giving it a comforting squeeze. 'I can imagine the sort of thing that they have told you about poor Sidonie,' he murmured. 'Athénaïs, your grandmother, was never very fond of her.'

I smiled then. 'I think that that must be an understatement.' I looked at him then, deciding that it was about time I heard the truth. 'Were you one of her lovers?'

He laughed. 'Ah.'

I looked at him, thinking how handsome he was for a man of how old? Thirty-five? Forty? He had not done a stroke of work in his life, of course and his face was as smooth and unlined as that of a man half his age. Yet there was something in his dark eyes that was weary, that looked out upon the world and found it wanting.

'Tell me.'

He turned to me then with a rueful smile. 'As I said, I thought she was the most charming woman in Paris. No one could have been more loveable, more desirable in every way.'

I nodded. 'What was she like?' The music had begun again and people were beginning to drift away from us, their short attentions already captured by some other tasty piece of gossip. I was no fool though and knew that this incident would be picked over in full in the morning when the court met in the Versailles chapel for Mass. I was already considering developing a headache so I could escape their vicious stares.

Lauzun reached across and took my hand. 'Your mother was perfect in every way and she loved you children more than she loved anything else in the whole world.'

'So why did she leave us then?' I asked, furiously blinking away tears. 'She can't have loved us all that much, can she? I can't even remember what she looked like.'

People were beginning to look again and I raised up my chin, proudly staring them all down.

He gently touched my cheek, wiping away a stray tear. 'Oh Cassandre, I think they must have lied to you about what happened. 'You should know that she did not go willingly, that they had to drag her from the house. She pleaded with your father to let her take you with her but he refused. So she went alone.'

I stared at him in shock. 'Is that true?' All my life I had been told by my father and Grandmère that Sidonie had left willingly, was glad to go and leave us with our father, and that she had had no desire to take us with her, not even Adélaïde, who was just a sweet little podgy baby at the time and whom she had clearly adored. I had hated her for this. Hated her for not loving any of us enough to stay, for not wanting us. Could it be that I had got it all wrong?

Lauzun squeezed my hand. 'Look into your heart, Cassandre. Surely you know that they were lying to you? Poor Sidonie never stood a chance.'

He put his finger to his lips. I looked up to see Aimée, the beautiful Duchesse de Fleury, walking towards us, her wide lavender blue silk skirts swaying provocatively. I had heard that Aimée, who at twenty years old was just two years older than myself, was Lauzun's latest mistress. But if it was true, they gave very little sign of it and greeted each other like distant acquaintances.

'I heard what happened,' she said to me without preamble, in her usual direct way, fixing me with pale green eyes. 'How perfectly shocking it must have been for you.'

I forced myself to smile. 'Yes, it was.'

She shook back long blonde ringlets, her glittering gaze resting on Lauzun for a long moment as she did so. So it was true after all. 'What do you propose to do now?' she asked.

I gave a shrug. 'What can I do? If I leave him, then I will be banished from court forever, and if I stay then I will have to endure his ridiculous behaviour for the rest of my days.'

Pathetically, I felt like crying. The rules at Versailles were strict and the Queen, so silly and inconsequential in many respects, had decreed that no woman who was separated from her husband could be received at court. If I left Eugène, then I would have to return to Paris, and my life here, which I loved so much, would be changed forever.

'You need to decide what is most important to you,' Aimée observed. 'Be warned though that it will be impossible to keep this incident quiet. The gossip queens are probably already vying to be the first to lay this particular titbit before Her Majesty.' She sighed and rolled huge eyes. 'And you know how much she adores the latest gossip. I have never known anyone so quick to dislike a person based only on a scurrilous and unproven rumour.'

She was right, of course. It took all of my courage to walk into the Queen's bedroom the next morning to take part in the ceremonial levée that marked the official beginning of her day. Whispers and stares followed me all the way down the Hall of Mirrors but I did my best to straighten my shoulders and shrug them off, keeping my gaze straight ahead and drawing courage from the sharp click clack of my high red heels against the shiny, polished parquet. I was under no illusions that the previous night's incident might not have come to the ears of the Queen, but I allowed myself a brief moment of hope as I sidled into her jasmine-scented bedchamber and took up a position by the windows. The toile curtains were resolutely closed against the bright autumn sun, which the Queen claimed to find incredibly unflattering to her complexion. Marie Antoinette was sitting in front of her enormous dressing table, staring miserably at her reflection and running a swansdown powder puff back and forth across her pale bosom, exposed by her low cut lace-trimmed negligé. Her expression was petulant and bored, which had the effect of drawing her mouth downward and accentuating the Roman bridge of her nose.

I breathed a silent sigh of relief that she did not yet appear to have noticed me.

The other ladies smirked and elbowed each other sharply. I forced myself to smile at them, baring my teeth, defying them to say something. Madame de Polignac, who stood in her usual position at the Queen's elbow, was the only one to meet my eye, shrugging apologetically and pursing her full cherry-red lips.

'Madame la Marquise de Vautière?' The Queen did not look at me as she said my name. I felt slightly sick as I stepped forward from my hiding place and made my way to her side.

'Your Majesty?' I dropped a curtsey while she hid a yawn behind her hand, dozens of pearl, ruby and diamond bracelets clicking as she moved her arm. 'You asked for me?'

I straightened up and waited as she fiddled with the very

feminine mess of bottles, jars, scraps of lace and pots of rouge that lay spread out before her.

'I heard about what happened last night,' she said at last, holding a diamond earring up to her ear and turning her head this way and that to admire it before casting it aside. 'Your husband's outburst is the talk of the court it would seem.' She looked up at me then, a frown between her blue eyes.

'I thought as much,' I said cautiously, remembering Aimée's warning. I heard the other ladies in waiting whispering and giggling and sighed. I wasn't popular here and most of them would be only too happy to see me sent packing back to Paris in disgrace. 'It was really nothing.'

'Nothing?' She tittered and after a pause the other women joined in, their laughter too high pitched and nervous to ever be considered natural. 'I heard that he slapped you, Madame la Marquise!'

I took a deep breath and forced myself to smile, making light of the situation. 'Oh no, it was the merest tap, your Majesty.' I lowered my voice as though about to impart a great secret. Unable to resist, the Queen leaned towards me. 'You know how passionate and wild my husband is,' I said with an expressive roll of my eyes. 'We are so in love, your Majesty, that when he saw me talking to the Duc de Lauzun, he quite lost control of himself, the silly boy.'

'Ah, Lauzun.' Marie Antoinette gave a tiny shrug. 'That man is a danger to all women.' She gave me a sharp look. 'I find it very odd though that your husband should have reacted in such a way to your merely talking to Monsieur le Duc.'

'I have known Lauzun ever since I was a little girl.' I fluttered my hands vaguely. 'You know how impulsive and romantic young men can be, your Majesty. They act before they think and are quick to take offence where none was intended.' I gave a sigh. 'My husband loves me so much that I fear it sends him a little mad sometimes.'

'I see.'

She turned away then and began to fiddle with her

diamonds and rouge pots again. It was a lie, of course, as she didn't see at all. Poor Marie Antoinette; she loved to surround herself with virile, handsome young men, with artists and poets who raved at length about her beauty and charm. But no man had ever been madly, insanely, crazily in love with her, least of all her husband. She had never had anyone stare at her hungrily across the room, had never been wept about, or kissed all over her body until she cried for mercy. She had all the trappings of romance: beautiful palaces, lovely clothes, friends, flattery and wealth but none of the reality. She was loved, but not adored. I looked around at the faces of her ladies, carefully composed into polite, docile smiles.

She made an impatient gesture with her hand and Madame de Polignac immediately stepped forward, her taffeta skirts rustling as she took my arm and led me away. 'Her Majesty has been fretful this morning,' she whispered. 'She thinks that she looks old and nothing can distract her from feeling sorry for herself.' She gave a tiny smile. 'You know how she can be.'

'Oh yes, I know.'

I had been at court all my life, ever since my first visit as a shy little girl hiding behind my grandmère's black and gold brocade skirts, round-eyed with amazement. She had led me up the crowded Hall of Mirrors to be introduced to the pretty new Queen who sat in a high backed gilt chair and blushed as she dipped her powdered white and pink head in greeting.

'I am truly sorry about what happened last night,' I added. 'It was shocking behaviour on Eugène's part.'

Gabrielle de Polignac shrugged and rolled her hazel eyes. 'He is young and hot-headed, so these things are to be expected.' She patted my arm. 'He will be a fine man one day, you know. Do not be too hard on him.'

I did not have to wait long before I saw Eugène again; he was waiting for me by the entrance to the royal chapel and stepped out so that I could see him as the Queen and her ladies swept past on their way to Mass. The liveried palace pages darted between us, carrying large velvet kneeling cushions with prayer books precariously balanced on top while our dogs ran freely underfoot, snarling and snapping at our long skirts.

'Please come with me,' he pleaded, his breath soured by wine. 'I need to talk to you.'

He looked terrible. His handsome face was pale and drawn, and there were dark shadows beneath his eyes. It was obvious that he had sent his valet away and dressed himself, tying his muslin cravat loosely and shrugging on a black velvet jacket with little care for how it looked.

I found myself nodding. We made our way back through the splendid reception rooms, empty now except for a few footmen and pages, who lounged on the velvet-covered chairs and stools and stood begrudgingly to attention as we walked past. The rest of the courtiers were at Mass in the chapel, determined to remain as close as possible to the King and Queen.

'I am truly sorry for what happened between us,' Eugène said, leading me into a sunlit window alcove that looked over the splendid gardens below. I could see a group of young maids making the most of the court being at Mass and splashing each other with water from one of the fountains. 'I have no idea what came over me, Cassandre. I wish with all my heart that I could go back and act differently.' He looked as though he was about to cry.

'And so you should,' I replied, more harshly than I had intended, dragging my gaze away from the girls below. How I envied them at that moment. 'Eugène, you behaved disgracefully and embarrassed me, not just in front of the entire court but also before someone who has known me since childhood. Have you any idea how mortifying that is?'

'Oh, Lauzun,' he said dully, rolling his blue eyes. 'I am sorry, Cassandre. I misunderstood how things are between you.' He tried to take my hand but I resolutely withheld it, pressing it close to my breast. 'I don't know why but I saw red and simply could not tolerate it for another moment.'

'Tolerate what, Eugène?' I demanded. 'I don't understand! Nothing happened!'

He pulled off his wig and cast it aside. 'I know that.' He

looked at me. 'I do know that, Cassandre, I swear. It is just that I love you so much, and yet ... '

I caught my breath. 'And yet?' I rested my back against the chill marble of the alcove and gazed out across the neat parterres again. 'What is it, Eugène? What is so dreadful, so utterly horrific about me that you just cannot find it within your heart to trust me?'

'Maman says ... ' Ah of course, his mother. I knew it. 'She says that I was wrong to marry you, that you are ... '

'Too much like my mother,' I finished for him. 'Of course.' I looked at him, bravely smiling as I met his eyes. 'It needed only that.' And I turned and walked away.

We remained married, of course, but in name only. I would appear at his side whenever etiquette decreed it, and whenever I had to stay in Paris, I would sleep in his house but at all other times we led separate lives. Most people guessed, but while we remained silent on the matter, they were too well bred to ever comment on it. And, to be frank, living apart from your spouse was hardly an unusual state of affairs at court.

Eugène never seemed fully reconciled to the situation but never again behaved as he did at Madame de Polignac's party, preferring to watch me from afar but say nothing. I should have been used to it but when I saw him watching me in the Hall of Mirrors that afternoon, my heart sank. I had a feeling that some sort of outburst was imminent.

'Why do you not reconcile with him?' Lucien asked, nudging me with his elbow and looking towards Eugène, who had turned away and was talking to the girl in pink with forced enthusiasm. I expected to hear in the morning that he had bedded her, one of the many silly little sluts that he had picked up then discarded since I rejected him. 'Or at least separate from him properly so that you can both begin again?'

I stared at him. 'Are you insane, Lucien? Do you not think that I would have left him years ago if only I was able to?' I lowered my voice. There was little privacy at court. 'If I leave him then, I will have to leave my post at court and be banished from

Versailles forever.' I grimaced. 'Can you imagine how awful that would be for someone like me?'

Lucien sighed. 'There is more to life than all this, Cassandre.' He gestured at the magnificent gallery and the beautifully dressed, spoilt people who stood chattering within it, their eyes darting here and there all the time, constantly searching for something new, for someone more important to distract them. 'This really means very little in the general scheme of things.'

'Does it, Lucien?' I asked, raising my eyebrows. 'Perhaps it means very little to you, but let me assure you that it means a great deal to me.'

There was no point trying to explain to him that this was all I had ever wanted in life, that I had listened, round-eyed and silent with awe to Grandmère's stories of the court under old King Louis and decided that I wanted to be a part of that beautiful, brittle, glamorous world. No point at all in trying to explain how thrilled I had been when I had first arrived after my marriage, surrounded by trunks full of splendid dresses and more than ready to take my place amongst the Queen's ladies-in-waiting.

'If your marriage was annulled, then you could get married again, have children.' My brother faltered when he noticed the expression of chill distaste on my face. 'Cassandre, the Bastille has fallen. Every single day our world is changing. Perhaps you should change with it.'

I was getting impatient now and looked over the heads of the crowd for the Vicomte de Barthèlmy but he was nowhere to be seen. 'I don't want to change, Lucien. My place is here at court.'

What was he talking about? I snapped out my fan and waved it in front of my face, my eyes darting around the room.

'There probably won't be a court for much longer,' Lucien muttered. 'Not at Versailles anyway.'

'What do you mean?' I stared at him now. Had he gone insane?

'Don't you read any newspapers, Cassandre? Or talk to anyone but the Queen and her stupid ladies-in-waiting?' Now it was Lucien's turn to sound impatient. 'It never ceases to amaze me how some people are so content to take so little interest in what is happening right in front of them.' He rolled his eyes. 'The Queen of course is simply in denial but the rest of you have no such excuse!'

I shrugged, still looking around for the Vicomte. Where had he gone? 'That sort of conversation bores me. If you want to talk about dull things like that, you would be better off visiting Adélaïde at Penthèmont.'

'Oh, Cassandre.' Lucien looked like he wanted to be cross but couldn't help but laugh. 'I would offer to send you some pamphlets about the latest news in Paris but what would be the point?'

I laughed. 'Lucien, there would be no point whatsoever.' I touched his cheek. 'Send them to Adélaïde instead.'

There was a discreet cough at my elbow. I turned to see one of the Queen's liveried footman standing behind me. 'Madame la Marquise, her Majesty requests your company this afternoon when she goes to the Petit Trianon.'

I looked at Lucien and raised an eyebrow. 'Now, there's a surprise.'

I had plenty of time to be alone with my thoughts that afternoon at the Petit Trianon. The Queen had gone off on her own to her little grotto, keen to enjoy the rare luxury of solitude. It was a beautiful day, sunny and bright with a few rain showers that sent the other ladies shrieking and giggling indoors. I had never cared about the rain though and settled myself on the stone steps that led down from the château to the gardens, pulling my soft cashmere shawl close around my shoulders and keeping my parasol close to hand, just in case.

I breathed a sigh of contentment as I looked around the gardens, enjoying the fresh air, the distant sound of birdsong and the piano music. It was a perfect day, a perfect moment. I wandered across the grass to the Belvedere, a small white pavilion beside the lake, decorated inside with pretty, fanciful arabesque designs on the walls and a painted sky with clouds on the ceiling.

It was a glorious day, the sun was dappled over the

marble floor, bees humming around the last of the fragrant summer roses. I sank down upon the green silk covered sofa that stood in the centre of the pavilion and idly pulled a discarded fashion magazine towards me, the corners of the pages dog eared and torn where they had been turned over.

I allowed the magazine to slip from my hand and leaned my head back against the sofa, closing my eyes as I breathed in the fresh autumn air and the voluptuous scent of the flowers that were everywhere at Trianon. It all seemed a million miles away from the troubles in Paris and the stresses of the past few months. Suddenly I understood why the Queen was so passionately attached to her little château and loved to spend so much time here, especially since the sad loss of her eldest son, the Dauphin, earlier that year.

The honeyed tranquillity of this scene was broken by a shout from the direction of the Trianon.

I sprang to my feet, my cashmere shawl falling to the floor as one of the Queen's young pages came running towards the Belvedere.

As the page ran, his hat fell off. He left it behind him, lying forlorn, a black splodge in the middle of the lawn.

I saw that he was absolutely terrified, his dark eyes wide with fear. With a cry of alarm I lifted up my white silk skirts and ran to meet him.

'What is it?' I cried, catching the boy as in his panic he fell towards me. 'What has happened?'

'Madame la Marquise, we must alert the Queen immediately!' The boy was sobbing now and clinging to my hands. 'The women of Paris are marching on Versailles. They will be here in only a few hours. Madame, they mean to kill the Queen and take the rest of the royal family back to Paris!'

I stared at him in uncomprehending horror. 'Mon dieu, it must be a mistake,' I breathed, knowing all the while that he spoke the truth and there was no mistake. It was not entirely unexpected after all – it was only due to our own complacent stupidity that everyone had forgotten the very real threat that the people of Paris posed to Versailles. I remembered what Lucien had said to me all those hours ago in the Hall of Mirrors and felt sick. Not everyone had been stupid.

'There is no mistake, madame,' the page replied, wiping away his tears with the back of his sleeve. All etiquette was forgotten at that moment. 'Monsieur le Comte de Saint-Priest himself sent me.' The Comte de Saint-Priest was one of the King's ministers and much respected at court. 'I have been instructed to bring the Queen back to Versailles as quickly as possible.'

He scampered alongside me as I turned and ran back, my heart beating painfully in my breast.

When we reached the grotto, I turned and put my finger to my lips. 'You should wait here while I go and fetch the Queen.'

He looked annoyed at being robbed of his moment of drama but, amidst much grumbling, complied and leaned against a tree while I pushed my way through the overhanging branches to the grotto. In the distance I could hear the shouts and screams of the other ladies as the news spread and they ran across the lawn towards us.

'Your Majesty?' It was gloomy inside and it took a moment for my eyes to adjust to the dim light.

'Who is that?' The Queen's voice rang out imperiously and faintly churlish. 'I thought that I gave orders not to be disturbed under any circumstances?' She stepped forward from the darkness, her pale muslin gown shimmering in the green and eerie sunlight that floated through the trees overhead. 'Well? What is it?'

'It is Cassandre, the Marquise de Vautière.' I took a deep breath. 'I am sorry, madame, but you have to return to the palace immediately.' She had seen me now and I dropped a hasty curtsey. 'Madame, the people are marching here from Paris.'

'The people are marching here from Paris?' she repeated, raising a hand to clutch the fine cashmere shawl around her shoulders. 'What do you mean?' She looked shocked, and peered at me as though she didn't quite understand what I was saying.

I felt suddenly impatient. 'Madame, they are coming to

Versailles and intend to take you back with them to the capital.' I stepped back and held the branches up so that she could walk through. 'You are in the gravest danger here and must return to the palace where you can be properly guarded.'

A carriage was waiting for us in the courtyard. I stepped aside as one of the footmen helped the Queen inside before clambering in myself, closing the door with a slam behind me.

'I have forgotten something...' Marie Antoinette murmured, putting her hand on the gilt door handle.

'Madame, there is no more time,' I said. 'One of the pages can come back for it.'

The carriage sprang away and I leaned back, gazing out of the window as we drove out of the gates for what might well be the very last time. I dared to steal just one look at my mistress' distraught face as we rolled away from the beautiful château that she adored so much and that had brought her so much happiness.

'Why do I have the feeling that I will never see my poor Trianon again?' she asked in a plaintive tone.

I forced a smile. 'I am sure you will be able to return tomorrow, madame,' I replied with a confidence that I did not entirely feel. 'It is bound to be a false alarm.'

I leaned my head against the seat and gazed out at the gardens, my thoughts not with the spoilt woman sitting opposite but with my sister and Adélaïde, both of whom were still in Paris. What was happening there?

It did not take long to reach the main château and the large groups of troops milling about in the Cour d'Armes and Cour Royale made it clear that the ominous news had already spread throughout Versailles. As the Queen's coach pulled up in the courtyard several liveried royal guards ran forward to surround it as Marie Antoinette and I were helped down and then hustled into the building, through the marble vestibule and up the ornate Queen's Staircase to her apartment, just as a heavy downpour of rain lashed mercilessly against the windows and sent the troops running for cover.

'Cassandre?'

I turned my head to see my brother, standing in one of the tall windows of the Queen's salon. He might have been dressed with his usual exquisite care in a suit of shimmering midnight blue silk with barely a lace or button out of place but I immediately noticed that his handsome face was careworn and anxious.

'Thank God that you are safe,' he said quietly, closing his arms around me as I rushed into his embrace. 'I have been waiting here since I first heard the news.'

'What is happening, Lucien?' We moved into the shelter of the window. The rain was still coming down heavily and I wondered about the army of women and how they were coping in the deluge.

'They must be soaked to the skin,' I murmured, gazing across the terrace, which was covered with troops, all standing about nervously and giving the appearance of not knowing quite what to do with themselves. In the distance I could see a small group of soldiers trying their best to close the enormous palace gates, which had become rusted to the ground through decades of standing open.

We stood for a while in silence, watching the stream of anxious courtiers as they made their way through the Queen's rooms, pausing every few minutes to plaintively ask every chance acquaintance if there was more news. 'The King is in a council meeting,' Lucien remarked at last. 'His ministers are advising him to withdraw to Rambouillet with his family but he is steadfastly refusing to abandon Versailles.' He sighed. 'Our only hope is the Queen. It may be that she will be able to persuade him to leave.'

I stared at him. 'You really believe it would be best to run away?'

'I do not think that there is anything to be gained from remaining here at Versailles.' My brother shrugged and helped himself to some snuff, its sharp cinnamon tang floating through the air. 'We are at the mercy of the canaille. I am told that there are several hundred women from the poorest faubourgs of Paris marching on the château,' he said, looking out of the window. 'If they manage to get past the guards, we will all be slaughtered.'

I gave a nervous laugh. 'Surely they are not savages?' I said. 'I refuse to believe that they have come all this way just to murder us.'

Lucien raised an eyebrow. 'My dear, they are telling all and sundry that they are coming for the Queen's head, and I, for one, believe them.'

I gasped and leaned back against the wall, suddenly faint. 'I do not believe it,' I whispered. 'I know that she is hated but I cannot believe that they actually wish to do her harm!'

I left him and went into the Queen's beautiful, luxurious bedchamber, which was usually so serene and relaxing but which was now filled with terrified courtiers. Their eyes were wild with fear as they chewed over the few scraps of information. The usually sweetly perfumed air had become sharp with the scent of sweat and pure, unadulterated terror. The Queen herself was seated in a comfortable armchair by the fireplace and looking very different to how she had looked only an hour earlier. Gone was the frightened, tearful, lost looking woman of the Trianon. In her place sat the composed and dignified daughter of an Empress. I no longer had any doubt that I was in the presence of a Queen. Never before had she looked so regal. Could it be that adversity would be the making of Marie Antoinette?

'I know that they have come from Paris to demand my head, but I learned from my mother not to fear death.' Marie Antoinette looked slowly around the assembled courtiers, who fell into a hush at her words. 'I shall await it with firmness, at the side of my husband.'

There was a flurry of activity as Madame la Princesse de Lamballe and several other ladies fell sobbing loudly to their knees in front of her, kissing her bejewelled hand and professing eternal devotion.

I made my way to the side of Aimée de Coigny, who was standing beside the door, looking impossibly beautiful as always and stifling a yawn behind her exquisite fan. 'Any news?' she asked, with a weary sigh. 'No one here seems to know what is happening. Perhaps it is all just a false alarm after all.'

I shook my head. 'I do not think so. I have just spoken to my brother. The King is being asked to withdraw to his château at Rambouillet but refuses to leave.'

'Ah,' Aimée said, barely troubling to lower her voice. 'And once again the King procrastinates while all around him France falls to its knees.'

In silent accord, we linked arms and walked out through the gilded salon next door to the Hall of Mirrors, where most of the court had assembled along with their children and a few of the servants. We were immediately assailed by a crowd of people desperate for any scraps of news but were unable to add much to what was already well known. As we pushed our way through, I heard a whisper that the mob of women had now reached Versailles and invaded the meetings of the National Assembly, where they were drunkenly causing havoc and loudly demanding to be taken to the King.

Aimée sighed. 'I hope that that will be an end to it.' She smiled at me and shrugged. 'It is not very likely though is it? Once they have caught the merest whiff of fear, they won't stop until they see blood.'

After several hours of waiting, the news spread that the King had finally listened to reason and agreed to leave for his château at Rambouillet.

His carriage had been ordered but it was discovered that the mob had cut the traces and stolen the horses. We were all trapped. Now suddenly, people whose only thought in life had been to reside amidst the splendour at Versailles were desperate to escape.

To my shame, I was one of them.

Everyone was hungry for news but it was frustratingly slow in coming. We were there when a small group of women picked out from the mob was escorted into the King's presence to make their demands in person.

Like everyone else, we covered our noses at the smell, stared in horror at how filthy they were, at the horrible rags that they wore, which barely covered their bodies and could have offered very little protection against the elements. It seemed inconceivable that fellow French women could be so destitute in appearance.

Again I felt a stirring of sympathy for the forces that had brought them here to Versailles.

Afterwards, we made our way through the huge, echoing state rooms to the salon d'Hercules. Its huge arched windows overlooked the rain-drenched courtyard, beyond which we could see the vast mob of women, baying incoherently and thrusting their hands through the locked gates.

It was a terrifying sight. I shivered as I looked down into their twisted, famished faces, their mouths pulled wide open as they screamed up at the château windows.

Night fell over Versailles. The footmen and pages walked silently from room to room, lighting lily-scented candles with long tapers, while the courtiers kept their vigil, desperate for news and too afraid to return to their rooms.

Aimée and I sat on stools in the dimly lit salon de l'Oeuil de Boeuf and ate stale bread rolls brought to us by one of the young château pages, who flitted freely from room to room dispensing food and valuable snippets of gossip.

'What do you think is going to happen?' I asked Aimée.

She sighed and looked around at the exhausted, drawn faces of the other courtiers. 'I don't know,' she said, swallowing the last morsel of bread. 'I have never felt so uncertain and it frightens me.'

At that moment the doors swung open and the Marquis de La Fayette strode in alone.

He was soaked through to the skin, covered with mud, and looked half dead with exhaustion. There was an excited stir at his arrival but he went straight to the door of the King's chamber.

I clutched Aimée's arm and hardly dared breathe. Had La Fayette come to save us all?

The door swung open and he vanished inside. A collective sigh ran through the room which then erupted into a chorus of conjecture and discussion.

'I would give anything to know what is being said,' Aimée remarked. 'The Queen detests Monsieur le Marquis de La Fayette and will never willingly accept his assistance.'

I sighed and nodded in agreement 'The Queen places rather too much importance on her likes and dislikes She should have learnt to be less childish about such distinctions by now. Her petty dislikes have already done her great harm.'

Aimée nodded. 'Just look at what happened with Rohan.' She winked. 'If the Queen had not taken one of her dislikes to him, then that whole absurd rigmarole with the necklace need never have happened, and perhaps we wouldn't be here now.'

The King's door opened again and Lucien appeared looking pale and exhausted. He ignored everyone else as they crowded around him, clamouring for attention and came straight to me. He kissed my hand, leading me into one of the alcoved windows where we could converse with some semblance of privacy. In the distance, I could see the tiny amber lights of the mob's campfires that blazed on the other side of the gates, while their drunken shouts and rowdy songs floated through the darkness.

'My darling girl, it looks like the crisis has passed,' he said in an undertone. 'La Fayette has brought several thousand troops with him from Paris and given his personal assurance that the château and its inhabitants will be safe from harm.'

I gave a little cry, then almost sobbed with relief. 'Thank God,' I whispered. 'Oh, thank God.'

Lucien gently touched my cheek. 'You look exhausted, petite.' He waved away a group of courtiers who were hovering nearby in the hope of catching some of our conversation. 'A message has been sent to the Queen. It will hurt her pride to accept help from Monsieur le Marquis de La Fayette but that cannot be helped. Not now. It is too late for such delicacies, I am afraid.' He took my hand again. 'Try your best to persuade her to be gracious.'

I laughed, a brittle sound that echoed uneasily in my ears

and made the others stare at us.

'She won't pay any attention to me.'

Lucien smiled. 'I know that she can be difficult but try your best.'

I gave Aimée a goodbye hug and walked through the splendid rooms to the Queen's bedchamber.

Marie Antoinette, quiet and clearly under a huge amount of strain, was in the middle of being prepared for bed. Her eyes gazed into the distance as her waiting women let down her blonde hair and carefully removed her pearl earrings and diamond bracelets. With the other ladies in waiting, I went through the slow, comforting motions of the centuries old ritual. But we were all aware that there was something different in the sweetly scented air, something that chilled us to the very bone. We looked at each other nervously behind Marie Antoinette's back and could hardly bring ourselves to meet her usually candid blue gaze.

The sense of something coming to an end was inescapable.

'That will be all,' the Queen dismissed us with a fleeting smile and a wave of her hand. 'Thank you.'

She went to the great canopied bed. Without removing her yellow and white silk dressing gown, she lay down upon the counterpane with its design of flowers and peacock feathers. 'I should like to be alone now.'

I went out into the large apple green salon next door to the Queen's bedroom and sank down with a grateful sigh on a chair next to the fireplace. I felt utterly drained and was in no great hurry to return through the dark and echoing staircases and corridors to my own small apartment. I stared for a while into the dying fire and wearily considered that day's events. It still seemed utterly surreal that we were under siege in such a way. La Fayette had promised to protect us all but was that really possible? I thought of poor Monsieur de Launey, who had been so horribly decapitated by the mob when the Bastille fell on Lucrèce's wedding day. They were clearly a law unto themselves. Bloodthirsty and untamed. Was La Fayette man enough to hold them back? I doubted it.

The rain continued to pelt against the windows. This gentle sound along with the glow of the fire finally silenced my racing, confused thoughts and lulled me into sleep.

I vaguely heard the Queen's waiting women tiptoe past at one point to take up their usual stations beside Her Majesty's door. But I could not rouse myself enough to speak to them, listening to their whispers as I floated in and out of sleep.

I was rudely awakened several hours later by a loud echoing banging noise and the sound of shouts and screams.

For a second I wondered where on earth I was, then realised that I must have accidentally dozed off before the fire. The banging and roar of voices came nearer. I sat up in alarm as it became clear that the noise was coming from within the château itself and was growing louder with each passing second.

'What is that?' I was still stupefied by sleep. 'What is happening out there?'

At that instant there was the distinct sound of a shot followed by a terrible scream. The Queen's two waiting women, Mesdames Auguié and Thibault, sprang into action and ran down the length of the long room to the door at the other end while I sprang up in panic from the chair and followed them, my heart beating loudly in my ears.

The shouting came closer and closer. I wondered what the time was; the pale blue light glimmering through the tall windows indicated that it was near dawn.

'Mon dieu, what is happening?' Madame Auguié cautiously opened the door to the antechamber. We all held our breath, fearing to be confronted by a terrible mob baying for our blood but the room was empty but for one solitary guardsman who was struggling to barricade the door with only his musket to assist him. His feet were sliding back along the floor as he pushed against the painted and gilded wood with all of his strength.

'Sauvez la reine!' he yelled over his shoulder, and I gave a scream of fright when I saw that his face was covered with blood, which dripped onto his once white muslin cravat. 'They are coming to kill her!'

The mob had somehow gained entrance to the château, made their way up the Queen's staircase and were now only feet away on the other side of the flimsy door. 'Go now!'

The guardsman was trying his best to keep the door shut against the oncoming tide but it was a losing battle. It was only a matter of time before they got in.

I turned and sped back across the salon to the Queen's door. 'Madame! Wake up!' I hammered on the door, fumbled with the latch, found it and then almost fell into the room. 'The mob are in the château! They are coming for you!' Marie Antoinette stared at me and sleepily sat up on the bed, which she had not even troubled to get into. 'Venez, madame! We must make haste!'

'Is this true?' The Queen pressed one thin hand to her throat and swallowed nervously as she listened to the noise of the angry mob. She sounded plaintive and faintly aggrieved. 'I heard a sound on the terrace beneath my windows. It woke me up.'

'Madame, there is no time to be lost!' I said impatiently, picking up the Queen's silk and lace dressing gown, which had been cast on to a nearby chair, and handing it to her. 'You must leave immediately!'

The two waiting women ran in and frantically locked the door behind them. 'Madame! For the love of God, get out of bed!' Madame Thibault shouted, in such a panic that all etiquette was forgotten. 'They are coming to kill us all!'

Marie Antoinette gasped then and scrambled from the bed. 'I must go to the King!' She threw her dressing gown on over her negligée, absentmindedly picked up some silk stockings, thought better of actually putting them on and ran to the concealed door that led to her petits cabinets and also the King's rooms. 'Quickly! Follow me!'

We lifted our cumbersome skirts almost to our knees and ran down the tiny little whitewashed corridor to the door at the end. Marie Antoinette clumsily tried to open it but the handle would not turn. 'Ciel, it is locked!' She tried again while the rest of us stared at each other in horror, unable to credit what was happening. 'Mon dieu, we are trapped!'

The Queen's voice rose in panic and frantically she began to scream and hammer against the door. 'Let me out! They are coming to kill me! Please, I beg of you, open the door!'

My heart was in my mouth as I also pounded on the door with all my strength and until my hands smarted with pain. I then tried to force it with my shoulder but it refused to budge. The sound of the mob came closer and closer until they were a loud roar only feet away. They had reached the Queen's bedchamber and it was only a matter of time before they discovered the little corridor.

'Hurry! They are almost upon us!' Tears of fear and frustration ran down my cheeks and I angrily wiped them away with the back of my hand. 'Open the door!'

There was a sound of scuffling, and miraculously the door opened. We fell into the salon de l'Oeuil de Boeuf only to be confronted by a frightened looking footman, his cravat untied and his wig askew. He had clearly been asleep until our screams awakened him.

Hurriedly, our fingers shaking with fear, we locked the door and then ran across the room, now empty and lit only by a few candles and the grey rays of approaching dawn, to the King's bedchamber. To our consternation, it was empty. A sleepy valet told us that the King had been informed of the invasion of the château and had gone in search of his wife. We then had no option but to sit and wait until he returned, Marie Antoinette staring straight ahead, still holding her crumpled stockings in her hands. I comforted the distraught Madame Thibault, who was sobbing and shaking with shock, while in the distance we heard the terrible roaring and screaming of the mob as they destroyed the rooms that we had just left.

The King returned soon afterwards, pale and trembling with relief at the sight of his wife. He had in his arms the little Dauphin, who clearly had no idea what was happening and stared at both of his parents in sleepy confusion.

'Maman, you don't have any shoes on,' the Dauphin

observed with a laugh, pointing at the Queen's bare feet.

Tenderly, the King put the little boy down on a sofa and took his wife in his arms. 'My darling.'

Whatever other faults Louis XVI might have as a King and a man, there was no doubting the enormous love he felt for his wife and family. For the first time, I felt almost envious of my mistress. Perhaps she was the lucky one after all?

'Thank God, thank God,' Marie Antoinette whispered into his chest, as he clumsily reached up to stroke her unbound and dishevilled fair hair which fell about her shoulders. 'I thought that I was going to be killed. I thought they were going to hurt me.'

Dawn arose. The first pink rays of the new day bathed the King's magnificent crimson and gold bedchamber in sunlight. I yawned and pulled my cashmere shawl closer about my shoulders before cautiously reaching up to pat my now collapsed and ruined hair.

'Maman, I am hungry!' The little Dauphin piped up in an imperious tone.

We all looked at each other in shellshocked horror, unable to comprehend the events that had taken place that night. He had been extremely patient so far but the hours were dragging and our little traumatised group had been left without sustenance for too long.

'When will I have my breakfast?'

The Dauphin's lower lip, so clearly inherited from his Hapsburg ancestors, pouted dangerously. He had been happily occupied playing with his sister's long fair hair but now his gentle plaiting was becoming painful tugs and she was beginning to wince with pain and gently protest.

Marie Antoinette turned back from the window and directed an abstracted gaze upon her son. 'Soon, chou d'amour.' She sighed and shrugged her shoulders. 'When all the people have gone away, then I promise that we shall have breakfast together.'

She touched his blond head, then turned away and continued to gaze out of the window at the immense, noisy crowd gathered in the courtyard below, which had become a seething mess of humanity in the hours since the intruders had been cast out of the actual building by Lafayette's brave troops.

'This is insupportable!' The King's obese younger brother, the Comte de Provence, paced the length of the room, punching his fist into his other hand. He had dressed in haste and his purple silk coat was stained with grease and wine. 'This is unbelievable! If I were King ...'

He stopped himself while his normally placid sister Élisabeth, ever the mediator in the troubled royal family, reached out and placed a restraining hand on his arm.

Marie Antoinette turned from the window. 'Yes?' She raised one eyebrow. 'If you were King, then what?' She pulled her dressing gown closer and held herself with immense dignity.

Her brother-in-law flushed and could not meet her eye.

The door opened. The King came in, followed by La Fayette, who looked flushed and mortified, his ears pink beneath his immaculate white powdered wig, because he had fallen asleep and missed all
he action and had therefore arrived at the château too late to prevent the invasion.

'I'm sorry, so sorry ...' Lay Fayette began.

The King spoke across him. 'Monsieur le Marquis believes that it might be for the best if I show myself to the people.' He went without pausing, as if he feared that he might lose his nerve to the windows which led to a small iron balcony, overlooking the courtyard. 'I must do my duty.'

He kissed his wife's forehead as he went past her. It was in vain that she caught at his arm and whispered his name.

I held my breath as the King pushed open the window and stepped out alone into the blindingly bright sunshine, half expecting him to be shot dead on the spot.

Instead he was greeted with cheers and even a few sparse shouts of 'Vive le Roi!', a sound which had not been heard for a long time, and which brought a buzz of relief and renewed hope to the room. He bowed and self-consciously waved to the mob.

When he returned, his wife and sister threw themselves

into his arms with relief.

'La Reine! La Reine!' The crowd suddenly roared in their thousands, to the horror of everyone assembled in the room. 'We want to see the Queen! Send her out on to the balcony where we can see her!'

The Marquis de La Fayette turned to Marie Antoinette 'Madame, do you feel able to show yourself?'

The Queen looked at him coldly. 'Of course.'

She straightened her shoulders proudly, took her children by the hand and looking for all the world as though she was about to take a stroll on the terrace, the most hated woman in all France stepped lightly out on to the balcony.

Everyone in the room held their breath. Overcome by the suspense, I dipped my head into my hands and silently prayed while beside me Madame Élisabeth did the same thing. There was a terrifying split second of silence before the shouts began again. 'No children! Sans les enfants!'

The Queen turned and gestured to me. I rose up from the floor and came shakily forward to took the sobbing Dauphin and Madame Royale by the hand and lead them back into the room. For one brief, breathless instant, I caught a glimpse of the huge crowd, a sea of hostile faces not so far below, and gave a shiver of fear, which I quickly hid in case the children noticed.

The little Dauphin released my hand and ran straight into the arms of his aunt, who held him close and kissed his forehead, while Madame Royale preferred to clasp hands with her father. All eyes were on the Queen, who stood alone and vulnerable in front of the hostile Parisian crowd. A few muskets were raised towards her, but miraculously no shots were fired. For a while, there was a breathless hush as she stood before them, her head proudly erect, her eyes gazing into an uncertain future.

'Vive la Reine!' The first lone cry was like a miracle and it was immediately echoed by a multitude of others. Once again the volatile Parisian canaille had changed their minds. They could always change them back again but for now we were all on the same side.

'Long live the Queen!' It was a long time since anyone had heard those words uttered with such enthusiasm by the Parisian populace and I saw that there was not a dry eye in the room. Even the Comte de Provence was openly weeping at that moment, daubing his fat tears with a grimy lawn handkerchief.

Her own eyes swimming with tears, Marie Antoinette graciously inclined her head and swept a low curtsey. La Fayette, regretting the slumber that had led to such disaster, now seized his moment and stepped out on the balcony to stand beside her, and to an ecstatic roar from the crowd he took the Queen's hand in his and lifted it to his lips in a theatrical gesture redolent of an almost forgotten chivalry.

'To Paris! To Paris!' The chanting was universal and impossible to ignore. The Queen and La Fayette came back into the room and immediately all of her careful poise deserted her and she staggered with exhaustion and had to hold on to the gilded gilt back of a chair for support. The Dauphin ran up to her and hugged her knees. 'Maman, are the noisy people going away now?'

'Soon, my darling, soon,' she whispered, lifting him up, kissing his rosy cheeks and hiding her tears in his shoulder so that he would not see her cry.

The King paced up and down the room, scene of so many court dramas over the centuries since it had been the bedchamber of Louis XIV. Outside the cries demanding that the King and his family come to Paris continued and he frowned with concentration. Always hesitant, he was uncertain how to act for the best. Should he leave Versailles, perhaps forever or remain? Which action would best ensure the safety of his realm and above all, his family? We all watched him closely, wondering what conclusion he was going to come to.

'I have made my decision,' he said at last, before waving away the ever present La Fayette, going out on to the balcony once more and raising his hands in a plea for silence. 'My friends,' he called, 'I will go to Paris with my wife and children; I entrust what is most precious to me to the love of my good and loyal subjects.'

His words were greeted with enormous cheers while behind him his wife sobbed uncontrollably.

'We are leaving Versailles,' she said. 'I wish to God that we had left last night when we still had the chance – at least then it would have been of our own free will instead of as prisoners.' At her words a chill fell upon the room.

Afterwards, I walked wearily back to my rooms that overlooked the Rue des Réservoirs, through silent rooms that had once hummed with vibrant, colourful, glamorous life. All the courtiers had given up their vigil and gone to bed, so that now the only sound to be heard was the tap tap tap of my high heeled shoes against the polished parquet. I paused for a moment and looked out of a window, admiring the pink and purple fingers of the dawn as it rose over the château gardens. It was a sight that I had seen many times before, usually while returning from another gaudy, drunken night at the Paris Opéra ball or a night gambling in Lauzun's smoky, red damask hung salon but never before had it taken on such a poignancy or appeared so bold or beautiful as it did on that final morning at Versailles.

'Madame la Marquise!' I turned and there he was.

'Monsieur le Vicomte de Barthèlmy.' I stopped and waited for him to come up to me, admiring the way that his dark hair fell about his shoulders and his clear grey eyes gleamed in the gloom. 'How did you know my name?' He was close enough now for me to be able to smell the clean lavender tang of his cologne.

'How did you know mine?'

I smiled. 'I hoped that you would come to me.' We were circling each other now, our eyes fixed on each other and the same half coquettish, half afraid smiles curling our lips.

He bowed then. 'How could I not? I have thought about nothing but you all day long.'

I laughed and raised an eyebrow. 'Even when we have a ragged crowd, baying for our blood at the palace gates?'

He grinned. 'Especially then.' He took my hand and pulled me closer. 'Men need something to fight for after all.'

I looked up at him quizzically. 'Do you fight, Monsieur le

Vicomte?' He did not look like a soldier.

His grip tightened on my hand, 'Madame, all the time,' and then he kissed me and more than just Versailles was lost.

1790

ADÉLAÏDE

Paris, July 1790

Everything had changed and at the same time, nothing had changed as life in Paris continued very much as it always had. The National Assembly had followed the royal family and court back to the capital and were now holding their meetings in the ramshackle and malodorous old riding school attached to the Tuileries, which had a leaky roof and pigeons roosting amongst the eaves. It was fashionable for a while to attend their meetings and sit in the gallery above pretending to earnestly listen to the debates while simultaneously discussing the latest gossip with one's friends and flirting with the more handsome deputies. Not that there were many to choose from - most were serious looking middle aged men from the provinces, who wore slightly too tight suits and looked up at us with expressions of mingled irritation and contempt.

'It's just like the Opéra, only far more dull,' Cassandre described it with a yawn. She had taken to carrying a fan bearing the hideously ugly countenance of the sexually voracious Comte de Mirabeau, who with his much avowed desire to found an English style parliament in France was considered to be the hero of the day and was fawned on and fêted wherever he happened to go. The novelty soon wore off however and after a while Mirabeau and the deputies were left in peace, Cassandre's vile fan was consigned to the back of a cupboard and along with the rest of the fashionable people of Paris, she returned to her usual pleasures of shopping in the Palais Royal or going for walks in the beautiful gardens of the Palais du Luxembourg, where the King's brother, the Comte de Provence had taken up residence with his ugly Italian wife.

Cassandre and Lucrèce reported back with miserable looks that court life at the Tuileries was just as dull and tedious as that at Versailles. The royal family had been housed together in a sprawling suite of small, shabby rooms at the top of a large and stately staircase, hastily furnished with cartloads of familiar items brought from their rooms at Versailles so that their apartment were cramped and uncomfortable. However, although the old courtly rituals continued just as they had always done, the new physical closeness of the royal family, who had previously been separated by countless staircases and galleries, meant that there was also a new budding sense of informality in the air. The little Dauphin in particular seemed to be flourishing and the dusty old palace rang with the sounds of his shouts and childish games as he played on the vast terraces with his sister, Marie-Thérèse and their mother's bevy of spoiled, obnoxious little dogs which had accompanied them from Versailles.

As for me, life was very different now. The Assembly had done away with religious worship, closing down the churches, religious houses and schools, Penthémont amongst them. I would never forget the evening that they gave us the bad news: the whole school had been gathered together for dinner and the huge, vaulted refectory had been filled with the buzz of conversation and laughter and the clatter of our spoons as we greedily ate our hot soup and ripped off chunks of fresh, soft bread from the large white loaves that sat on the centre of the tables.

A hush had fallen on the room when the Abbesse had pushed back her chair and stood up, clapping her hands together and looking around the hall, seeming to fix every single last one of us with her piercing, dark eyed gaze so that we all shuffled our feet, blushed and looked down at our plates in mute embarrassment.

'Pénthemont is closing,' she said without preamble and I saw the other nuns glance at each other sharply behind her back; clearly this is not how they had expected the news to be broken. 'The National Assembly has spoken and we must bow to their will. All classes are immediately suspended, your parents and guardians have all been informed and you will be returning to your own homes as soon as proper arrangements have been made to collect or transport you.' Another swift look around the room, taking in each of our faces. 'May God bless and protect you all, my poor girls.'

We stared at each other in aghast amazement, absolutely unable to believe what we had just been told. I looked around at the faces that had been a part of my everyday existence for almost eight years, most looked shocked and stunned like myself but some were openly sobbing while others laughed and gave the appearance of delight.

'Adélaïde...' I turned to look at Hortense and saw that she was pale and visibly shaking with dread. 'I don't want to go home. I had hoped that I could stay here until I was married.' She wiped away a tear. 'Why couldn't they leave us all alone? Why must everything change?'

I shook my head and rubbed her back through the thin red linen of her dress. 'I don't know, Hortense. I wish that I did.' I thought of my father's house on the Rue des Francs Bourgeois and felt cold and sick at the prospect of returning forever. I may not have been popular at Pénthemont but at least I felt at home there.

'Will you write to me, Adélaïde?' Hortense asked now, smiling through her tears. 'Let me know if you find your mother?'

I smiled back and squeezed her hand, feigning a bravery that I did not feel. 'Of course I will.'

Our trunks were already waiting on our beds when we got back to our rooms after dinner and shortly afterwards our maids arrived to help us pack away our belongings for the final time. It did not take long as we were not allowed to have much with us, but I hugged every single thing to my breast before folding it and putting it away, dreading the final moment when the trunk was closed and fastened and there was nothing left to do.

In the morning, my father's carriage arrived along with several others and after one final tearful embrace with Hortense, whose own vehicle had not yet arrived, I climbed up inside and was driven away for the last time. It was February and a flurry of snow had fallen overnight so that everything was coated with a heavy cloak of crisp, glittering white. Normally I loved this time of year but my heart felt heavy as I pulled my woolen cloak close and gazed miserably out upon the world, staring unsmilingly at the grinning men and women who clustered around the glowing braziers that had been erected on the street corners.

It didn't take long for us to cross the Seine and reach the busy, noisy Rue des Francs Bourgeois, where street traders looked curiously into the carriage and offered me gingerbread biscuits, fresh warm bread or a cup of mulled wine, all of which I waved away without even a cursory glance. 'Suit yourself, my fine lady!' they called jeeringly as we rolled past but still I ignored them, unable to think about anything but my own unhappiness.

My heart sank in my breast as the carriage turned through the stone gateway that led to my father's house and I looked up at the Hôtel windows with a sigh. 'It might not be so bad,' I told myself, not really believing it. They had never been actively cruel, I had never returned to school with dark pinchmarks up my arms like Hortense, for example, but I knew, had always known that I was not wanted here.

'Mademoiselle de Saint-Valèry,' a new tall, good looking footman that I had never seen before came forward to pull the door open and let down the carriage steps. 'It is good to have you home again.'

'Thank you.' I let him help me down and stood for a moment in the ankle deep snow, looking about me and delaying the moment when I would finally have to go inside. 'Is my father well?' The chill, damp snow was beginning to seep through the thin leather of my shoes and I was starting to lose all feeling in my toes.

He looked confused. 'Very well, mademoiselle.' There was an awkward pause as I hopped from foot to foot, trying to keep the cold at bay. 'Would you like to come inside, where it is warm?'

I sighed, pulling my cloak closer around myself. 'I suppose so.' He led the way into the house and I cheered up a bit at the sight of a welcoming fire burning in the huge marble fireplace in the entrance hall. I went thankfully towards it and held out my pink, frozen hands, closing my eyes rapturously as the fire's warmth slowly spread through my chilled bones.

The footman cleared his throat. 'Your father asked to see you in his study as soon as you arrived,' he said. 'I should take you to him now.' He gave me a sympathetic look. 'There is a fire in there as well.'

I reluctantly followed him to my father's study and almost implored him not to leave when with a final smile and wink, he held the door open so that I could walk inside.

The door closed softly behind me and for the first time in many years I found myself alone with my father. I looked around the room, which looked exactly as it had always done from the large paintings of hunting scenes on the walls to the way that he liked to arrange the paper and huge gold ink wells on the desk that stood between us.

'Ah, Adélaïde.' He couldn't have sounded more disinterested, more disappointed. 'How nice to see you again.'

I tried to remember the last time that I had seen my father. A month ago? Two months? 'Thank you, papa.' I looked at him curiously, wondering as always what I had done to make him dislike me so much.

He cleared his throat. 'I expect that this is a great surprise to you,' he said, fiddling with the papers that lay in front of him. The large ruby ring that he wore on his little finger glinted in the bright winter sunlight that filtered in between the blue brocade curtains, sending shards of red light glimmering around the room. 'I myself did not expect you to come home for many years.'

'I'm seventeen,' I said, shocking myself by speaking more loudly and angrily than I had meant to. 'How long did you think that you could leave me there for?'

'Seventeen.' My father looked surprised. 'Ah. Yes. I suppose that you must be.' He stood up and went to the window. 'We will have to start thinking about your future,' he said with a sigh. 'Times may have changed, but I am sure that a suitable match can still be found for you. I know that your grandmother already has someone in mind.'

'I'd rather not...' I began, quivering with indignation as I imagined the sort of person that Grandmère would cheerfully marry me off to. One of her gambling cronies no doubt, some nasty old Marquis with snuff stained nostrils, an outmoded wig and debts up to his ears. I thought, briefly and wistfully of the handsome lawyer, Xavier de Saint-Benoît but then just as quickly dismissed him from my mind. What was the use after all?

'Silence,' my father interrupted me. 'You will do as you are told, mademoiselle.'

And so it began. I climbed the stairs up to my room on the top floor with a heavy heart, remembering the days when my sisters and brother had been at home and the beautiful, light filled rooms had been filled with their noise and chaos. I had always been the observer to their games, too young to be of interest and too quiet to be much fun and had all too often wished that they would either go away or be quiet. Now though the silence unnerved me and I found myself missing them all.

My room was just as I had left it, with the same bright yellow walls, faded prints of scenes from English history and scratchy embroidered counterpane that had been there ever since I could remember. It was a little girl's room, not that of a young woman and as I sank down upon the narrow bed and looked around myself, it just seemed to serve as yet more proof that no one here was the slightest bit interested in me.

'I don't like them either,' I reminded myself, blinking away hot, angry tears and kicking irritably at my trunk, which lay on the floor at my feet. 'I just wish that I was someone's favourite.'

And as soon as I had said it out loud, I found that it was impossible to hold back my tears any longer.

I sat alone in my room until one of the footmen came to tell me that it was time for dinner. Wearily, I got up from the bed, brushed down my crumpled grey cotton skirts, patted my hair then followed him down the stairs to the dining room on the ground floor where Papa and Grandmère were already waiting for me.

Grandmère's critical gaze swept across me. 'Pray don't make an effort on our behalf,' she remarked caustically. 'Honestly, we have spent a fortune on school fees and for what?'

'I'm sorry,' I mumbled, instantly abashed, just as usual. 'I fell asleep. It won't happen again.' I took my place at the dining table in between them and stared down at my plate, moving aside slightly as a footman poured wine into my glass.

'The girl needs to be married,' Grandmère said to Papa, pointing her fork at him. 'Although heaven knows who will have her now. I had thought that perhaps Monsieur de Vitry but....' she shrugged, the unknown Monsieur de Vitry having apparently proved dissatisfactory in some way.

Papa cleared his throat. 'There is a substantial dowry...' Oh really? I continued to stare down at my plate but I was all ears now, waiting to hear more.

Grandmère snorted. 'Ridiculous profligacy! There is certainly no need for family money to be squandered in such a way!' She speared a piece of chicken with her fork and glared at me, even though I had not spoken and was trying my best to shrink as far as possible into my seat. 'I absolutely do not approve, Claude.'

My father smiled wanly and took a sip of red wine from an exquisitely crafted glass. 'Nevertheless, that is how things are.' He glanced at me then just as quickly looked away again.

My days soon fell into a familiar, even comforting pattern with solitary mornings spent reading or writing in my room or walking in the Hôtel gardens followed by afternoons filled with lessons with the art, languages, dancing and music tutors that my father had engaged for me. He had decided that my lessons with David could no longer continue and had instead hired a miserable faced spinster to teach me how to paint with watercolours, much to my disgust.

In the evening, Grandmère would come for dinner and I would sit between them in awkward silence, picking miserably at my food as they talked about me over my head. Their conversations always took the same course: Grandmère would criticize everything about me and Papa would try his best to change the subject. Sometimes Lucien or one of my sisters would join us and then things would be much more pleasant as they would chatter about other things and tell jokes until the mood was softened and the sour edge had been taken off Grandmère's tongue.

'Don't mind her,' Lucien whispered to me once with a comforting squeeze of my arm as we walked to the salon after dinner, where Lucrèce was already sitting at the harpsichord, playing an air by Grètry as her husband leaned over her and slowly turned the pages of her music, all of his attention focussed entirely on the top of her gleaming auburn head while she sent soft looks from beneath her long eyelashes at his handsome cousin, Sébastien who had caught Grandmère's fancy thanks to his skill at sedately vicious card games and so was often invited to dine at our house. 'She has always hated all of us. I think that it must be habit now.'

I pulled my gaze away from Lucrèce and smiled at him. 'I know you are lying, Lucien,' I said with a tiny shrug. 'But thank you.'

I had been at home for three months when preparations began to be made for the enormous fête that was to be held to celebrate the first anniversary of the Bastille's capture and all of Paris gave itself over to a feverish and optimistic expectation of good times ahead. Hundreds of people gathered daily on the Champs de Mars to assist in preparing the ground for the grand parades and celebrations and it became de rigueur for fashionable ladies to join them in digging up weeds and pushing wheelbarrows full of soil while cheerfully singing patriotic songs alongside people that they would hardly have deigned to look at a year previously.

My sister Cassandre, keen as always to be at the forefront of any trend was to be seen there every day for several weeks, until finally she confided to me that she rather feared that she might be getting a freckle from being outside so often. At first though she found it absolutely hilarious to call in to see us afterwards, with an artfully placed smudge of dirt on her lovely nose.

'Oh, call for some wine, Adélaïde!' she would exclaim, collapsing on a sofa and dabbing her forehead and cheeks with a handkerchief scented with rosemary and lavender. 'It is such hard work being a patriot.'

I too longed to help of course, but father would not allow it. My future was still uncertain after all and a prospective suitor may well be turned off by what could be seen as an unwomanly interest in politics. Married women like my sisters, however, could act as they pleased, free of the constraints that burdened we single girls.

I was at liberty however to look forward to the forthcoming celebration, and when the morning of the fourteenth of July finally dawned, I leapt from my bed and ran to my window to look out. The Journal de Paris had predicted rain and to my disappointment, this had indeed come to pass as the skies over Paris were leaden and heavy and the cobbles beneath my window were still slick and gleaming after a recent downpour.

'It might brighten up later on, mademoiselle,' my maid, Henriette said with a smile, noticing my disappointment, which she must surely have shared as I knew that as soon as we had left for the day she was planning to change into her very best pink dress, meet up with her fiancé, a handsome footman from the neighbouring Hôtel de Montellier and go to the Fête as well.

I dressed with care in my favourite deep blue silk dress, with a fine yellow cashmere shawl that Lucien had given me as a birthday present arranged around my shoulders and tied behind my waist. Then I sat listlessly in front of my tiny dressing table and tried to ignore the rattling of the rain against the thin window panes as Henriette arranged my hair and held it back with a red silk ribbon then fastened some coral beads around my neck.

'I should get my ears pierced,' I remarked, thoughtfully touching the lobe of one of my ears with a finger. Most of the fashionable ladies, including my sisters wore large gold or silver hoops in their ears and I was frankly envious of the way they rattled noisily whenever they moved or spoke.

'It would look very becoming, mademoiselle,' Henriette said, holding my thick dark hair back for a moment and regarding me thoughtfully. 'Would you like me to do it for you now?'

I winced, suddenly nervous. 'Maybe later?' I looked at myself in the mirror and smiled. For once I was quite pleased with my appearance - I looked fashionable and at the same time a little unusual. I would never be a beauty like Cassandre or Lucrèce but perhaps, maybe, I could be a little bit pretty?

'You look nice,' Papa remarked as I took my place at the breakfast table. 'You should wear your hair like that more often, Adélaïde.' He finished his coffee and carefully replaced the tiny jade green and gold Sèvres cup on its saucer. 'You are no longer a child after all.'

I looked at him cautiously, unused to praise of any kind from him. 'No, I'm not.' I helped myself to a roll and began to butter it, allowing the awkward silence to hang and grow between us. 'I must admit that I do not feel very grown up though,' I hazarded at last, thinking of my narrow bed in the old nursery.

'No, that is understandable,' he agreed, not quite looking at me. 'Perhaps it is time that you moved into one of your sister's apartments on the first floor.' He sighed. 'I will make the arrangements.'

'Thank you,' I quickly looked down at my plate so that he could not see how pleased I was.

I could hardly contain my excitement as after breakfast I rattled and bumped in one of father's carriages to the Hôtel de Saliex on the Rue de Grenelle and even our slow progress through streets that were jammed with carriages and huge throngs of merry makers could not abate my high spirits. When we finally arrived at the Hôtel, I could hardly wait for the footman to let down the steps and open my door before I jumped from the vehicle and ran up the marble steps to the door.

Lucrèce was waiting for me in the hallway and looked very beautiful in a dress of shell pink silk, tied at the waist with a wide black taffeta sash and with her red curls tumbling about her shoulders and down her back. She embraced me quickly, surrounding me with a delightful scent of lilies and violets.

'The streets are packed with people,' I said excitedly. 'I've never seen so many!' We made our way arm in arm to the salon where the Duc was waiting for us. 'How thrilling it all is!' I felt like a different person in my sister's house, more lively and interesting and absolutely less in the way.

'I hope you don't mind...' Lucrèce whispered with a squeeze of my arm, as a footman opened the salon door.

'Don't mind what?' I stepped into the room and greeted my brother in law, the Duc with a smile, which slid from my face when I realised who was standing beside him. 'Oh.'

If Xavier de Saint-Benoît noticed my dismay, he was too polite to give any sign of it. 'Mademoiselle de Saint-Valèry,' he murmured, bowing low. 'How enchanting to see you again and looking so wonderful too.'

'Monsieur.' I looked enquiringly at my sister, who blushed and laughed, shrugging her thin shoulders. 'What a surprise.'

'I met Monsieur de Saint-Benoît at a party last week and invited him to join us,' she whispered as she took my arm and led me away. 'I thought you would like it if he came with us to the Fête. I can easily send him away if you don't want him though.'

'You don't have to do that.' I looked back at Xavier, who was standing by the fireplace and watching me with a quizzical expression. 'I am delighted that he will be coming with us.'

Lucrèce clapped her hands. 'Now we are just waiting for Cousin Sébastien and then we can set off! I thought that we could walk there rather than take the carriage? What do you think, Monsieur de Saint-Benoît?'

Xavier made a gallant bow. 'I think that a most charming idea, madame,' he said. 'There is a little rain but that shouldn't trouble us.'

'No, indeed,' my sister agreed with a laugh. 'I must confess that I do like to be caught out in the rain sometimes. It makes me feel so wild and free. Do you not find that, monsieur? Adélaïde?'

'Absolutely,' I said with a smile and a squeeze of her hand. 'Although there is nothing better than being indoors and listening to the rain outside. It is such a cosy, contented feeling.' I thought with a pang of my old room at Penthémont and the night that Hortense and I had spent there together, sitting up in our beds and eating secret supplies of chocolate bonbons while outside a storm raged, lighting up the dark sky with flashes of mauve, azure and lilac. I blushed when I looked across at Xavier de Saint-Benoît and realised that he was watching me with a smile on his handsome face.

'Were you somewhere else, Mademoiselle de Saint-Valèry?' he asked in a friendly way, that made me blush even more.

'Yes,' I replied, deciding to be candid with him. He would never be interested in me as anything more than Lucrèce's silly younger sister so why not say whatever I pleased to him? It's not as thought I ever had any hope of impressing him. 'I was remembering my old school and how happy I was there.'

'Ah, yes of course,' he smiled politely before turning to Lucrèce, who had produced a basket full of tricolor cockades and after attaching one to her hair, was trying to fasten one to the lapel of his russet silk jacket.

Not long after this, Cousin Sébastien arrived, smiling gently around the room, and trying his best to hide the light that came into his pale blue eyes whenever he looked at my sister. He blushingly accepted the cockade that she pinned, gravely and without an ounce of flirtation to his lapel, raising her wide hazel eyes just once, fleetingly to his face.

'It is always pleasant to see you, Mademoiselle Adélaïde,' he said with a smile. 'How are things with you?' His fingers played nervously with the cockade as he spoke, smoothing out and crumpling the ruffled red, white and blue striped silk.

'Same as usual,' I replied with a laugh. I was very fond of Cousin Sébastien and had fallen into the habit of addressing him just as I would an old friend. 'Has your mother found you a wife yet?' His mother's matchmaking efforts were the bane of his life.

He slid me an amused sidelong glance. 'Alas no.' It was time to go and he tucked my hand under his arm to lead me from the room. 'You do realise, Mademoiselle Adélaïde, that it is only a matter of time before my mother and your grandmother encounter each other and decide to combine forces?'

We were just about to leave the Hôtel when the doors burst open and in bustled Cassandre and the Vicomte de Barthèlmy, both soaked to the skin thanks to the rain and grinning like devils. 'You weren't going to leave without me!' Cassandre exclaimed in accusing tones.   Lucrèce sighed and stepped lightly forward. 'Of course not, but I thought you were attending the Queen this afternoon?' She lightly hugged our sister and acknowledged the Vicomte, whom she didn't really like, with a nod which he received with a grave smile and bow.

'That was the plan,' Cassandre admitted, going to a mirror and straightening her enormous, flamboyant hat on her head, twirling her damp red curls around her fingers. 'However, at the last minute, Her Majesty decided to dispense with my services for the day and so here I am!'

'How are things at the palace?' Xavier asked in a low voice.

Cassandre sighed. 'Not good,' she replied. 'The Queen is nervous and this makes her pick fights with everyone. I swear that she almost slapped me yesterday just for stepping on the hem of her dress. It's very unlike her.'

Lucrèce laughed. 'Surely not, Cassandre,' she murmured, with an anxious look at Xavier, who we could never forget was the god son of the King's cousin and most bitter enemy, the Duc d'Orléans.

'You weren't there!' Cassandre retorted, as usual not caring who heard her. 'You should take up your duties, Madame la Duchesse, and see for yourself how things are!' She swept a mocking curtsey.

'Perhaps I will,' Lucrèce replied, with a quick look at her husband, who nodded approvingly. She had been invited to join the Queen's ladies shortly after her marriage but had refused, believing that she would quickly fall pregnant. Clearly she had given up hope of having a child anytime soon and I felt a pang of sadness for her.

The rain had stopped by the time we went outside and we walked at a brisk pace through the streets to the Champs de Mars, which was not too far away. When we saw that the roads were at a standstill thanks to the dozens of carriages that were trying to get to the same destination, we congratulated ourselves and Lucrèce, who walked ahead arm in arm with her husband, on the good idea of walking instead.

I held onto Cousin Sébastien's arm and looked around me with delight at the busy, crowded, bustling streets, which teemed with people and music and noise. Everyone was shouting, laughing and singing at the tops of their voices and there was even dancing as young men grabbed passing girls and whirled them around to the sound of violins and drums that surrounded us.

'What a glorious day!' I said to Sébastien. 'How wonderful to be a part of something so joyous.'

'Indeed.' He smiled at me, but he didn't exactly looked thrilled to be there. He peered anxiously up at the sky. 'I hope that the rain holds off for a bit longer.'

The parade ground was full of people by the time we arrived, all clambering over the turf seats that had been erected and yelling across to their friends. Dozens of street vendors, selling everything imaginable wandered through the crowds, hoarsely shouting about their wares and flirting with the passersby. I saw Cassandre slap her Vicomte's arm with her fan when he exchanged a lazy smile with a buxom passing orange seller.

'Mademoiselle de Saint-Valèry?' A melodious male voice that I remembered all too well murmured my name and with a shocked sharp intake of breath I whirled around to face the actor, Monsieur Bertrand. Our paths had not crossed since that wintry day at David's studio in the Louvre, but he had not changed at all and was just as magnificently tall and handsome as ever in his green and black striped silk coat and flamboyant cravat.

'Monsieur Bertrand,' I said, giving him my hand and ignoring the curious looks of my sisters who had both clearly recognised him and were exchanging incredulous looks, wondering where I had made the acquaintance of such a celebrated personage. 'How nice to see you again.'

'You remember me?' He looked oddly pleased and the smile in his dark eyes as he gazed down at me was warm and genuine. 'I have often wondered if we would ever meet again.'

I stared at him, totally confused. 'Monsieur Bertrand, I do not think that I quite understand.' I struggled to think of the right words. 'I am flattered, of course by your interest in me but I don't...'

'Bertrand, I presume?' Cassandre had stepped between us and was smilingly extending her hand towards the handsome actor. 'I can't believe that we have never met!' She looked up at him flirtatiously. 'I am such a great admirer of your work!'

'Madame la Marquise,' Bertrand gallantly lifted her hand to his lips. 'You remind me very much of your mother. She was the most beautiful and exquisite woman that I have ever had the good fortune to meet.'

'So gentlemen keep telling me,' Cassandre replied dryly, with a look that I couldn't quite fathom.

'You knew my mother, monsieur?' I asked, suddenly breathless. 'What was she like?'

Bertrand looked at me then, his expression sad. 'Your mother, mademoiselle, was charm personified.' He reached out and gently touched my blushing cheek. 'You are very like her.'

I gazed up at him, the noise and activity of the immense crowd that surrounded us fading to nothing as I looked into his dark eyes and admitted to myself that which I think I had known deep within my heart ever since that day at David's studio: that he and not the Comte de Saint-Valèry was my true father. 'I think that we should talk properly,' I whispered, my throat dry. 'Not here, it is too noisy.'

He took my hand again and kissed it fervently, immediately understanding. 'Of course, yes,' he murmured in his rich, dramatic voice. 'It is all that I wish for.' He reached into his pocket and produced a card with his name and an address on the Rue du Bac printed on it in ornate black script. 'Can you come to me later?' he asked, his dark brows knitted together in concern. 'I will make sure that I am totally alone.'

I took the card from him and smiled. 'I will do my best.'

The rest of the day passed in a blur. Afterwards I would only be able to remember the shouts and cheers of the crowd as the King stepped forward to swear his allegiance to the nation, the dyed red, white and blue plumes in the Queen's powdered hair and the way Cassandre and Lucrèce whispered and giggled together whenever Monsieur de Talleyrand forgot the words of the Mass that he was celebrating, while Cousin Sébastien and the Vicomte looked on in resigned disapproval. 'They are so childish together,' I heard one of them whisper to the other with a sigh.

After the ceremony, we returned to the Hôtel de Saliex for dinner, then donned our cloaks once more and set forth into the darkening night, where an immense street party was just beginning. The stately roads of the Faubourg Saint-Honoré were lit up with brightly coloured paper lanterns strung from the branches of the trees, torches hanging from the walls of the houses and bonfires in the roads while thousands of people roamed at will, dressed up in their very best clothes, keen to flirt, dance and enjoy themselves while eating and drinking delicious wares purchased from the gaudily decorated stalls that had been set up on the street corners. The atmosphere was light hearted, with

110

every heart full of optimism that the Revolution was at an end and that peace, prosperity and happiness would be the lot of every man, woman and child from that moment on.

I linked arms with my sisters and tried my best to dance and laugh alongside them, but my mind was elsewhere, as I considered how best to get to the Rue du Bac. Xavier de Saint-Benoît alone seemed to realise that I was not myself and he came close to me and tucked my hand under his arm. 'Are you quite alright, mademoiselle?' he asked with the laughing, sidelong look that I had grown to love.

I forced a smile and nodded. I looked at him speculatively, wondering if I could take him into my confidence: it would make it so much easier if someone knew the truth. 'Could you tell me where the Rue du Bac is?' I asked. 'I have an old school friend there that I should like very much to see and I do not often get opportunities to go to places...'

He smiled. 'I understand, mademoiselle.' A horrible suspicion crossed my mind that he might think that I was planning to meet a lover. 'It is close at hand; would you like me to accompany you?'

I was about to refuse when a quick glance around me at the hundreds of revelers, now rapidly getting drunk on cheap wine and brandy and dancing together in the most provocative and rowdy manner while singing at the tops of their lungs made me change my mind. 'That is very kind of you, monsieur.' I put a hand on his arm as a rowdily dancing young couple jostled against me then shouted their apologies. 'Do you think we will be missed if we go now?'

He looked over at my sisters, who had joined in the dancing while the other men watched in amusement. 'I doubt it, don't you?' He offered me his arm and we walked briskly away, pushing our way through the crowds and smiling and nodding at the people who shoved their faces in ours and with breath soured by cheap vinegary wine, shouted 'To liberty!'

'Here we are,' Xavier said as we turned onto the Rue du Bac, a street of stately houses with tall, secretive windows all set back behind the traditional gated courtyard which led out onto the road. I slipped the card out from my pocket and swiftly checked the address, fearful that Xavier should see Bertrand's name and come to entirely the wrong conclusion. 'It is this one,' I said presently as we walked down the street and came to stand outside a huge gate, its bright blue painted doors surmounted with a huge stone bust of Medusa, hideously grinning with bulging eyes and carved snakes for hair.

'This one?' Xavier looked nervously up at the house's windows, all of which were brightly lit with a red glow beyond the elaborately swagged and fringed brocade curtains. 'Are you sure?' He looked at me curiously, clearly wondering what sort of company I had been keeping.

I nodded, suddenly sick with nerves. 'This is the one.' I anxiously patted my hair, which was untidy as usual and escaping from the wide ribbon that I had tied around it. 'Would you mind waiting for me, Monsieur de Saint-Benoît?' We both stared up at the windows again.

He smiled down at me. 'Of course I will, mademoiselle.' He led the way to the front door with me trotting rather timidly behind him. 'I promise to wait here for as long as it takes and then restore you to your sisters.'

I swallowed and squared my shoulders. 'I should just get it over with, shouldn't I?' I lifted the heavy brass dragon shaped knocker and let it fall. 'I promise not to be long.'

The door was opened by a very grand looking black footman dressed in a rich purple silk livery. 'Who is it?' he asked, peering at first Xavier and then me. 'Do you know whose house this is?'

'I'm here to see Monsieur Bertrand,' I said as clearly as I could, ignoring Xavier's start of surprise. 'It's Mademoiselle de Saint-Valèry.' I took a deep breath. 'I believe that he is expecting me.'

The footman nodded but did not smile. 'Yes, he is waiting for you.' He held the heavy wooden door open. 'Come inside, mademoiselle.' He looked beyond me to Xavier. 'You can wait inside, monsieur. No need to stand on the street.'

'Thank you,' Xavier replied courteously, before taking hold of my arm and adding in an undertone: 'Are you sure about this, Adélaïde?'

My heart leaped within my breast as I looked up and saw the concern in his eyes. If I had been Cassandre, I would have wasted no time and kissed him at that moment, but it was me, Adélaïde, the youngest and least favoured of the Saint-Valèry girls and so instead I smiled and did nothing. 'Yes, I'm sure. I have never been more sure about anything in fact.'

We followed the footman across the paved courtyard, where purple bougainvillia grew thickly up the walls, filling the air with their luscious, heady scent and two huge lavender filled terracotta pots, shaped like chimeras flanked the steps leading up to the glossy, red front door.

'Follow me,' the footman said over his shoulder as he pushed open the door and led us across a huge, incense scented marble floored hall to some double doors at the far end. 'You can wait in here, monsieur,' he said to Xavier, pushing the doors open to reveal a sumptuously decorated sitting room with vast mirrors set into the blue brocade covered walls. It was clearly a room designed for pleasure and revelry and I found myself blushing as I peered up at the lavishly painted ceiling, with its profusions of frolicking pink naked female flesh. 'I will bring you some refreshments presently.'

Xavier took my hands in his and looked down earnestly into my face. 'Adélaïde, I don't know what has brought you here, but I wish you good luck,' he whispered. 'I will be waiting for you. Do not be afraid to call for me if I am needed.'

I nodded and squeezed his hands, so thrilled by his use of my first name to be able to speak, then turned quickly away lest my resolve, already fluttering, falter entirely. I followed the footman silently back through the hall, where I now realised that the heavy scent of incense was wafting in plumes of smoke from huge jade green and gold porcelain burners placed on red marble plinths in the corners of the room.

'Up here,' the footman said, leading me up the imposing red marble staircase that dominated the hallway. He looked back over his shoulder and smiled, his teeth white and gleaming in his dark face. 'Do'nt be afraid, mademoiselle. My master won't hurt you.' He softly scratched at a door at the top of the stairs then pushed it slowly open. 'Monsieur, Mademoiselle de Saint-Valèry is here.'

I took a deep breath and stepped into the room, which was as opulently gloomy and richly decorated as the rest of the house, with huge gilt framed paintings hanging on crimson silk and the only light coming from two huge crystal chandeliers that hung overhead, their translucent droplets tinkling slightly in the draught as the footman bowed and closed the door behind me.

'Adélaïde!' Bertrand was reclining at his ease on a crimson silk covered sofa but stood up abruptly as I entered the room and came towards me with his hands outstretched. 'You came!'

I curtsied, rather more primly than I liked. 'Of course.' I looked him over curiously, taking in his unusual height; his thick dark carefully arranged hair, which he wore pomaded with rose oil and brushed forward towards his face; his blue and gold silk dressing gown which he wore open over his fine linen shirt and puce taffeta breeches. He must have been at least fifty but he was still a very handsome man, with smooth olive skin, dark eyes and a sensual mouth that was smiling with honest pleasure as he took my hands in his and raised them to his lips.

'You're just like her,' he murmured. 'You have the same lovely eyes and pretty ways.' He released my hands and put his arm around me, leading me to the sofa. 'She would have been very proud of you, my darling girl.'

I sat beside him, suddenly tongue tied and unsure of what to say. 'I wish that I could have known her,' I said at last. 'She went away when I was just a baby.'

He sighed. 'I know and I am sorry for it.' He took my hands again. 'You must have so many questions for me.'

I nodded. 'Yes, many, but I dare not stay too long in case

we are missed.' I looked around at the lavishly decorated room in which we sat. 'This is a lovely house,' I said politely. 'Did my mother come here?'

He laughed. 'Alas no, I was not nearly so rich when I knew my poor Sidonie. If I had been, then who knows what might have happened?' He released my hands, stood up and went to a table by the window, where he proceeded to pour himself a glass of red wine. 'And for you, mademoiselle?' he asked politely.

I hesitated for a moment. 'Yes, please.' I stood up as well and went to take my glass from him. 'How long have you known about me?' I asked, taking a sip of wine.

Bertrand sighed. 'I have always known, Adélaïde,' he replied, with a regretful shake of his handsome head. 'Your mother, Sidonie, came to me as soon as she found out that she was expecting a child.' He put down his glass and wiped his hand across his eyes. 'I asked her to come away with me, to leave Paris behind and live with me as my wife, but she refused.'

'Why?' I asked curiously. 'Didn't she love you?' He was such a glorious contrast to the Comte that I couldn't imagine any woman not preferring him.

He sipped his wine again. 'She didn't want to leave Paris and your brother and sisters,' he said after a long pause. 'She also didn't want me to ruin my career for her sake. The scandal if we had left together, would have destroyed both our lives forever.' He looked at me then. 'And your's, once it became publicly known that you were my daughter and not that of the Comte.'

I took a long draught of my wine, which made me feel curiously and not unpleasantly light headed. 'What happened when she went away?' I asked.

He sighed. 'She didn't go willingly, Adélaïde,' he said. 'The Comte and his mother arranged it between them that she should be taken away at night and driven to a convent far from Paris, there to live out the rest of her days.' He took my hands. 'I don't know for sure what happened that night, but I absolutely believe that if she had been allowed to do so, then your mother would have taken you with her.'

I stared at him. 'Really? I have always believed, always thought...' I sat down heavily on a chair. 'No one loves me, monsieur and I believed that it has always been so.'

He smiled. 'No, it has not always been so and is not so now.' He reached into his shirt and produced a small diamond surrounded miniature, which he gazed at sadly for a moment. 'Your mother loved you more than anyone else in all the world, Adélaïde,' he said at last, as I stared up at him. 'She used to tell me that your brother and sisters were Saint Valèry's children whereas you, my beauty, were entirely hers.' He handed me the miniature, which depicted a beautiful blonde girl with huge eyes, holding a smiling baby on her lap. 'She often spoke of her plans for you. You were going to be the most lovely of her girls, she said.'

I looked down at the miniature. Here she was at last. Sidonie. 'She was even more beautiful than I imagined,' I said, tracing the contours of her perfect face with my finger. 'I had no idea.' I sighed. 'Am I the baby?'

He smiled. 'Yes, that's you, Adélaïde. She had the painting done for me in secret just a few weeks before she was taken away.'

I took one last glance, feeling inexpressibly sad, then handed the picture back to Bertrand. 'Monsieur, where is she now?'

He sighed, his fingers closing around the miniature. 'I do not know,' was the reply. 'I have spent a fortune trying to find her but have discovered nothing at all. I knew that she was in a convent but had no idea which one.' He looked at me and I saw that his dark eyes were shining with tears. 'I had thought that perhaps she would come back once the convents were all suppressed but have heard no news at all, despite my best attempts to find her.'

I looked at him. 'You have never forgotten her,' I said, taking his warm hands in mine.

He squeezed my fingers and gave a rueful smile. 'No, and I never will.'

1792

LUCRÈCE

Paris, August 1792

The long expected war between France and Austria broke out in April and almost overnight Paris became rife with suspicion and turmoil as the government began to recruit troops and everyone wondered if we were were about to be invaded by blood thirsty foreign armies who would storm the capital, burn down our homes and slit our throats as we slept. The skillful orators of the Jacobin and Cordeliers clubs, Danton, Robespierre and their supporters whipped up frenzies of paranoia against the aristocracy and the émigrés, who were regarded as the enemies of France and popularly expected to return at any minute, massacre all good citizens and seize control of the country. The happy, optimistic camaraderie of 1790 was very definitely at an end.

The pleasant, balmy Spring gradually became an unbearably hot and oppressive Summer and tensions rose as the heat became ever higher. By June the streets were full of rioting, sedition and fear as the inhabitants of the poorest Parisian faubourgs vented their anger and frustration as they had always done by burning straw effigies, attacking the well dressed with handfuls of horse excrement scooped up from the filthy streets and smashing windows. On the twentieth of June, matters came to a head and the mob invaded the Tuileries – the royal family came to no real harm but were left shaken, anxious and awaiting the next blow.

For the wealthy inhabitants of the faubourg Saint-Germain, where we continued to live quietly at the Hôtel de Saliex, life continued much as it had always done with the usual round of intimate supper parties, salon evenings and trips to the theatre. There was a new sense of hush and reticence to our activities as we locked away our jewels and dressed as plainly as we could in plain white muslin and silk gowns with our hair hanging unbrushed and unpowdered about our shoulders. And all the while our numbers dwindled every day as friends either emigrated in panic and secrecy from a city that was clearly on the brink of explosion or either, more terrifyingly vanished into the rapidly swelling prisons.

The already inflammatory situation was worsened in July by the publication of the Duke of Brunswick's 'manifesto', written by the Duke of Brunswick, who was in charge of the joint armies of Austria and Prussia, which were camped at Coblenz and poised for action against France. This ill judged document made the aims of the armies very clear and threatened violent and hideous reprisals against the French people should the King and his family be harmed in any way.   The manifesto, as it was called, was made public by monarchist groups, who assumed that it would frighten the government into submitting to the Austrian demands. Instead it immediately caused a huge and wholesale panic in the capital and a greater distrust and loathing of the already hated émigrés, the royal family and their friends still in France.

'The city of Paris and all its inhabitants without distinction shall be required to submit at once and without delay to the king, to place that prince in full and complete liberty, and to assure to him, as well as to the other royal personages, the inviolability and respect which the law of nature and of nations demands of subjects toward sovereigns... Their said Majesties declare, on their word of honour as emperor and king, that if the chateau of the Tuileries is entered by force or attacked, if the least violence be offered to their Majesties the king, queen, and royal family, and if their safety and their liberty be not immediately assured, they will inflict an ever memorable vengeance by delivering over the city of Paris to military execution and complete destruction, and the rebels guilty of the said outrages to the punishment that they merit...'

It was impossible to read this and not be afraid for the future and as the summer passed from July into August so too did the atmosphere in the capital became ever darker and ever more fearful. Everyone regarded everyone else with suspicion and the Austrian army was daily expected to appear at the gates of the city, sweeping all before them in a storm of fire and blood.

It was at this time that the so called 'domiciliary visits' began and people began to disappear from their homes, vanishing into the prisons that began to spring up all across the city. Former schools, private buildings and religious houses were hastily converted in order to accommodate the rapidly increasing amount of prisoners. The visits were intended to be as alarming as possible and so took place at the dead of night, when a group of ten armed and doubtless drunk citizens carrying flaming torches would hammer on the door then ransack the house before dragging their cowering prey into the darkness, never to be seen again. The people of Paris barely slept through that long, intensely hot, sultry Summer – they lay awake and frightened in their beds with the windows wide open, waiting for the sound of the Ça Ira being drunkenly sung in the streets below as the mob came ever closer. To make matters worse, there seemed to be no way of protecting oneself either as people seemed to be imprisoned for the most spurious of reasons – from plotting to rescue the royal family to drunkenly ranting about the government to unapologetically bearing an ancient name.

Like everyone else in Paris and with perhaps more reason than most, I lay awake at night on my little sofa by the window, propped up on cooling linen pillows and restlessly wondering if the mob that I often heard passing noisily down the Rue de Grenelle was going to stop at the Hôtel de Saliex and tear us all from our home. I hardly dared to breathe until I could no longer hear them and knew that we had all escaped for another night.

At my husband's insistence, we all did our best not to provoke any suspicion – we dressed as plainly as possible, wore a tricolor cockade at all times and generally tried not to draw any attention to ourselves. At first Cassandre rebelled against this but in the end, even she bent her head to his dictates and cheerfully fastened a red, white and blue rosette from Rose Bertin's shop to her fashionable hats. With an expression of absolute sincerity, she even addressed all and sundry as 'Citizen' and 'Citizeness'.

At the start of August the hot, dusty streets filled with hundreds of troops from Marseilles and their catchy and bloodthirsty marching song, la Marseillaise was soon to be heard on all lips. At the same time 'insurrection' became the mot du jour and the Assembly and fashionable salons were all abuzz with talk of the planned assault on the Tuileries and overthrow of the monarchy. No one knew quite when it was to happen but it was expected that the blow, when it did fall, would be bloody and decisive.

The ninth of August started much like any other day with attendance at the once thronged but now sadly quiet and depleted Queen's lever and then a long, dreary Mass in the shabby Tuileries chapel. The prevalent mood at the palace was never very cheerful, especially since the royal family's ill fated and ultimately humiliating attempt to escape the capital a year earlier and so when I entered the Queen's rooms and saw that everyone was looking pale and anxious, I thought nothing of it and quietly went about my duties as usual. I tried in vain to amuse the downcast, tearful Queen, played with the two royal children and took Marie Antoinette's spoilt little dogs for a walk in the gardens before returning to the palace for a strained, silent dinner with the other ladies in waiting. I thought wistfully of my own home and family as I dispiritedly spooned in some weak, brown soup and listlessly crumbled a hard bread roll onto my chipped and slightly grubby plate. There had been a time, long ago, when we had all laughed joylessly together about how very different it all was to Versailles, but those days were long gone now.

The afternoon was spent doing needlework and idly listening to the stale gossip that still floated around the bored court before I heard from Madame Campan that there was talk of an attack on the palace in the next day. At first, I did not know whether to panic or dismiss the news as yet another false alarm – there had been so many after all.

'Are you quite certain, madame?' I asked incredulously, hardly bothering to look up from my embroidery. 'There is talk all the time of yet another assault on the Tuileries.'

Madame Campan looked rather affronted to have her word doubted and roughly jerked her head in the direction of the window. 'See for yourself, Madame la Duchesse,' she said. 'The troops are already massing in front of the palace.'

I sighed and laid aside my embroidery, then made my way to the window which overlooked the Cour Royale, where I was astonished to see that hundreds of soldiers had gathered with both the blue of the national guards and the red of the King's famous Swiss guards in evidence. I wondered if my sister's lover, the Vicomte de Barthèlmy was somewhere amongst the throng – his own regiment had been recently been disbanded as a result of being considered 'too aristocratic' but regardless of this, he had vowed to fight for his King. This was much to Cassandre's dismay as she wanted him to remain safely at her side instead of risking his life for what she believed to be a lost cause.

I sighed and turned back to Madame Campan, feeling quite shaken by the sight and now wondering if this time the end really was coming for us all. 'What happens now?' I asked, trying my best not to sound afraid.

'Now?' Madame Campan gave a grim smile. 'Now, we sit and wait.' She shrugged in the superior way that made her so unpopular at court. 'You are of course at liberty to return to your family but I prefer to remain by the side of my Queen.'

Never before had time slipped away so slowly. The Queen's state coucher, when she prepared for bed, was more sparsely attended than I had ever known it with only a handful of yawning, distracted ladies in attendance. This struck me quite forcibly as it used to be one of the central acts in the great drama that was Marie Antoinette's official day and the fact that there were so few people there on what could well be our last day in the palace made me feel both sad and alarmed in equal measures.

Afterwards, I went with the other ladies to one of the huge, shabbily elegant palace salons, where we threw ourselves down on the threadbare pink and gold sofas and talked quietly amongst ourselves. Darkness fell upon the palace and its grounds and the liveried footmen walked silently around the room, carefully pulling the heavy brocade curtains closed and lighting the cheap wax candles in the tall candelabras that stood on every surface.

Bored with the endless chatter, I stood for a while by one of the windows, staring out across the city and wondering where the people I loved best were at that very moment. I had managed to send a messenger to the Hôtel de Saliex with a note for my husband and another to the Hôtel de Saint-Valèry for my father, Cassandre and Adélaïde but had hesitated over the third note, to Cousin Sébastien that I ended up kissing then hiding inside a drawer. There was nothing I could do now but pray that I would see them all again soon.

I was dozing on one of the sofas with my head on Madame de Tourzel's pretty daughter Pauline's shoulder when the church bells began to ring out across Paris. I immediately jumped to my feet and ran to the window, from which I could glimpse the little orange fires that marked the soldier's makeshift camps but nothing else, thank God. I turned back to the room, where the other ladies in waiting were beginning to sit up, smoothing down their crumpled, petal coloured silk skirts and patting their messy hair. As the terrible, discordant, urgent sound of many church bells filled the air, we stared at each other in horror and knew with a sudden certainty that we were doomed. The Princesse de Lamballe, melodramatic as ever, immediately dropped to her knees and began to pray.

The sky was a vivid blood red when dawn finally rose over the sleepless city and we were all up and watching anxiously from the windows when at five o clock the King went out to inspect the troops and defences of the palace. I turned away, unable to watch when he hastily retreated indoors after being greeted with catcalls and jeers from the national guards.

'How dare they behave in such a way?' Marie Antoinette muttered as she watched her husband come up the grand staircase, which was now swarming with troops – he looked crumpled and defeated with his wig slightly askew, his green waistcoat unbuttoned and a shadow of stubble on his chin. 'We are all lost. It would have been better if he had not shown himself at all than be exposed to such indignity!' She turned and swept away, not bothering to greet her husband, who watched her go with tears in his eyes.

I stood for a long time with Pauline de Tourzel at an upstairs window, watching the angry populace as they screamed abuse up at the palace and fired shots into the air. There looked to be several thousand people outside and I felt almost sick with fear as I looked down into their angry, hate filled faces and recalled the events of October 1789. I wished with all my heart that Cassandre was with me, but at the same time was glad that she was almost certainly safe in her own house on the Rue Saint-Honoré.

Little Pauline, a pretty girl with beautiful brown eyes and long chestnut coloured hair shyly slipped her hand into mine. 'Do you think that we are going to die, Madame la Duchesse?' she asked in a timid voice. The girl was only sixteen and had everything to live for.

I swallowed down my own dread and forced a brave smile. 'No, I don't.' I squeezed Pauline's hand. 'Let's come away from the window and see if we are needed elsewhere.' We walked through rooms filled with soldiers; brave men who were fully prepared to lay down their lives for their monarch and his family. I looked anxiously for tall, dark haired Alexandre de Barthèlmy, who always strode so confidently in the midst of the other men but couldn't see him anywhere. Perhaps he had got out in time and was with Cassandre in the house that they discreetly shared, far from the prying eyes of gossips of the Faubourg Saint-Germain.

Discussions raged in the royal apartment as their advisers tried to persuade the stubborn Louis and Marie Antoinette that it was in their best interests to vacate the palace as quickly as possible and seek refuge in the Assembly, whose meetings in the ménage were only a short walk away. However the Queen had a complete and almost romantic faith in their brave troops ability to defend the Tuileries and was determined to remain despite everyone's advice to the contrary.

'Madame, do you really want to make yourself responsible for the massacre of the King, your children, yourself, to say nothing of the faithful servants that surround you?' the deputy Roederer, who was Procurator General of the Paris region, was demanding of the Queen as Pauline and I quietly entered the room. The younger girl immediately shrank back with a small cry, frightened by the blunt language but I pulled her close and hugged her tightly until she had quietened, imagining for a moment that she was my sister, Adélaïde, who was hopefully safely at home on the Rue des Francs-Bourgeois.

The Queen flushed crimson at the harsh words. 'On the contrary, what would I not do to be the only victim,' she retorted in a low voice, her blue eyes burned with emotion and sincerity. Roederer pressed on with his attack, this time turning to the King. 'Sire, your Majesty has not five minutes to lose. There is no safety except in the National Assembly. The opinion of the Department is that you go immediately. You do not have sufficient men in the courtyards to defend the palace, and besides they are not well disposed. The gunners have even unloaded their guns.' He sighed, as had done many others when faced with the taciturn stubbornness of Louis XVI. 'Sire, they have twelve cannons and several thousand men coming from the faubourgs of Paris. You are vastly outnumbered. There is no option but to go to the Assembly.'

Finally, the Queen capitulated and it was agreed that the royal family would leave the Tuileries and place themselves under the protection of the National Assembly. There was an audible sigh of relief as the King stood up and announced their decision before vaguely waving his hand towards the door. 'Let us go. There is nothing further to do here. Marchons, marchons.'

'What about us?' Pauline whispered, voicing what was uppermost in every mind at that moment. 'Do we go with them?'

'I don't know,' I replied, my heart pounding alarmingly in my breast. We could hear the clamour of the mob outside and it took every ounce of self control not to turn and run screaming from the building as it was only a matter of time before they broke in and then who knew what would happen?

'We are to remain here,' Madame Campan said to us with a curt nod. 'Only Madame la Princesse de Lamballe and Madame la Marquise de Tourzel are to accompany their Majesties to the Ménage.' She looked in her short sighted way at Pauline who went pale when she heard that her mother was leaving her and going with the royal family. 'You will be remaining here with us, child. We will take good care of you.'

There was crying as Marie Antoinette embraced each one of her ladies in waiting and said goodbye. 'We will be back,' the Queen said, smiling through her tears as she kissed my cheek. 'We will all be reunited soon. If the King's downfall is decreed by the Assembly, he will accept it and then things will continue as they have always done.'

I nodded mutely, not knowing what to say. It was so clear that they were never going to come back and at that moment I doubted that I would ever see the Queen again as there was such an air of martyrdom and hopelessness about her as she moved slowly around the room.

Those who remained stood aside as the pitiful little procession left the state apartments and made its way downstairs. It seemed incredible and unbelievable that the French monarchy could end in such a way – shabby, downtrodden and hounded by its own people.

'We are never coming back,' the Princesse de Lamballe whispered, echoing everyone's thoughts as she walked past. Her long blonde hair was escaping from its pins and falling in profusion down her back and her eyes were black with exhaustion.

We, the final, shattered remains of the once huge and magnificent court all watched in weary, frightened silence until the slumped and defeated royal party vanished out of sight then turned to each other in panic, not knowing what to do next, while all the while the palace began to fill with the noise of hammering, stamping, screams and shouts as the mob broke inside.

'What shall we do? ' Pauline wailed, rooted to the ground in horror as the terrible noise came ever closer. 'They are going to kill us all.'

'We should run and hide,' I said, taking her hand and pulling her from the room. 'This palace is huge. There must be somewhere we can go.'

We made our way swiftly through once splendid rooms, now decaying and gloomy, with plaster falling from the walls and the splendid ceilings stained and denuded of their gilt decorations. All was chaos and confusion as swarms of soldiers, servants and courtiers also ran aimlessly from room to room, clutching makeshift weapons and staring about themselves in wild eyed terror.

It wasn't long before we heard the first volley of shots from below and we clung to each other helplessly behind a shabby crimson velvet sofa in one of the deserted salons, listening in terror to the overwhelming, furious roar of the crowd outside, the frantic volleys of gunshot and the shrill screams of the wounded.

'The Swiss Guards must be ordered to retreat at once!' some one yelled close by. 'The King should have left orders when he left! They are totally outnumbered and are going to be massacred out there!'

I pulled away from the sobbing Pauline and went to the window which had been hit by bullets and was riddled with holes. I pulled aside the tattered crimson brocade curtain then shrank back in horror from the terrible scenes being enacted outside as the Parisian mob slaughtered the brave Swiss Guards. There was blood running all over the dusty cobbles below and I covered my mouth in shock and disgust as men clearly begging for their lives before being ruthlessly despatched by the gory axes, swords and knives carried by the mob. It was horrible and I put out a hand to prevent Pauline getting up from her hiding place and seeing anything of the massacre. 'No, don't come any closer.'

I went back to her and we sank to our knees behind the sofa and hugged each other, sobbing and terrified as the sound of cannon fire and mayhem floated in through the window. The minutes dragged on until finally the noise came to an end and there was an uneasy silence broken only by the pitiful shouts and the groans of the wounded.

'We must find somewhere to conceal ourselves before the mob gets in,' I said as we stared at each other, not knowing what to expect next. 'With the Swiss Guards gone it is only a matter of time before the attackers find us.' I pulled the frightened and unwilling Pauline to her feet and we ran from the room, lifting our now grimy skirts above our ankles and making our way down corridors and staircases crowded with frightened, weeping servants and courtiers until we arrived at the Dauphin's apartment, where we found the other ladies in waiting huddled together and sobbing as they listened to the confusion and mayhem. Someone had lowered the blinds so that the room was in darkness and the small group of women presented a sinister sight. It was another blisteringly hot day and the room was unbearably over heated as no one dared to open the blinds and windows.

'We must leave the door open and have light in here so that they do not mistake us for soldiers,' I said at once, seeing that someone needed to take charge. 'It is hell on earth out there and in the darkness and chaos they might well mistake us for guardsmen and slay us where we stand.' I went about the room, pulling up the blinds and tying back the curtains before throwing up some of the windows, letting in some much needed fresh air.

I went to Pauline's side and held her hand, biting my lip and trying my best to remain brave and not break down and weep with fear as the sounds of screams and looting came ever closer. The tumult was terrible and we could only imagine the horrors that were speedily coming our way. I thought again of my sisters and brother, praying silently that they were safe from harm and that my messages of reassurance had reached them.

Madame Campan whispered prayers over and over, as we all stared at the door, dreading the inevitable moment when someone would step through it. My grip on Pauline's hand tightened as I heard the sound of running footsteps coming ever closer.

It was almost a relief when there was a terrible shout near at hand and a crowd of bloodstained men carrying swords and guns rushed into the room. Madame Campan drew herself up and stared at them. 'I trust that you will not slay innocent women!' she cried in a thin, nervous voice but her words were lost in the tumult as the men filled the room and grabbed at the fleeing, screaming ladies in waiting.

I shrieked as someone's filthy hand gripped my shoulder, staining my once pretty pink and white dress with blood. I strained against my laughing, grinning captor until my dress tore and I was free from his clutches. The furniture was smashed and splintered all over the floor and the heavy curtains were dragged from the windows, filling the room with choking, swirling motes of dust. I looked around but could not see Pauline anywhere in the violence and confusion. 'Pauline!' I yelled over the shouts and screams. 'Where are you?' I ran swiftly to the door and slipped out, almost crazed with terror and with no idea where to go. Quickly, I lifted my skirts and hurried down a debris filled corridor to the staircase. It was like a terrible nightmare – everywhere that I looked there were bloodstains, bodies and over turned furniture.

'Lucrèce! Over here!' I turned and to my astonishment saw my brother-in-law, Eugène de Vautière. He was looking very bedraggled, his once cream silk breeches were stained with blood and dirt and his fair hair hung messily around his face. 'You startled me! What are you doing here? I had no idea that you were in the palace!'

'I came here to see the King,' he replied, roughly seizing my arm so that I yelped with pain. 'I beg your pardon for hurting you, Lucrèce, but you have to get out of here!' He started to lead me further down the corridor.

We stumbled over an inert body of a man that lay across the corridor and I gave a little scream. I could not see the face but there was blood everywhere, all over the walls and floor. I took Eugène's hand and swallowed down the sickness that threatened to overcome me while he listening intently to the clatter, gunfire and roar of the mob which suddenly seemed louder and closer at hand. 'Here, take this.' He took off his long, dark cloak and bundled it into my arms. 'It might be the only chance that you have.' He led me swiftly down some stairs that led to a door that opened out to the gardens.

Still unable to speak, I wrapped the cloak around herself, hiding my dress and auburn ringlets which had fallen out of their chignon and now fell tangled and loose to my waist. I could not help trembling with fear, although it was oppressively hot in the Tuileries, and my fingers were clumsy as I fastened the cloak and removed my diamond rings, necklace and earrings, which would have marked me out instantly as an aristocrat.

'Now, keep your head down, don't speak to anyone and keep walking until you are clear of the palace.' He stood aside and kissed my hand. 'God speed, chérie, give my best regards to your sister.' He smiled. 'Tell her that I love her still and will always do so.'

I stared at him in horror. 'Are you not coming with me, Eugène?' I caught his hands. 'You have to come with me! They will kill you! You said yourself that we could not remain here! Please, Eugène, come with me!'

He resolutely shook his head and gently shook his hands free from my grasp. 'My place is here beside the King. I must stay and fight for him.'

'Eugène, you can't stay here!' I pulled at his lapels. 'There is nothing left to fight for!'

'Au revoir, Madame la Duchesse!' He pulled away, bowed and strode quickly away, leaving me alone in the corridor.

I hesitated for just a moment, sadly watching him as he went before I turned and ran out of the door into the sunlight. It took a moment for my eyes to adjust to the sudden brightness but then I pulled the dark cloak close and ran as fast as I could across the slippery blood covered parterres towards the Pont Tournant, a little swing bridge that led to the Place de Louis XV. However, troops had rallied in the gardens and begun to fire upon each other so I was forced to turn and run back towards the palace so as not to be shot. I ran up some steps that led to the terrace and wildly thought about jumping over the wall that separated the palace gardens from the Quai and Pont Royal but the drop was too deep and the bridge was clearly impassable thanks to the incessant volley of fire coming from the insurgents upon it.

'Here!' I turned to see the Dauphin's valet Cléry, a kind hearted man who was devoted to the royal family, beckoning towards me. 'Madame la Duchesse, we might have a chance of escape if we head towards the Dauphin's garden.'

I nodded and followed him down the terrace, pausing only once to look back over my shoulder at the palace, which was surrounded by thick black smoke. Furniture and bodies were being thrown wantonly out of the windows, falling in a twisted heap on to the ground below and I wondered where Pauline and the other women were, silently praying that they had survived the attack and were safe from harm.

'Don't look back!' Cléry took my hand and led me on. 'We have no time to lose!' We came to the garden and then shrank back in horror as we turned a corner to come upon a large group of armed men who were busily stripping the red uniforms from a pile of slaughtered Swiss Guards. The men were clearly drunk and were mocking and slapping their victims in between swigs from a bottle that they passed between them.

Cléry backed away. 'There is a stable adjoining this

garden,' he said, pointing towards a building behind some trees. 'I beg you to conceal yourself there and I will come as soon as I am able.'

I nodded, bundled up my skirts and running as noiselessly as possible from the scene, just as one of the drunken men caught sight of Cléry and advanced upon him with a sword that was dripping with blood.

'What, Citizen! Without arms? Take this sword and help us to kill!' The man had clearly mistaken Cléry for a compatriot and thrust the hideous weapon into his hand. I did not stop to see what happened next but instead slipped behind the trees until I came to the stables. The door was stiff and I had to push my shoulder against it to make it open. Inside, all of the horses had gone, presumably stolen and everything was gloomy and silent. I hid in one of the stalls, pulling a blanket and straw over myself and waited for Cléry to arrive, which he finally did after a few breathless, terrifying minutes, which had stretched on like hours.

'Madame la Duchesse?' he whispered into the gloom.

'I'm here, Monsieur Cléry,' I whispered back, crawling out of my hiding place so that he could see where I was. 'What is happening?' There were the sounds of screams and shouts close at hand, frighteningly close at hand in fact and I expected to be dragged out and killed myself at any minute.

Cléry sat down heavily beside me and dropped his head in his hands. 'I took the sword and walked beside those men for a while but then they came upon a small group of Swiss Guards hiding in another part of the stables,' he swallowed and looked as though he was going to cry so I awkwardly reached out and patted his shoulder until he had composed himself. 'While those villains fell upon the Swiss and beat them to death I took the opportunity to slip away and come to you.'

'Will they come for us next?' I asked, going cold with fear. 'What should we do? Is there anywhere for us to go?'

Cléry shook his head. 'The Pont Tournant was our only hope but it is swarming with hostile National Guardsmen.'

I sighed. 'Then we are trapped here.'

There was more shouting outside and Cléry suddenly went very alert then put his finger to his lips and went to the door. 'It is Monsieur Le Dreux, the manager of the stables,' he whispered. 'He is sending those brigands away.'

'Will he help us?' I whispered.

'I think that he might,' Cléry replied, beckoning for me to follow him. 'He is a good man and I believe he might well give us shelter until the killing has stopped.' We pushed open the stable door and fell, blinking into the bright sunlight. Monsieur Le Dreux, a small plump man with an amiable face, was clearly astonished to see us but quickly understood the situation we had found ourselves in and immediately offered us shelter in his own home, which was attached to the stables. 'My wife will be only too happy to care for you, madame la Duchesse,' he added as an aside to me, putting his strong arm around me as I came perilously close to fainting with stress and fatigue. 'Come inside and rest. You will be safe with us.'

'Thank you, monsieur,' I replied, trying hard not to look at the murdered guardsmen who lay on the ground. I had already seen more than enough blood and carnage that day and did not think that I could bear to see any more. 'I hope that sheltering us will not endanger you?'

'Not at all,' the gallant Le Dreux replied. 'I am not afraid of those scoundrels!' He led the way into his house, where his wife immediately took charge of the situation. She ordered brandy and food for us and briskly but not unkindly took me off to her room in order to exchange my sadly torn and blood stained silk gown for a plain blue cotton one of her own. At first I refused to accept her offer, conscious that for most women dresses were precious belongings and not something to be parted with lightly. 'I cannot accept this!' I stammered. 'You cannot part with your own clothes!'

'Nonsense!' Madame replied. 'You will be set upon at once if you set foot aside in your own pretty dress and so please, I beg you to accept my own dress instead! It is not as nice, I know, but we are much the same size and it may well save your life.'

The killing continued throughout the day and after a

while I could no longer fight off my exhaustion and lay down upon the overstuffed red sofa in the Le Dreux's sitting room to sleep. When I finally woke up it was dark and it took me a moment to recall where I was and how I had come to be there. I jumped up and went to the window, which overlooked the elegant Place Louis XV, where gangs of drunken, filthy women were stripping the corpses of the fallen.

The door opened behind me and Madame Le Dreux appeared, smiling and holding a glass of water. It was intolerably hot in the sitting room and I accepted it with gratitude. 'I hope that you slept well?' She pushed the window open and a slight breeze filled the room, which went some way towards relieving the stifling heat. 'The killing has stopped now and the bridges should be open again. My husband will escort you as far as you wish to go.'

'Thank you,' I said, wishing that I could refuse my generous host's help after they had already done so much to help me but I had never crossed Paris on foot before and was afraid that I might get lost. 'I should probably set out as soon as possible.'

After a small meal of cold meat, cheese and bread, I donned Eugène's black cloak over my dress and set out with Monsieur Le Dreux. It occurred to me that it might be wiser and easier to head towards Cassandre's house on the much nearer Rue Saint-Honoré rather than walk all the way to the Rue de Grenelle and so we turned our steps back towards the Tuileries. The guns and cannons had gone and it was swarming with people – both ordinary citizens trying to get home and doing their best not to meet anyone's eye and drunken, blood splattered rabble who linked arms and sang La Marseillaise defiantly while dancing around the corpses that still littered the blood soaked ground. I pulled my skirts up as high as I could and tried my best not to wince or look afraid as I stepped over the dead bodies, many of whom missed their heads and other limbs.

'Keep close, madame,' La Dreux whispered as I slid on a pool of blood and cried out in alarm, thinking that I would surely fall over. 'Keep your head down and don't make a sound. There is still violence in the air and we must be careful.'

I did as he said and pulled Eugène's heavy, dark cloak even closer, wondering where he was now and what had happened to Pauline and the other ladies in waiting.

'Lucrèce?' A familiar male voice close at hand made me stop and cautiously turn around.It was Cousin Sébastien, my Sébastien, dressed in sombre black, with his dark hair loose and tangled about his shoulders and a shadow of stubble on his chin. He looked exhausted and worried.

'Sébastien!' I ran to him and flung my arms around his broad shoulders, almost weeping for joy as I rubbed my hot, grimy face against his plain coat. I smiled up at him through my tears.

He stroked my tangled hair and kissed my forehead as I clung to him thankfully. 'My darling girl, ma belle,' he murmured, holding me close. 'I went to the Hôtel de Saliex as soon as I heard that something was afoot and have been looking for you ever since.' He looked down at me and gently stroked my hair away from my face. 'I could not rest until I knew that you were safe from harm.'

I gazed up at him, clutching his hands with mine and sobbing. 'You could have been killed.'

'I could not rest,' he repeated hoarsely, pulling me to him again. 'I had to find you, no matter what.'

And in that moment, everything was forgotten as he dipped his handsome head and kissed me on the lips as I clung to him and ecstatically returned his embrace.

CASSANDRE

Paris, August 1792

And where was I on the day that the world as we knew it came to an end? Where indeed. In fact, I was at my old friend Germaine de Staël's elegant house on the Rue du Bac when I first heard about the insurrection at the Tuileries. One minute we were idling on her sugared almond hued sofas, chatting about what to wear to the opera that night and the next we were on our feet and rushing to the windows, straining our eyes to see the smoke from the burning palace drifting over the rooftops of the city while shouts and screams of panic and fear filled the streets.

The blood splattered and exhausted messenger sent to Germaine from her lover, the Comte de Narbonne, told us what was happening mere yards away from where we were standing. My thoughts immediately flew to my sister, Lucrèce, who was at the palace that day and to my Alexandre, whom I knew would have gone recklessly to the defence of the King that he had sworn to serve until death. His valiant loyalty to the monarchy was one of the things that I loved best about him but at that moment I wished with all of my heart that he was a measly coward and anywhere but at the Tuileries. Never in all my life had I loved anyone as much as I loved that man, a fact that was both a source of wonder and also torment to me.

'We must go there immediately,' Germaine exclaimed in her usual decisive way as she paced up and down her exquisite salon, hampered somewhat by the fact that she was six months pregnant and beginning to waddle in the most ridiculous and inelegant way. 'I must know what is happening.' Her thoughts were clearly all with her lover and father of her unborn child, the handsome and charismatic Narbonne, who had been denounced as a traitor by the all powerful political Jacobin club and was now in hiding in a secret location in Paris that not even I knew.

Like my poor Alexandre, he was a fervent monarchist and had vowed to fight for his King no matter what, despite being wanted by the authorities. It was entirely typical of him to sneak off to the Tuileries to fight, just like all the other impatient, hot blooded aristocratic young men who had been bred up to serve their king and country and were now denied that honour.

'I shall come with you,' I said, knowing that I could not possibly remain there alone when I was needed by those I loved. I needed to be doing something while I waited for news. I stood up and embraced my terrified friend, who was shaking terribly. 'I cannot believe that it has come to this, at last.'

'We always knew that it was just a matter of time,' Germaine said, pensively, her dark eyes turned towards the ground as she chewed her nails and considered the situation. 'I had just hoped for a few more months grace.'

There was a scratch on the door and a nervous looking footman entered bearing a sealed letter on a silver tray. Germaine, hungry for news, snatched up the missive, ripped it open and then after a cursory scan of its contents, screwed it up and flung it to the floor. 'It is from my husband,' she remarked with a shrug. 'He wants me to leave Paris immediately and use my travel permits to go to my parents in Switzerland.' She sighed. 'There can be no question of that, however. I am not leaving Paris until I know that all of my friends are safe from harm.'

We donned plain dark cloaks and went in one of Germaine's carriages to the Pont Royal, where we were stopped by a huge gang of armed, drunken men and prevented from going any further.

Germaine got out of the carriage and did her best to persuade them to let them past but to no avail – they were quite adamant that no one was crossing the river and made horrible cut throat gestures
to demonstrate what was happening at the Tuileries.

'Have you news of Citizen Narbonne?' Germaine asked each one in turn, in an agony of suspense. 'Has he been found yet?' The men all spat on the ground and shook their heads and she wandered off in search of anyone else who might have news of Narbonne, while I dismounted from the carriage and stood alone on the quay, which had an excellent view across the Seine to the Tuileries. The beautiful, old palace was on fire and covered with a heavy swathe of thick black smoke while the sounds of shots and screams were still clearly audible and drifted across the Seine to the thousands of Parisians who stood in silent, watchful horror on the opposite bank. It was intolerable not to know what was happening and I could scarcely believe that the two people that I loved best were both somewhere in the midst of such horror, while I had no way of helping either of them.

Germaine came to stand beside me and we linked arms and stood in silence for a moment, staring across the water and inwardly praying for those caught up in the fighting 'I wish that I was there with him,' she whispered, resting her head on my shoulder. 'I would gladly have picked up a sword and fought to the death at his side.'

I nodded, my eyes still fixed on the black plumes of smoke that were beginning to drift across Paris.

'If only we were men,' I said with a rueful smile, echoing the silent despairing cry of a hundred thousand other women in the city that day. We turned and walked slowly down the quay, making sure to keep in sight of the Tuileries and keeping watch for anyone who looked like they might have news.

We waited at the quay for two hours, pacing wearily backwards and forwards, staring across to the Tuileries and sitting in the carriage until finally we found a friend who was able to tell us that Narbonne and his brave associates had taken part in the rout before being forced to return to hiding. Of Alexandre and Lucrèce, however, there was no news as yet and with that we had to be content. Germaine burst into tears and almost fainted when she heard that Narbonne was safe and I had to put my own troubles aside to support my prostrate friend and lift her into the carriage. 'Come now, chérie, at least he is still alive!' I said, kissing my friend's cold, pale cheeks and rubbing her hands. 'We must try to find him and then see what we can do to get him out of Paris.'

Germaine nodded weakly, still overcome with the shock and relief. 'I must see him.' She looked ashen and sank into the corner of the carriage. 'I will not believe that he is entirely safe until I see him for myself.' She sighed and closed her eyes as the carriage lurched forward and took us back to the Rue du Bac. I sat in silence, watching my friend and gazing out at the crowded Parisian streets as they rushed past. I did my best to be brave for Germaine but my heart and mind were still with Alexandre and Lucrèce, wherever they might be and I knew that I would not be able to rest until I knew what had become of them both.

As soon as we had returned to the Rue du Bac, Germaine put a dark shawl on over her head and went out on foot in search of her lover. 'I can think of several houses where he might have gone and I will go to each and every one until I find him or at least learn where he is.' She drank some red wine that I silently handed to her and the colour slowly returned to her cheeks so that she looked less alarmingly pale. 'Would you be so kind as to stay here in case he sends a message?'

I nodded, relieved to be staying behind in case Alexandre sent word also. 'Of course, chérie.' I frowned. 'You shouldn't go out alone.' The enraged shouts and screams of the mob floated up to us through the open window of the salon and I shuddered to think of my friend wandering alone amongst them.

Germaine smiled as she artfully arranged her shawl over her bonnet and then tied the loose ends behind her. Despite everything, she still contrived to look utterly delightful. 'I am making my maid come with me. She is very faithful and utterly trustworthy. I will come to no harm with her beside me.'

I could not afterwards recall how long I sat alone in Germaine's beautiful, blue and gold salon. I heard, as if far away in the distance, the shouts and screams from the street below and the murmuring sounds of servants going about their business within the house, their heels gently clip clopping on the wooden floors, their cotton skirts whispering past the paneled walls. The elaborate clock, surmounted with a gilt Venus and Adonis on the mantle piece chimed on the hour but I barely heard it, so deep and complete was my reverie. Darkness began to fall beyond the window and still I did not move to close the heavy blue brocade curtains but instead sat alone and still, with my hands folded neatly in my lap and my eyes gazing far into space while all the while my thoughts were of nothing but Alexandre and Lucrèce.

I heard the front door bang and did not move, thinking that it must be Germaine returned from her quest. Then the door to the salon flew open and I looked up in astonishment to see Alexandre standing before me He looked pale and dirty and disheveled but was very much alive. With a cry I sprang up and ran into his arms.

'You are safe!' I buried my face into his shoulder, which smelt strongly of gun smoke and clung to him as though I would never let go again. 'I was so frightened, Alexandre.' We kissed for a long time and I could taste salt, smoke and wine on his lips. 'Next time, take me with you!' I said, smiling up at him, unable to take my eyes off him now that he was safely beside me again.

Alexandre grinned, his teeth gleaming white in his grimy face. 'Germaine came to the house where I had taken refuge and told me where you were,' he said presently. 'I can't stay here for very long though – I have been told that I was seen today at the Tuileries and there is now a warrant for my arrest..'

I grasped his coat collar. 'Must you remain in hiding then?'

He looked at me sadly. 'Yes, I must, until I am able to return home to Brittany.' He must have seen despair flash across my face as he took hold of my hands in a firm grasp. 'Cassandre, I must set my mind to going home. My family and our people need me now more than ever.' He sighed. 'They write to me often. Times are hard for them and they need me to come back.'

'What about me?' I cursed myself for being so selfish but could not help it. 'How can you leave me here like this?'

He sighed and stroked my hair. 'Please, Cassandre, I have already been away from Brittany for far too long.'

'Then take me with you!' I spoke recklessly and in fact had no idea what I was offering to him. I only knew that I must not let him leave me like this. 'You can't leave me here in Paris without you!'

He smiled fondly and kissed my forehead. 'No, my darling, I will not do it.'

I went to him and put my arms up around his shoulders as I gazed up into his face. 'I will make you change your mind,' I said with a smile. 'In the meantime we must find somewhere for you to hide until we are able to leave Paris. The Hôtel de Saliex would be ideal, of course, but I fear that my brother-in-law would be less than pleased if I took you there.' I considered for a moment, chewing my nails as I did so. 'Ah! Of course! My father has a small house on the Ile de Saint Louis, which is never used any more. I could take you there.'

We heard the front door close and a few moments later, the salon door opened and our erstwhile hostess bustled in, pulling the shawl from her head and throwing her gloves on to a table. 'My dear, my dear!' She advanced towards me with a dejected expression on her face. 'I am so sorry. Have you heard the news?' She looked at Alexandre enquiringly and he gave a small shake of his head.

'What has happened, Germaine?' I jumped up and went to my friend, suddenly feeling sick with dread. 'Is it Lucrèce? Please God let it not be her!' My hand went to my throat and I wobbled a little on my feet, making Alexandre move swiftly to my side and support me. How could I have forgotten about her?

Germaine embraced me. 'No, it is not Lucrèce! I have not seen her but by all accounts she is safe and well.'

'Thank God,' I breathed, passing a hand across my forehead. I looked at Germaine, who was still looking worryingly sombre. 'If not Lucrèce then who?'

Germaine took my hands. 'Your husband was arrested at the Tuileries and taken to prison.'

I sank down on to the sofa, hardly daring to meet Alexandre's eye. 'I can't believe it.'

'I'm sure that they will free him soon,' Germaine said, sitting down beside me and taking my hand. 'I promise that I will find out where he is being kept and then make arrangements for you to go and see him.'

I nodded but did not know what to say. I felt a sudden lash of terrible shame that my only thoughts all day had been with my sister and lover, whilst all the while my husband, the man that I had promised to love and obey forever more had been in mortal danger and I had not spared a single thought for him.

Once Alexandre had been safely conveyed to the empty, dust and spider filled house on the Rue St Louis-en-l'Ile and left there with the parcel of wine, bread, cheese and meat provided by Germaine, I found that I could not bear to return to our home on the Rue de Saint-Honoré and so instead I directed the coachman to take me back to the Rue de Grenelle, motivated by a need to reassure myself that my twin was truly unscathed by her adventure.

Lucrèce greeted me with delight when I arrived at the Hôtel de Saliex and we clung together, crying in the hallway for a long time, unable to believe what was happening in our city and the extreme danger that people close to us now found themselves in. I waited until we were alone in her pink and silver boudoir before I told her about Alexandre and her hazel eyes widened in shock and wonderment when I told her that he was currently a fugitive and that I fully intended to go with him when he left Paris. 'Only, he doesn't know it yet,' I added ruefully.

'Are you quite sure?' Lucrèce asked. 'It sounds very dangerous, Cassandre.'

I nodded. 'I am absolutely sure,' I replied. 'You cannot

imagine how frightened I was today when I thought that he might have been killed by the mob. I don't think that I could bear to go through that again.' I looked at her and took her soft hand in mine. 'I'm sorry, Lucrèce, but if I do not go with him, I'm afraid that every day will be like today.'

She nodded, but I could see tears welling in her eyes. 'I understand, Cassandre, I really do.' My sister opened her mouth again as if about to add something else but then she gave a little shake of her head and covered it with a nervous laugh as I looked at her curiously. 'What now?' she asked after a moment.

'Now, I must work out how to get Alexandre out of Paris and at the same time do my best to get Eugène out of prison,' I replied with a rueful smile. 'Never let it be said that I like my life to be uncomplicated.'

The next few days were amongst the most difficult and exhausting that I had ever lived through. Lucrèce and I woke early and immediately set to work, writing endless letters to everyone we could think of, outlining Eugène's sadly not unusual predicament and begging unashamedly for assistance. After this we set off for the Ile de Saint-Louis, where Lucrèce pretended to visit to a friend couple of streets away, while I slipped into the little house on the Rue St Louis en l'Ile and crept up the stairs to the small salôn at the back of the building, where Alexandre was hiding.

After only a few hours in each other's arms, I would wrench myself away, meet up with Lucrèce and we would go together to the Palais Royal to stroll arm in arm through the public gardens just as we had always done in the past, relishing a chance to pretend that life was just as tranquil and carefree as it ever was.

'I imagine that your position at court is at an end,' I said on one occasion. 'You must be relieved.'

I cast my sister a sidelong smile, knowing how much she had disliked her duties as a lady in waiting to the Queen. I had hated it too, after all.

'I have not been officially dismissed but I think we can safely assume that my services are no longer required,' Lucrèce replied with a sad shrug. After accepting the protection of the Assembly, the royal family had been taken first to the convent of the Feuillants and then on to the Comte d'Artois' Parisian residence, the fortress of the Temple in the Marais, where they were lodged in the forbidding mediaeval tower and not in the pretty little palace that had been scene of some of the most decadent parties of the ancien régime. Madame de Tourzel and the Princesse de Lamballe had accompanied them but the rest of their attendants had been sent away. The pretense that the royal family were not prisoners in their own capital was at an end and I knew that Lucrèce wondered if she would ever see them again – she had wanted to go to the Feuillants to wait upon the Queen, as others had done, but Saliex had refused to let her go as he believed that it was too dangerous.

'He says that a king who has been taken prisoner does not have long to live and that he has no intention of sharing his fate,' she said morosely.

I looked across at Lucrèce as she paced alongside me through the lovely gardens with a gloomy expression on her lovely face and reached across to give her arm a reassuring squeeze. 'I am glad that I do not have to go to the Tuileries any more but at the same time wish that things were still as they once were,' she continued. 'I am so afraid, Cassandre. Do you remember what it was like only a few years ago when we thought the revolution was such a marvellous and exciting thing?'

I nodded. 'It seems impossible to imagine that only a few years ago we were all at Versailles with not a single inkling of what was about to happen and now look at us all!' I sighed. 'I wonder if we will ever be as happy again as we were in 1789?'

'I wonder that too,' Lucrèce said.

It did not take long for replies to arrive to our letters, although many of the recipients clearly deemed it safest not to respond at all. The charming aristocratic lawyer Hérault de Séychelles, a cousin of Madame de Polignac who had nonetheless wasted no time in allying himself with the National Assembly was not amongst them, however and sent a violet scented and elegantly worded missive that rather recklessly recalled 'happy evenings spent dancing at Versailles with the lovely Marquise de Vautière'. He would be only too delighted, he said, to be of service to me now in my hour of need and so had made arrangements that I should be allowed to visit my husband in La Force the very next day.

Enclosed was an official signed order from Hérault and a brief note explaining that if there were any problems then we must let him know immediately and he would go to his friend Danton, who had been appointed Minister for Justice on the eleventh of August.

The next morning Lucrèce and I both dressed in our plainest dark gowns and went by carriage to the Rue Pavée, which lay just off the Rue des Francs Bourgeois. The prison of La Force was a large and forbidding building surrounded by stone posts with chains, that prevented approach and with a circular peristyle that was large enough to allow carriages to turn beneath it.

We cautiously descended from our carriage onto the filthy street outside, which had gained its name as a result of being one of the very first in Paris to be cobbled, not that you would realise this from the thick layer of mud and ordure that covered it.

Despite the warmth of the day, I shivered as I gazed up at the building. 'This is indeed a prison.' I had been expecting a mere house of detention – basic but not as positively fearsome as the dank, forbidding building that loomed over us. I slipped my hand into Lucrèce's, which was shaking with fright. 'Are you sure that you want to come with me, dearest?'

'Quite sure,' Lucrèce replied with a nod.

I felt quite faint and frightened as we passed through the main gate and then through two more smaller gates, each one manned by a group of slovenly looking guardsmen and citizens, who scanned the letter signed by Hérault that I produced for their inspection, spat on the ground and then let us pass, with an abundance of crude comments about our appearance that made us look nervously over our shoulders lest they followed.

We came to a large, damp, stinking records hall where

new prisoners gave their details before being swallowed up by the dark cells beyond. I once again produced my now dirty and crumpled letter for the irritable looking clerk behind the table. 'Citizen Hérault has requested that I be allowed to see my husband,' I said with barely a tremble in my voice although Lucrèce, who still held my hand, must have known that I was shaking like a leaf.

The clerk sighed and shrugged. 'It is not usual for prisoners to be allowed visitors,' he said with a bored expression.

'Citizen Hérault is a close friend of Citizen Danton,' Lucrèce said now. 'What possible harm could it do for my sister to be allowed to see her husband for a few short minutes?'

'It is not usual,' the man repeated with a yawn, although we could both see that Danton's name had had some effect upon him.

'We don't want to go back to Citizen Danton to tell him that this small request has been refused,' I said, pressing home our only advantage. 'I think that he would be very displeased to know that his friend's order has been rejected. You have heard of Citizen Hérault have you not?'

The clerk shrugged. 'Of course. Who hasn't?' He was clearly wavering and was no longer looking quite so bored. 'Very well, Citizeness. Ten minutes only and there will be guard present at all times so no funny business.' He looked me up and down in the most impertinent fashion. 'Your husband is fortunate indeed to receive visits from such a tasty piece as yourself.'

He summoned forward one of the hovering guards and gave him some whispered orders. The guard looked us up and down appreciatively, nodded and then, with his huge bunch of keys jangling loudly at his hip, led us down a series of cold, dank corridors to a small, airless cell which appeared to be in the very bowels of the prison.

We stepped into the horrible, stinking little room and looked about ourselves in horror. 'Wait here,' the guard said with a jerk of his unshaven chin. 'Make yourselves comfortable, Citizeness.' He smirked as he swung the heavy door shut behind him and then locked it.

Lucrèce shivered at the hideous, scraping sound of the key turning in the lock then turned to me. 'Do you suppose that they intend to keep us here?' she remarked with an attempt at lightness.

I closed my eyes and shuddered. 'Do not joke about such a thing,' I muttered.

We waited in the gloom for what seemed like forever, listening with fear in our hearts to the distant murmurings, clankings and groans of the prison. Finally, just as I was beginning to feel quite afraid and wonder if we had been tricked or forgotten there came the heavy tread of a guardsman outside and the horrid sound of the key grating once again in the lock before he appeared, this time with Eugène. His dark breeches were grimy with dust and dried blood, his once white linen shirt was ripped and stained and his hair was tied back loosely with a thin black ribbon. We looked at each other for a moment in silence as I took in his pale face, the slight shadow of stubble on his jaw and the lingering traces of what had once been a virulent black eye.

'What did they do to you?' I asked, gesturing to his eye.

He smiled ruefully. 'I'm afraid that I was somewhat unwilling to go with them,' he said, stepping towards me. 'It is good to see you, Cassandre.'

I smiled. 'I could not stay away,' I said. 'I am still your wife after all.'

He nodded. 'After all that we have done,' he murmured musingly. 'Still, I am glad that you are here.'

The next moments passed in awkward conversation as we faced each other across the chill little cell, while the guard and Lucrèce turned their backs to afford us a little privacy.

'I wish that things had been different for us,' he said suddenly as I told him the latest news of the royal family. 'I have often thought about it since coming here.'

I shook my head, feeling suddenly uncomfortable. 'I wish that you would not,' I said.

'What else do I have to do here, Cassandre, but regret that

which I no longer have?' he asked, his face filled with a despair, a misery that I had never before seen. 'We could have been so happy together but I ruined it all, didn't I?'

I looked at him. 'Yes, you did.' I sighed. 'We were young, Eugène. It was not all your fault.'

'I should never have said those things to you,' he carried on. 'I should have trusted you absolutely.'

I reached out and took his hand. 'Don't dwell on it, Eugène,' I murmured. 'It is too late for us.' I looked at him sadly, thinking how handsome he was and remembering how much I had liked him when we were first married, how desperate I had been for his approval. 'We should not talk about this. It serves no purpose.'

He shrugged, his fingers tightening on mine. 'Of course.' He looked at me through a strand of his fair hair that had fallen across his face. 'I know that you love someone else now and I accept that, but that doesn't stop me loving you too.'

I pulled my hand away. 'Please, Eugène, don't.'

'No, listen to me,' he whispered urgently. 'I've been mulling it over and I think that it would be best if you divorce me.' He took my hands again. 'If we are no longer married then there is a chance that you might be able to protect yourself from sharing my downfall.' He looked quickly at the guard, who was clearly doing his best to eavesdrop on our conversation. 'New prisoners are arriving here every day, many of whom have committed no other crime but being related to someone who has already been arrested.' He looked at me. 'Do you understand me, Cassandre? You must do everything you can to protect yourself and if that means ending our marriage, such as it is then so be it.'

I nodded, feeling a troubling mixture of both relief and sorrow, that my marriage, a source of bitter resentment for so long, could be over within weeks. 'I understand, Eugène.'

The guard gave a hoarse cough and rattled his keys in an impatient manner that made it clear that he was bored and that our brief interview was at an end. 'Time's up, my fair lady,' he barked, grinning nastily. 'You've seen yourself what good care we

149

are taking of him.' He unlocked the door and another equally filthy and villainous looking guard came in and took hold of Eugène's arm.

'Remember,' Eugène whispered to me as they pulled him away. 'I love you so much, Cassandre. Please don't think harshly of me.'

'God be with you, Eugène,' I whispered as they led him from the room, his eyes fixed on mine until the very end. I was suddenly very sure that I would never see my husband again. Lucrèce came to stand at my side and put her arm around me comfortingly, saying nothing but rubbing my back until I felt able to follow the guard from the cell.

'He loves you so much, Cassandre,' she said. 'I wish that things had turned out differently for you both.'

'I wish it too,' I said, leaning against her as we walked nervously down the long, dimly lit corridors, trying our best to avoid meeting the eyes of the guards as we went past so terrified were we that they might decide to arrest us and keep us there forever.

Never before have I been so pleased to see daylight and we both stood in the street and breathed in great gasps of air, almost crying with relief to have made it back outside. Suddenly Lucrèce touched my arm. 'Look!' She pointed to a plain black coach that was pulling up outside the columned entrance to the Petite Force, which was designated a prison for women 'It is Madame la Princesse de Lamballe, Madame de Tourzel and little Pauline,' she whispered, aghast. 'They must have been taken prisoner as well. I thought they were with Her Majesty.' We watched as the Princesse was helped down from the carriage and stood for a moment blinking and shaking in the sunlight, looking about her as though she did not where she was or what was happening. 'You must remember how frail Madame la Princesse is,' Lucrèce murmured. 'I don't t know how she'll cope with a place as this.'

I nodded. 'Do you remember how she used to have palpitations at the mere sight of a prawn and then fainted away when Madame de Polignac had a painting of a lobster on her fan? So funny!' I laughed. 'I remember wondering at the time if Yolande had done so deliberately.'

We turned away and went back to our own carriage. 'What do the authorities propose to do with all these prisoners?' Lucrèce remarked. 'They can't keep them all locked up forever and I am sure that the prisons must be running out of space. It seems like everyone in Paris knows at least one person that has been arrested now.'

We made our way to the Hôtel de Vautière on the Rue de l'Université. Xavier had written to warn Lucrèce that there were plans afoot to seize the property of prisoners and that although Eugène's beautiful, perfect house was so far unmolested it was only a matter of time before we lost all of our possessions. Lucrèce and I had therefore resolved to remove as many of the best items as possible to the attics of the Hôtel de Saliex which was not as yet under any threat. My maid had already collected all of my remaining clothes and jewels and a covered cart had already removed much of the best furniture so there was very little left for me to do other than walk through the deserted rooms, picking up this and that object and sighing to myself.

Exhausted, I dropped into a chair in one of the salons and listened to my sister's high heels as they echoed through the almost empty rooms. I remembered the many happy hours that I had spent here, including the night of a wonderful ball shortly after my wedding when I had been so young and still eager to please. I remembered dancing with my husband, Eugène, and how dazzled I had been by him back then.

'Shall we go?' Lucrèce was back again, followed by a pair of footmen struggling beneath the weight of a large painting. 'They forgot to take Madame Vigée-Lebrun's portrait of you so I thought that I ought to rescue it.' She shrugged. 'I know that you never did like it very much but I would hate to see it fall into the clutches of the government as they will probably either sell it to some English lord or use it as firewood!' She smiled and helped me to my feet.

'You might as well keep it,' I said with a smile. 'I don't see the point in owning a portrait of myself and I know that you have always admired it.'

We linked arms and wandered out to the courtyard, where the carriage waited for us. 'I have already arranged with grandmère that our horses will be stabled at the Hôtel de Saint-Valèry until all of this is over. They went this morning, I believe.' I shrugged. 'It is intolerable that we are being made to resort to such measures but still we must submit or lose everything.' I gestured back to the beautiful golden Hôtel. 'It is dreadful to imagine all of this in the clutches of some commoner from the provinces.'

There was an uneasy calm across the city in the weeks that followed. I did everything I could to secure my husband's release but without success. I approached Danton, Desmoulins and Robespierre countless times but they wouldn't do anything to help me. At the same time they could not tell me what grounds there were for keeping Eugène under arrest, other than the fact that he was an aristocrat and known to be sympathetic to the monarchy. They were his only crimes and were apparently enough to condemn him.

The handsome lawyer, Xavier de Saint-Benoît, object of a ridiculous crush on the part of my youngest sister, Adélaïde, visited the Hôtel de Saliex every day and brought with him the papers that I would need to divorce Eugène, but I couldn't quite bring myself to sign them. I no longer had any love for my husband but the foolish and sentimental memory of how he had once been was just enough to prevent me.

My nights, however, were spent in the little house on the Ile de Saint-Louis with Alexandre, who was preparing to return in secrecy to Brittany, not knowing that I fully intended to go with him. We drew the heavy crimson brocade curtains and filled the tiny back bedroom with the light of dozens of candles before lying together on the ancient, mouldering bed and giving ourselves up to love and despair. I dug my nails into his shoulders, desperate to keep him as close to me as possible, weeping silently into his chest as he entered me over and over again.

ADÉLAÏDE

Paris, September 1792

The carriage came to a halt in front of Notre Dame and I felt tears prick behind my eyes as I gazed up at the beautiful twin towers that loomed overhead. There was nothing so lovely or so comforting, to a Parisian, than the familiar sight of Notre Dame on a sunny day, when the sunshine cast a mellow golden glow over the old stones and even the famous gargoyles seemed to smile benignly down.

'Mademoiselle.' A footman pulled open the carriage door, unfurled the steps and helped me descend.

I smiled at the man, ordered my maid to remain in the vehicle and then covered my head with a black veil before entering the cathedral through the richly carved Portal of the Last Judgement, the central of the three doors. It took a few moments for my eyes to adjust to the gloom but then I was rewarded with the sight of the sun's rays flooding through the exquisite stained glass windows, covering the cold stone floor with a myriad swirls of light and colour.

I dipped my fingers in the water in the font, crossed myself and made my way swiftly past the giant pillars, down the nave to the transept, where I stood for a moment beneath the

153

famous rose window, admiring how beautiful it looked when backlit by sunshine. After this I walked rather more slowly to one of the small side chapels, where I knew that I would not be disturbed. Here, I crossed myself before a statue of the Virgin and child and then knelt in silent prayer for some time before crossing myself again and taking a seat on one of the benches and allowing the tranquillity of Notre Dame flow over me. The heavy scent of incense in the air was a great comfort and never failed to transport me to memories of happier times when I had first come here with Grandmère and my sisters as a little girl to hear Mass. Later I had come alone as an ignored and unhappy adolescent to pray and be alone with my thoughts in one of the many silent little chapels.

As always and despite all of my good intentions it did not take long for my thoughts to return to the secular world that lay beyond the great doors of the cathedral. I thought first of my brother Lucien, who had recently managed to escape the capital after the terrible events at the Tuileries and had sent word that he was safe and well in London, along with half of his acquaintance. I missed him terribly - his light hearted, happy presence had made life with Papa and Grandmère almost bearable but now there was no one to save me from their bad moods and barbed conversation.

Life had become even more unpleasant recently, now that Grandmère with her usual relentless ill will towards me, had decided that I should be married with all haste to the uncouth and spotty son of one of her oldest friends, the Vicomte de Sallèry. 'How old are you now, Adélaïde?' she hissed nastily over the dinner table. 'Eighteen? Nineteen? Twenty? No one has wanted to marry you so far, and who can blame them?'

I stared at my plate, feeling the hot colour rise to my ears. 'I am nineteen.'

'Nineteen!' She was triumphant. 'I was married with two children by the time I was your age!'

'Times are different now,' I ventured, putting down my knife and fork, no longer hungry.

She laughed and jabbed at me with her thin finger. 'Men have not changed though and none of them want you.' She looked at my father with an expression of smug self satisfaction. 'As it is, your father will have to pay Sallèry a handsome dowry to get him to accept you into his family.'

I sighed. 'I don't want to marry him,' I said, as I had done a dozen times before.

'You will do as you are told.' And so it went on. I thought about the revolution and the way that it was changing all of society, creating liberty and freedom where previously there had been none, and yet here was I, just the same as ever, trapped with Papa and Grandmère and longing for someone to come along and rescue me.

I had thought that perhaps Bertrand would help me escape, but beyond meeting me in secret every few weeks, he had given so sign that he was ready to proclaim me his daughter. Any dreams that I may have had of his coming to the Hôtel de Saint-Valèry, striking Papa down for his bad treatment of me and then bundling me into his carriage to take me away to his own house had long since vanished.

'Mademoiselle de Saint-Valéry?' A voice close behind me made me jump and hastily whirl around, crimson with embarrassment. 'I'm sorry; I didn't mean to startle you.' Xavier de Saint-Benoît stepped out of the gloom, running his thin fingers nervously through his fiery hair and clearly mortified by his faux pas. 'I ought not to have said anything. Forgive me, mademoiselle.'

I forced a smile, cursing the way that I always blushed with embarrassment whenever I saw him. 'There is no need for forgiveness, monsieur.' I stood up and straightened my veil. 'I was about to take my leave anyway. I am expected at a friend's house.'

'Don't leave on my account,' Xavier said. He stepped towards me and smiled. 'I could not resist seizing the opportunity to speak to you.' He blinked at me in the bright light that streamed through the tall stained glass window. 'I have not been alone with you since the night that I accompanied you to the Rue du Bac,' he said, remembering that strange evening so long ago when he had come with me to Bertrand's house then silently escorted me back to my sisters, listening in attentive silence as I tearfully told him the truth about Bertrand. He was still the only person who knew. 'Please, sit with me for a while.'

'Very well.'I folded my trembling hands on my lap. 'I have never properly thanked you for the service you rendered to me...' I began, rather more formally than I had intended.

Xavier shook his head. 'It was nothing, really,' he said gently. 'Have I done something to offend you, mademoiselle?' he asked suddenly. 'You are always so formal with me, so correct.'

I looked up quickly at his face, then swiftly looked away again. 'Am I?'

'Yes, you are,' he took my hand then and pretended to examine it, smiling a little as he did so. 'And yet at the same time...'

'I don't know what you mean,' I whispered, suddenly breathless. 'I like you very well, Monsieur de Saint-Benoît.'

Xavier released my hand. 'I'm glad to hear it,' he said softly. 'I like you too, Mademoiselle Adélaïde.'

Suddenly frightened, I stood up. 'I must go now,' I said, stumbling over the words.

'Would you do me the honour of walking with me? ' Xavier asked after a moment's hesitation. I was standing against the light, and he screwed his face up amusingly as he peered up at me. 'I should like to talk some more with you.'

I sent the carriage on ahead and we strolled across the Pont Neuf and then walked down the Rue André des Arts towards the Boulevard Saint-Germain. It was a lovely day and despite the definite atmosphere of tension the streets were filled with people going about their business and children playing on the pavements. I heard and saw very little though, as I was floating on clouds of happiness, my hand on Xavier's arm and my eyes shyly downcast as he murmured words that I had never even dared to dream to hear him say.

'I wish you had some idea how enchanting you are,' he said, stopping for a moment and looking down into my face, while I looked quickly away, too embarrassed to meet his intent gaze. 'I wish that you could see how you appeared to me that night on the Rue du Bac, with your dark hair falling about your shoulders and your enormous, beautiful eyes shining in the moonlight.'

I blushed. 'I've never looked that way,' I murmured. 'Please, monsieur, do not tease me.'

Xavier sighed. 'I'm not teasing you,' he said. ' Ridiculous girl. I'm trying to tell you that I love you.'

I stared at him in shock and was just opening my lips to reply when suddenly screams and shouts came from the direction of the huge, turreted prison Abbaye de Saint-Germain-des-Près, which faced us at the end of the Rue Sainte-Marguerite.

Xavier pulled me down the street. 'Come on!' He led me towards a large crowd that had gathered around six bloodstained carriages that had drawn up outside the prison gates. As we approached, someone pulled the vehicle doors open and the terrified priests cowering inside were dragged out before vanishing beneath a torrent of blows from fists and makeshift weapons. The shrieks were dreadful as the unfortunate men threw their hands in front of their faces in a desperate effort to protect themselves.

'Xavier, get me away from here!' I stumbled away, unable to believe what I had just seen with my own eyes, even though I could still hear the vile encouraging shouts and jeers of the baying crowd.

Xavier was beside me, taking me gently into his arms and leading me away from the terrible scene. 'Come away now.' He looked down at me anxiously. 'I am sorry that you saw that.' He put his arms around me and drew me close protectively. 'Can you ever forgive me?' He sighed. 'I'm afraid to say that this has been inevitable for a long time now. Marat, Hébert, Fréron and their supporters have been calling for the prisons to be... cleared for some weeks. It needed only the panic generated by the fall of Valmy for the sparks to ignite and all hell to break loose.'

'They were only priests!' I said, pulling away from him in disgust, thinking of the gentle nuns who had taught me at

Pénthemont. Were they next to be slaughtered like animals in the street? They had done nothing wrong! Why did they need to be killed in such a way? They are not the enemies!'

'In the eyes of the common man, they are very much the enemy,' Xavier pointed out patiently as if instructing a child. 'Priests, nuns, aristocrats, royalists, émigrés – they are all the same to the man in the street.' He pointed to a placard that had just been pasted to a wall on the Rue André des Arts. 'Aux Armes, Citoyens! La Patrie En Danger! There is your answer. The people of Paris are desperately afraid – they are constantly being told by the pamphleteers and rabble rousers that they are in danger of imminent slaughter at the hands of the enemy. They've been told to defend themselves but against what?' He gestured back at the Abbaye. 'The prisons are highly visible and are well known to be filled with the enemies of France. What would you have them do?'

I stared at him, feeling as though I did not know him at all. 'This is not you speaking, Xavier!' I cried. 'This is Danton's doing!' I turned away, ignoring him as he took hold of my arm. I thought of the nuns at Penthémont, of my mother, and wondered what was to become of them.

'Listen to me, Adélaïde!' he sounded desperate. 'This was not Danton's doing! It was inevitable with or without his sanction!' He lowered his voice, aware that we were attracting curious stares from passersby. 'Don't blame him. Blame the true enemies of France, whose plots and counter plots have spread fear and suspicion throughout the nation.'

'You can't possibly mean any of this,' I hissed. 'Listen to yourself, Xavier! Have you lost your mind?' I took his arm and shook him. 'This is all wrong! People should not be dying in the streets like this! This is not what the Revolution was meant to be about! Do you remember how it felt in 1789 when the Bastille fell and everything was new and exciting and full of hope? Well, do you?'

He shrugged my hand from his arm. 'You don't know what you are talking about, Adélaïde.' His face was cold and stonier than I had ever seen it. 'I will take you home to the Hôtel de Saint-Valèry and then go back to the Ménage.'

'But, Xavier...' I tried again to touch him but he shrugged me off.

'I don't want to discuss this matter any further.' He looked down at me and to my relief his gaze softened. 'Do not hate me. It was not of my doing.'

The massacres continued for the next five days. When the massacre at the Abbaye had finished, the mob hurried down the Rue de Rennes to the Carmes and when they had finished their terrible work there, moved on to the next prison and then the next. Prisoners were summoned before a makeshift 'tribunal' where they were asked to take an oath to the constitution. Each one that bravely refused was handed over to the mob who fell upon them with swords, pikes and axes.

Like everyone else, I tried my best to remain indoors and ignore what was happening outside, fortified by notes from Xavier de Saint-Benoît, which were delivered to my bedchamber every evening with a knowing smile by my maid, Agathe.

'One day soon I will come for you,' he wrote in his slanting handwriting, 'and I will accept no refusals, Mademoiselle Adélaïde. If I had ever suspected that we were destined to be together, I am now absolutely certain of it.' I crushed his letters to my breast and threw myself back onto the bed, giving myself over to rapturous, delightful imaginings.

On the third morning, I was sitting alone at my luncheon, crumbling my bread on to my plate and daydreaming about Xavier, when suddenly my thoughts were interrupted by a frantic hammering on the front door of the Hôtel. Immediately fearing the worst, I stood up, knocking my plate to the floor and scattering the crumbs across the carpet. 'Have they come for us?' I cried in alarm, swiftly crossing the room and wrenching open the door to the entrance hall where my father's footman was hurrying across the marble floor, a look of alarm on his corpulent face.

'Mademoiselle, you should step back into the dining room,' he ordered. 'This could be unpleasant.'

I lifted my chin, made bold by the secret letter from

Xavier, which I had secreted between my corset and the thin summery white muslin of my gown. 'I will remain here. My father has gone out and I am the only member of the family still at home.' I swallowed and hid my shaking hands at my sides. 'Now, open the door or I will do it myself.'

He gave me a stiff bow. 'As you wish, mademoiselle.' He pulled open the door and instantly I relaxed, all terror gone when I saw my sister Cassandre standing there, a look of terror on her lovely face and her red hair falling in untidy ringlets down her back.

'I didn't know where else to go,' she said simply, stepping into the hallway and pulling off her gloves, looking about her as though to reassure herself that here at least everything was normal. 'The mob has attacked La Force and I need to know what has happened to Eugène.' She looked at me with some disappointment. 'Is Papa here? Is it just you?'

I shook my head, feeling suddenly helpless. 'He has gone to see one of his friends.' I took her arm and led her into the dining room, where I knew that the maid had brought some freshly brewed coffee. 'He thinks that we have lingered in Paris for long enough and is talking about getting permits so that we can go away to Vienna or perhaps London,' I whispered. 'He has gone to see someone about it today.'

Cassandre nodded bleakly. 'Anyone with any sense would want to leave Paris now.' She gratefully accepted the cup of coffee that I handed to her. 'It has been taken over by bloodthirsty lunatics, who have no respect whatsoever for human life.' She put down the cup and went to the huge mirror that hung between the windows, patting her disordered hair back into place and rubbing at her pale cheeks.

'We will go as soon as I am ready,' I said, ringing for my maid. 'La Force is only a short walk away from here.' I thought with a shudder of the horrible deaths of the priests at the Abbaye and wished with all my heart that Xavier was there to help us. 'I'm sure that Eugène is safe,' I said, awkwardly patting my sister's arm and not knowing what else to say.

160

Once I was ready to leave, we left the Hôtel on foot and hurried down the Rue des Francs-Bourgeois until we came to the turning for the long and twisting Rue Pavée. We could hear the sound of shouts and screams far ahead and I reached across and took Cassandre's hand in order to provide her with some extra strength as we headed towards La Force, which lay at the furthest end of the street, on the corner of the Rue du Roi de Sicile. It took us some minutes to get there, and we walked in silence, hardly daring to imagine what lay in wait for us and not knowing what to say to each other. I kept thinking that I should say something comforting to my sister, but I just didn't have the words.

As we drew closer we could see that the crowd was made up of all manner of people – well dressed men and women watching silently, presumably in the hopes of saving their loved ones and shrieking, foul harridans and bloodstained, drunken murderers who brandished their gory weapons in the air and cheered every time a new victim was delivered to them.

'What's happening?' I took the opportunity to ask of a soberly dressed man who was standing a little apart from the scene. 'Where are the prisoners?'

The man turned to us and I saw that his grey eyes were red rimmed from weeping. 'They are being taken one by one to face a tribunal and then are being forced out into the prison yard, where the savages await them.' He angrily wiped away his tears. 'It is inhumane, unjust.'

'Have any been set free?' I asked, taking the unusually mute Cassandre by the hand and leading her forward. 'We are looking for my sister's husband. He is a prisoner here.'

'I am waiting for news of my son, Charles Villemain.' The man shrugged. 'A few prisoners have been released but most have been dispatched by the mob.'

I nodded, blinking away my tears and taking him by the hands. 'I will pray for your son.'

Villemain nodded. 'Prayer is all that is left to us now.'

There was a loud cheer and we turned to see a young man being carried out on the shoulders of a pair of blood

161

splattered, rough looking men. The mob, who would have been baying for his death had he been condemned now pressed close and joyously yelled 'Vive la nation!' at his release.

'I feel sick,' Cassandre murmured before sitting down heavily on a doorstep. I went to her side and pressed her hand.

'Have courage!' I whispered. 'It's not as hopeless as we originally thought! Look, see, they are setting some prisoners free so why not Eugène as well?' I took her by the hand, pulled her unwillingly to her feet and led her through the mob to the prison entrance, where a group of slovenly looking National Guardsmen lounged against the walls smoking their clay pipes and ogling the women in the crowd.

I forced myself to be brave and spoke to one of the guardsmen, who looked cleaner and rather more approachable than the others. 'I am looking for Monsieur le Marquis de Vautière. He is imprisoned here.'

The guardsman removed his pipe and looked thoughtful. 'Vautière?' He turned to one of his companions. 'Vautière? Does that name sound familiar, Jacques?'

Jacques spat on the floor. 'Who wants to know?' He peered suspiciously at Cassandre and I.

'We're his friends and would like to be able to convey some news to his family,' I said carefully, wishing more than ever that Xavier was with us. He would have known exactly what to do. 'Is he still here?'

Jacques laughed. 'Oh, he is still here alright!' He jerked his thumb over his shoulder to a pile of mangled, naked bodies that lay on the blood soaked cobbles. 'Over there.'

My heart leaped into my throat as as I followed his gaze. 'No!' I gave a cry of alarm and tried, too late, to shield Cassandre from the sight, catching her arm as she pushed past me to get to the pile of corpses. I could clearly see Eugène lying on his side beside the pile with his eyes gazing sightlessly up at the sky and a terrible gash across his face.

'Eugène!' Cassandre had fallen to her knees on the blood stained cobbles and was cradling her husband's ravaged body in her arms as she sobbed over him. I went to her side and put my arm around her as she wept. 'This is murder not justice,' she whispered.

I looked up and saw that some of the mob were watching us and muttering amongst themselves. 'I think that perhaps we should leave now,' I murmured. 'It is too dangerous here and we are making ourselves conspicuous. They're all staring at us.'

Cassandre shrugged me off angrily. 'I don't care,' she said. 'I am not leaving him here.'

'Cassandre, we have to go.' I looked up again at the mob, more of whom were glaring at us and clutching their makeshift weapons in a menacing manner. 'Eugène would not have wanted you to endanger yourself like this.' I pulled at her arm again. 'Come on, let's go now. We can't help him any more.'

My sister pulled his body even closer, his blood seeping into her dress. 'I'm not going anywhere, Adélaïde.' She looked at me haughtily. 'You can run away if you are so afraid, but I'm not leaving him.'

'What have we here then?' A man's heavy hand fell on my shoulder and I looked up to see an enormous, toothless butcher with a blood covered apron covering his ragged clothes and with a shabby red cap covering his greasy black hair. 'Two little aristo whores, groveling together in the mud where they belong.'

'Leave my sister alone,' Cassandre ordered sharply. 'How dare you lay your hands on her!'

'Cassandre, no...' I shook my head at her, desperately willing her to be silent as a small crowd gathered around us, staring down at the tableau that we made with harsh, uncaring eyes. 'She doesn't know what she is saying,' I said to them, trying to appeal to their better natures. 'She has just lost her husband.'

'He was an aristo,' a woman called out. 'He deserved to die!' The crowd closed in and I struggled to my feet, while behind me Cassandre began to scream, a horrible, ear shattering sound of despair and distress. The butcher released my arm and slapped her hard across the face, knocking her onto the cobbles.

'I'll make the bitch shut up,' another man snarled, stepping forward with his blood covered sword held aloft.

I pushed him away. 'Don't touch her! She doesn't know what she is doing! Please, citizen, have a heart!'

'I'll give you a taste of this as well, you little whore!' He shoved me angrily, spitting in my face as he shouted at me. 'You should have left while you still had a chance!' He lifted his sword and I closed my eyes, waiting for the blow to fall, while all around the mob screamed and shouted their approval.

'What's all this?' I opened my eyes at the sound of a familiar, beloved voice and turned to fling my arms around Xavier, sobbing into his neck as he held me close with his free arm. 'What is happening here? This lady is my betrothed and the other lady is her sister.' He pulled himself up and looked around the mob, who shuffled back. 'I demand an explanation.'

'I am sorry, Citizen Saint-Benoît,' the butcher mumbled, shuffling backwards. 'I didn't know who she is. We thought they were aristocrats.'

Xavier reached down and pulled Cassandre to her feet then pointed at Eugène's body, which was now sprawled across the cobbles. 'I want you to wrap this man up decently and take him to wherever Madame la Marquise requests.'

Cassandre gave Xavier a smile of gratitude. 'Take him to the Hôtel de Vautière on the Rue de l'Université,' she said. 'His servants there will know what to do.'

'Thank you,' I whispered to Xavier. 'How did you know where we were?' I reached up and touched his cheek, still amazed that he had saved my life once again.

'I heard about what was happening here and was on my way to your house make sure that you were safely indoors,' he said with a rueful smile as he pulled me tightly against him again. 'I might have known that you would be in the thick of it,' he murmured into my hair.

The next day, in the dead of night, a trio of black clad figures stood with heads bowed beneath the beautiful painted ceiling of the church of Saint-Sulpice as the body of Eugène Louis

Charles, Marquis de Vautière, joined that of his father and grandparents beneath the floor of the church. It had cost Cassandre a great deal of money to acquire a priest (who had had to come out of hiding for the occasion) and bribe some workmen to come in and bury the body. But I believe she considered it money well spent as she watched his coffin being carried away.

'Adieu, Eugène,' Cassandre briefly reached down and touched the cold stone pavement, under which he would shortly be resting. 'I wish that I could have been a better wife to you.' She let a single red rose fall to the floor and then turned away, her beautiful face stricken beneath the thick veil.

Xavier was waiting for me outside the church doors, smiling sadly as he offered me his arm and walked with me to my carriage. I sneaked a look at him from underneath my eye lashes, admiring the way his auburn hair curled in its ponytail, the curve of his mouth and the decisive set of his jaw.

'I can't thank you enough for what you did for us yesterday,' I said in a low voice. 'We all owe you an enormous debt.'

'It was nothing, Mademoiselle Adélaïde,' he said. 'It was a pleasure to be of service to you.' We stood for a moment in awkward silence before he cleared his throat and spoke again. 'You remember what I said outside La Force?' he ventured, a slight blush warming his cheekbones. 'This is not how I wanted to ask you, Adélaïde, but I did not want you to think that I had forgotten.'

I looked up at him in shock. 'You mean about getting married?' I asked breathlessly, my heart hammering within my breast. 'You really mean it?'

He smiled down at me. 'Yes, I really mean it.' We both looked up at the mismatched towers of Saint Sulpice, that loomed above us, outlined against an azure, cloudless sky. 'I will speak to your father tomorrow morning,' Xavier said, pressing me close again and kissing my forehead.

I was so nervous and excited that I could hardly sleep that night. When my maid came in the next morning to open my curtains and bring me my breakfast of hot chocolate, bread and jam, she found me already wide awake, if a little bleary eyed. I'd dressed myself in a simple gown of white muslin, pulled in at the waist with a crimson silk sash but had been defeated as usual by my long, curling hair and had impatiently tied it back with a red ribbon.

'You're up early,' she observed, putting her tray down on the little table beside my bed before busying herself fluffing up my white linen pillows, while casting me suspicious looks. To mollify her a little, I poured myself a cup of hot chocolate and took a tiny little sip, but as soon as I heard voices in the marble hallway below, I put the cup down, smoothed down my skirts with shaking hands then flew from the room and down the stairs.

'Is Monsieur de Saint-Benoît here yet?' I asked the footman standing by the door, trying my best to seem unruffled and unconcerned but betrayed by my red cheeks and the dark rings beneath my eyes.

The footman nodded. 'He is with your father in his study,' he said with the whisper of a smile.

I sat down heavily on the bottom step of the sweeping staircase that dominated the hall, feeling the chill of the marble gradually seep through my thin skirts as I dropped my head in my hands and prayed. I couldn't see what Papa could possibly object to in the match - he had never liked me anyway and Xavier was a good prospect as a son in law. On the other hand, Grandmère would almost certainly oppose the betrothal out of spite and Xavier was not nearly so prestigious a match as those made by my elder sisters, which may go against him.

The tall grandfather clock behind me, that had stood on the landing for as long as anyone could remember counted down the minutes as I stared at the closed door to Papa's study and waited. Finally, just as I was beginning to wonder if they were going to stay in there all day, the door opened and out stepped Xavier, dressed in a green and black striped silk suit. The frown between his eyes disappeared as soon as he looked around the hall and saw me, pale faced and anxious, slowly rising from my perch on the stairs.

'Well?' My throat was dry and my voice came out as a sad little croak. 'What did he say?'

Xavier strode towards me and took my hands in his, lifting me to my feet. 'My darling girl, my Adélaïde,' he murmured, kissing me gently on the lips. 'It took all of my not inconsiderable powers of persuasion, but he agreed in the end.'

I stared at him in amazement. 'Really, Xavier? He said yes?' I stood on tiptoe and threw my arms around his neck, kissing his cheek, his ear, the corner of his mouth and anything else that I could reach. 'I can't believe it!'

'Adélaïde!' My father's voice rang out across the hallway, causing every last bit of joy to slowly ebb away. 'You forget yourself.'

I turned to look at him, the man who had been my father for as long as I could remember. I took in every detail of him as he stood framed in his study doorway, a thin, elderly figure in black watered silk with an old fashioned white powdered wig on top of his head and a dissatisfied expression on his once handsome face. 'Father,' I murmured, sweeping a curtsey, my heart swelling again as I realised that from that moment on my days at the Hôtel de Saint-Valèry were numbered and that I would soon be far away from him.

He coughed delicately. 'I'd like to speak to you, Adélaïde,' he said, beckoning me forward with one elegant, thin hand.

I turned briefly to Xavier, squeezing his hand and smiling up at him. 'Wait for me?' I whispered.

He returned my smile and lifted my hand to his lips. 'Always.'

I almost skipped across the hall towards my father, who held the door open for me as I stepped lightheartedly into his study, scene of so many painful scenes throughout the years. Now though it seemed different, light filled and almost cosy and I myself felt braver than I had ever done before, emboldened by the nearby presence of Xavier and the knowledge that we were soon to be together always.

'I must confess that I am surprised,' my father said as I sat down in his habitual seat behind his desk, as usual putting an expanse of wood between us. 'I had no idea that you and Monsieur de Saint-Benoît had such intense feelings for each other.'

I blushed. 'Nor did I until quite recently,' I replied.

He looked at me coldly for a moment, playing almost nervously with the thin ivory letter opener that lay on the desk in front of him. 'My first instinct was to refuse Monsieur de Saint-Benoît's proposal,' he said. 'He may well come from a wealthy family and his godfather, as he was at some pains to tell me, may well be the Duc d'Orléans, but he has no title and as a younger son in our present times, no hope of acquiring one either.'

'I don't care about that sort of thing,' I said with a smile.

'You will,' he prophesied gloomily. 'Women always care about that sort of thing, sooner or later.'

1793

LUCRÈCE

Paris, January 1793

On a beautiful afternoon at the end of October, Xavier and Adélaïde, blushing and sweetly pretty in pale pink silk with white roses in her hair were married in a brief and unromantic civil ceremony at the Hôtel de Ville. Adélaïde warned us beforehand that the new civil weddings were very different to the beautiful old church ceremonies that we were all used to, but even so, I was shocked by how short and serious it all was, like agreeing on a business transaction, not celebrating a marriage.

Adélaïde looked delighted though, as she looked up with starry eyes at her new husband and even Cassandre seemed to wipe away a tear. Knowing that she hated to be seen crying, I pretended not to notice and instead looked around the room, taking in the smiling faces of men that I had started to think of as our enemies: Danton and Desmoulins were there with their pretty, blonde young wives, as well as the handsome Hérault de Séychelles, who had helped us visit Eugène at La Force and Xavier's godfather, the Duc d'Orléans, who arrived dressed in a tight fitting coral silk jacket and made crude jokes, that only he laughed at throughout the ceremony.

'Adélaïde looks beautiful,' I whispered to Papa, who

stood rigid and silent beside me throughout the ceremony. Grandmère was absent of course - Papa and I had made a half hearted attempt to persuade her to be there but she had refused, preferring instead to remain alone at home. If Adélaïde noticed or cared about her absence then she showed no sign.

Afterwards we all went back to the Hôtel de Saint-Valèry for a modest wedding breakfast. Papa had left all the arrangements to Cassandre and I and we had been at some pains to ensure that our Republican guests were not offended by any inappropriate ostentation, while at the same time Adélaïde had the beautiful, festive wedding that she deserved and that was her due as a bride.

We need not have worried - Xavier's political crones fell with alacrity upon the champagne and oysters and were soon drunkenly toasting the bride and groom, while our old family friends looked on in well bred horror, shuddering as they rubbed shoulders with the men that they blamed for the bloody outrages of the last twelve months.

Adélaïde stood by the window, looking beautiful and so happy as she watched her new husband walk in between the different groups, accepting their congratulations and grinning at their jokes. I went to her and took her hands in mine. 'How does it feel to be a married lady?' I asked.

She laughed with sheer joy. 'There are no words for how happy I am at this moment. I wish that it could always be so.' She smiled a little sadly. 'I've always loved him, you know, ever since the time he rescued us on the bridge on the day that the Bastille fell.'

I smiled and kissed her cheek. 'I know,' I murmured, remembering that day and casting a surreptitious look across the room at my own husband, Armand, who was standing alone by the mantlepiece, sipping a glass of champagne and clearly wishing that he was somewhere else. I sighed and turned back to my sister. 'That's a very pretty locket,' I remarked, lightly touching the one that hung from a red silk ribbon around her neck.

Adélaïde blushed then put her hands behind her neck to

untie the ribbon. 'I wanted to show this to you,' she whispered to me, handing the locket to me. 'Bertrand sent it to me as a wedding present. He couldn't come to the wedding today, but wanted me to know that he is thinking about me.'

I looked at her in surprise then opened the locket. Inside there was a beautiful miniature of a pretty girl holding a baby. 'Is this...' I stared at the picture, a vague remembrance of a pair of laughing grey eyes and soft, lily scented coils of blonde hair coming back to me. 'Why did Bertrand send this to you?' I stared at her. 'What is he to you, Adélaïde?'

'He is my father, Lucrèce,' Adélaïde said. 'He loved Sidonie and wanted her to run away with him, but Papa had her sent away instead.' She looked at me. 'But you already knew all about it didn't you?'

I shrugged. 'I don't know very much, Adélaïde. Grandmère told me that Sidonie was a bad wife and so had to be sent away - the rest I picked up from being in society after I was married.' I took her hand. 'I didn't tell you because Papa made me promise not to and because I knew that you would find it all out for yourself in due course, just as I did.'

'Do you know where she is now?' Adélaïde asked, tears in her eyes. 'Bertrand has been searching for her but doesn't know where she is and now that the convents have been closed...'

I shook my head. 'I don't know, Adélaïde,' I whispered. 'I wish that I did.'

After the party had ended and Adélaïde and Xavier had been sent amidst much cheers and laughter to their new house on the Place de l'Odéon, which was being rented to them by the Duc d'Orléans, Cassandre and I donned our cashmere shawls, linked arms and went for a walk around the garden, reminiscing together about all the happy and not so happy times that we had spent there.

'Do you remember the time you kissed Fabrice de Montfauchon in the arbour?' I asked with a laugh, as we strolled around the fountain, where golden and russet leaves floated serenely on the still water. 'I had such trouble distracting

Grandmère when she would have walked that way.' Cassandre laughed, but I noticed that she was looking unusually pensive. 'Is there anything wrong?' I asked. 'Is it Alexandre?' Over two months had passed since he had gone into hiding and I knew that the situation was taking its toll on my sister as she waited for him to leave Paris forever.

Cassandre sighed then turned to me. 'Lucrèce, he is leaving Paris tonight,' she said, 'and I am going with him.'

I stared at her in horror, unable to believe what I was hearing. 'Cassandre, you can't do this!' I took her hands in mine. 'It is so dangerous in Brittany at the moment! Stay here with me!'

She laughed then and kissed my cheek. 'And Paris is so safe is it?' She shook her head sadly. 'I cannot bear to be apart from him, not even for so much as a day.' She looked back at the house. 'Something good has to come out of all this, Lucrèce.'

I sighed. 'This is not going to end well,' I said. 'You should wait here in Paris for Alexandre to come back. I can't believe that you are considering anything else.' I took her arm again and we carried on walking.

'My mind is made up,' my sister, my beloved twin whispered brokenly and I realised that she was crying. 'I keep thinking about Eugène lying broken and dead on the cobbles and about how little I loved and appreciated him when he was alive.' She angrily wiped away her tears, clearly furious with herself as usual for showing any weakness. 'It made me realise that life is too short and too fleeting to be spent waiting for something to happen or to lose sight, even for a moment, of the people that you love.'

'And what about me?' I cried, seizing her arm. 'You would be leaving me behind, Cassandre! Don't forget that!'

Cassandre smiled then and briefly touched my cheek. 'You have Cousin Sébastien to love you,' she said, as I blushed and fell silent. 'Do you seriously expect me to believe that if he was to leave Paris, you wouldn't find a way to go with him?'

I thought for a moment, longing to deny it, prepared to say anything that would keep her there beside me but in the end I had to shake my head. 'No, you are right.' I looked back at the house again, where I knew Cousin Sébastien was - last time I had seen him, he was deep in conversation with Camille Desmoulins' pretty wife, Lucile who was keen to know all about his trips to London before the war. 'I would find a way.'

I went to the Ile de Saint-Louis that night to say goodbye. Cassandre tried to persuade me not to come but I couldn't stay away - after all, who knew when I would see her again? Cousin Sébastien insisted upon coming with me and, telling Armand that I was visiting my Grandmère, I went to his house on the Place Dauphine in my carriage first before we set out again on foot, swathed in dark cloaks and shivering slightly in the sudden chill in the air. A gang of armed citizens went past us at one point, clearly on their way to arrest some unfortunate soul, and Cousin Sébastien pressed me against the wall and hid our faces with his cloak, kissing me until they had gone away.

Cassandre and Alexandre were just about to get into their carriage when we arrived. 'I was afraid you weren't coming,' Cassandre whispered to me as she ran forward for a hug. She produced a sheaf of papers from inside the simple pale green cotton dress that she was wearing, teamed with a black woollen shawl and a plain white muslin cap. 'From now on we are Citizen and Citizeness Fouchard,' she said with a smile, showing the papers to me. 'A good, honest linen merchant and his modest little wife, on their way home to the countryside.'

'Where did you get them?' I asked, frowning.

'Xavier,' she replied with a shrug. 'You should ask him to do the same for you, Lucrèce. He's part of the family now, after all.'

I looked back at Cousin Sébastien and shook my head. 'My place is here.'

Alexandre stepped forward then and took my sister's arm. 'I'm sorry, Cassandre, but we have to go,' he said with a look of regret. 'We have a long journey ahead of us.'

Cassandre looked frightened then, for the first time and took hold of my hands, bringing them up to her lips and kissing them. 'I will write as often as I can, Lucrèce,' she promised. 'Pray for us, won't you?'

I nodded through my tears, unable to believe that this was really happening and that I was standing here in the middle of the night in a cold Parisian street, saying goodbye, perhaps for the last time to my sister. 'I will miss you so much.'

'I love you,' she whispered as she kissed me for the last time before allowing Alexandre to gently lead her away. 'I will be back soon, I promise.'

Cousin Sébastien held me in his arms as we watched her carriage drive slowly away, then gently stroked my hair as I sobbed into his shoulder. 'She will come back soon,' he murmured. 'Don't worry, my love, ma belle, you will see her again.'

Not long afterwards, on a bitterly cold day in the beginning of December, Louis Capet, formerly known as Louis XVI was brought to trial at the Manège. Myself, Adélaïde and Cousin Sébastien were present in the crowded, noisy upper gallery as the former King of France made his entrance and took his seat below us, apparently oblivious to the jeers and catcalls and the shower of orange peel and apple cores that cascaded through the air like confetti towards him. It was the first time that I had seen the King since that dark day at the Tuileries on the 10th of August and prison life had done Louis no favours. He was just as shambling, plump and scruffy as ever with dark shadows beneath his eyes and several day's worth of stubble (seeing my look of disgust, Adélaïde leaned across and whispered that he had had his razor confiscated by the authorities) and an air of peevish annoyance. He was not an impressive sight.

A hush fell upon the hall as the Convention President Barère, a handsome man with melancholy dark eyes and a gloomy demeanor ordered the former King to be seated before the lengthy list of charges was read aloud – a list that ranged from the obvious to the ridiculous and covered a multitude of plots, schemes and betrayals.

'Louis, the French Nation accuses you of having

committed various crimes in order to re-establish tyranny on the ruins of liberty; the National Convention has decreed that you shall be tried – and the members who compose it are to be your judges.' At this point, Xavier who was sitting beside Danton and Desmoulins on the benches below us looked up and exchanged a tight lipped smile with Adélaïde.

Louis listened without any change in his expression, which was a great disappointment to most of the spectators, who had been hoping for some sort of undignified outburst like tears and pleas for clemency. They shifted uneasily in their seats and began to talk amongst themselves as the lengthy litany of charges continued and the former king murmured his responses to each one.

'I can hardly believe my eyes,' I whispered to Adélaïde, horrified. 'How on earth did it come to this? Something must have gone terribly, badly wrong.'

Adélaïde sighed and shook her head. 'I know just what you mean. It seems unbelievable doesn't it? I can still remember seeing him at Versailles, dressed in mauve silk and covered with diamonds and orders and now...' She shivered again and lowered her voice even more. 'My fear is that once they have dispensed with Louis then they will turn their attentions to the Queen.'

'Why?' I could feel the colour draining from my cheeks 'She is just a defenceless woman and has done nothing wrong.'

'Madame de Lamballe was just a defenceless woman as well,' Adélaïde gently reminded me.

'That was the mob, the vile canaille of the streets not the Convention,' I whispered back, feeling sick as I recalled the horrible fate of the gentle Princesse that I had known so well at Versailles. 'It's not the same thing!'

Adélaïde raised an eyebrow. 'Isn't it?'

The trial of Louis XVI dragged on for over a month until finally at the start of January, the Convention was ready to vote on his fate. Each member was expected to stand at the rostrum and give a speech giving his opinion and answering the following three questions: Is Louis guilty of plotting against the Nation's

177

freedom and of a criminal attempt on the general security of the state? Shall the sentence be sent to the people for ratification? What is the penalty to be?

'It's all very exciting!' I whispered to Xavier over dinner at the Hôtel de Saliex - since Cassandre's departure, Adélaïde and her husband had been coming to our house for dinner twice a week. 'Are you nervous? I think that I'd be terrified if I was called upon to give my verdict on such a grave subject.' I looked across at my husband, who glanced quickly away. 'What do you think, Armand?'

There was an awkward silence, which was broken by Adélaïde leaning across and kissing my flushed cheek. 'I think that it is only human to be nervous at such a time.' She turned to her husband and took his hand, smiling at him as she did so, while I marveled at how lovely she had become since her marriage. She was dressed that night in a gown of shimmering teal silk, with her dark hair hanging in loose curls around her shoulders and topaz earrings swinging from her ears. 'However, I have absolute faith in Xavier.'

He smiled back and squeezed her hand. 'I wish that I could agree, my love!' There was a burst of laughter at this, which he waved away. 'No, I'm being serious! This is a historic moment and a huge responsibility; I really hope that I can do it justice.'

'Justice?' Armand spoke then, raising an eyebrow at his brother-in-law. 'What a curious word to use at such a time.' I put my hand on his arm, but he pulled it sharply away without even looking at me. 'Oh let me be! I think my position as an avowed royalist is well known by now!'

Xavier nodded. 'And I have absolute respect for it,' he said, with a discreet and reassuring squeeze of Adélaïde's fingers while my cheeks flamed with embarrassment. 'Besides, it would be ill mannered indeed for me to disagree with a man at his own table.' He grinned and raised a glass to Saliex.

'There is no point, I suppose, in asking you what you intend to say to the Convention?' Cousin Sébastien asked with a smile as I looked at him under my eyelashes. Under the table his foot snaked towards mine, rubbing it reassuringly.

'No, none whatsoever,' Xavier replied with a grin. 'And even less point trying to change my mind.' He released Adélaïde's hand and looked around the table. 'I'm sure that my views are sufficiently well known by now for you to be able to guess how I plan to vote. I make no apologies and have nothing to say other than that I am acting entirely as I think right and that I am motivated by what I
believe to be the very best course of action for the nation.'

'So Louis must die?' my husband said with a frown.

Xavier paused then nodded his head. 'Yes, Louis must die.'

The meal came to an end shortly after this and we all wandered into the salon for more champagne. Armand, keen to argue about politics some more, cornered Xavier by the fireplace while Adélaïde went to her usual post at the piano and began to play a lively air, smiling with contentment as she did so.

Left alone, Cousin Sébastien and I smiled at each other and walked to the window, which overlooked the frost covered gardens of the Hôtel. 'I always think that things look so much more beautiful after it's been snowing,' I whispered with a sigh, leaning against him discreetly. 'I will never forget my first ever glimpse of Versailles when I was a little girl and my grandmother took Cassandre and I there for one of the Queen's children's parties – it had been snowing that day and I thought it looked like the Snow Queen's Palace gleaming at the end of the avenue.'

Cousin Sébastien smiled. 'I imagine that the snow hid the hideous architecture admirably.' He turned aside and accepted a glass of champagne from a footman. 'I never thought Versailles very lovely, I am afraid.'

'It's very ugly but you must at least agree that it is impressive.' I grasped my champagne, enjoying the feel of the cold, hard stem of the glass against my fingers, which itched to reach across and touch his face.

'I will agree that it is an impressive monument to one man's insane and absurd egotism,' he said with a smile. 'I think that the one good thing to have come out of all this is that we are no longer expected to dance attendance there and can instead remain here in Paris.'

After the convention had voted, overwhelmingly in favour of Louis' death, any possibility of a reprieve was swiftly rejected and it was decreed that the former King of France was to be executed on the twenty first of January. At this news a strange silence fell upon the city as the citizens digested this information and prepared ourselves for what was about to happen. There was almost a sense of collective shock; as though we had never meant matters to go as far as this and could not quite believe what was happening. Above all, everyone was worried about the reaction of foreign powers to the news as the King's execution would make war inevitable.

On a cold and frosty morning, Adélaïde, Cousin Sébastien, my husband and I all dressed as warmly and plainly as possible and made our way on foot through heavy mist from the Ile de la Cité to the Place de la Révolution, which had formerly been known as the Place Louis XV. It was still as magnificent as ever with its beautiful houses and sweeping view of the Tuileries gardens.

I gasped in horror when I caught my first glimpse of the guillotine, which had been erected on a black scaffold in the centre of the square. The guillotine had been in use for almost a year now but as only a very few people had been executed upon it this was the first time that most had seen it in action.

'How ugly it is!' Adélaïde murmured.

We pushed our way through the immense crowd that was already beginning to form, held back from the scaffold itself by several rows of mounted National Guards. 'Stay close to me,' Armand barked over his shoulder when the movement of the crowd threatened to tear us all apart. 'I don't want to lose you in this mob!'

We found a spot which commanded a decent view of the scaffold and prepared to wait. Xavier had decided that he could not bring himself to actually witness the execution that he had voted for, which Adélaïde thought understandable but Armand was rather scathing about. 'Could it be that he is ashamed of himself?' he wondered aloud now to Adélaïde's annoyance.

'Of course he is not ashamed!' she cried. 'Why should he be? Xavier acted as he believed best and has no reason to reproach himself!'

'Then why is he not here?' Armand enquired with a raised eyebrow. 'His accomplices also seem to be tellingly absent from the scene of their crime,' he said after a pause, during which he had scanned the crowd immediately around the scaffold. 'I had imagined that Robespierre, Danton, Marat and Saint-Just would be here in person, preparing to celebrate their victory!'

'You don't know what you are talking about,' Adélaïde replied stiffly. 'And stop talking about accomplices and crimes.'

Again that maddening eyebrow raise. 'Oh? Is that not how it is?' Armand placed a hand on Adélaïde's arm as she looked away from him indignantly. 'My dear child, do not allow your wifely obedience blind you to the true facts of this case.'

'For God's sake, Armand, lower your voice!' Cousin Sébastien interposed with an angry grimace before turning with concern to Adélaïde who was looking very pale. ' Would you like me to take you home?'

Adélaïde shook her head, as a distant drumbeat announced that the King and his final cavalcade was almost at the square. 'I am just a little cold.'

We watched in silence as the former King's rather shabby black carriage went past, it was covered in mud, presumably slung by the hostile crowd and surrounded by hundreds of mounted and marching troops. The Convention was clearly expecting some sort of last minute rescue attempt and had pulled out all the stops in order to ensure that Louis wasn't going anywhere other than to the scaffold.

It was a moving and tense moment as amidst drum rolls and the shouts of the crowd, he descended from the carriage and there was a brief pause during which he was seen to actively prevent his guards from removing his coat and hat. He then straightened his shoulders and, with his hand on his priest's arm, climbed up the steps on to the platform, which looked across the Tuileries gardens. I wondered what he was thinking of as for a brief moment he gazed across at his former palace before turning resignedly away.

The drummers obediently fell silent as he began to speak. 'I die innocent of all the crimes laid to my charge; I pardon those who have occasioned my death, and I pray to God that the blood you are now going to shed may never be visited upon France, and you, unfortunate people...'

A wave of panic went through the crowd as they realised the sinister import of his words and with a curt gesture one of the mounted officers ordered the drummers to resume drumming and drown out the rest of his words, whilst the executioner and his assistants advanced upon the former King, took hold of him and tied him to the guillotine's plank. Cousin Sébastien and I exchanged horrified glances and without saying a word I slipped my hand into his and closed my eyes as the plank tipped over and the blade began its descent.

There was a loud cry and a sound like a sword swishing through the air before an almighty crash. Adélaïde surreptitiously crossed herself as a young guardsman ran forward, lifted Louis' gory head from the basket and began to walk around the scaffold, displaying it to the crowd who recoiled in horror.

An eerie silence, broken only by a few screams and cries fell across the spectators as they fully comprehended what had just occurred before them. The King was dead. There was no going back now.

A few random shouts of 'Vive la République!' rang through the air and within minutes, after a hesitant beginning, the entire square rang with shouts and cheers whilst the sky was dark with thrown hats. Complete strangers flung their arms around each other and danced on the spot – overcome with joy and jostling us as we stood still amidst them, a silent group, rooted to the ground in shock and disgust. The heavens had not opened after all; they had not been struck down by God. Everything was just as it had always been.

'Shall we go?' Cousin Sébastien whispered to me as Adélaïde and my husband began to push their way through the crowd. 'You are looking very pale and I have no further desire to be in close proximity to this stinking mob. I think that we should be able to fight our way back to the quay now.'

I shook my head and stood for a moment and looked back at the guillotine, which stood dark and brooding against the bleakly grey January sky. It still seemed incredible and unreal and I could not quite connect the splendidly dressed King of Versailles with the overweight, shivering man who had met his death that day. I turned to look at Cousin Sébastien who was also gazing into the distance and no doubt thinking along similar lines.

'It hardly seems possible,' I murmured, shaking my head. 'I still can't believe it.' We made our way through the crowd, many of whom were now surging forward to dip cloth in Louis' blood, which had splattered across the cobbles. Cousin Sébastien regarded them with disgust. 'Nothing will ever be the same again.'

My husband and I dined alone that night, facing each other across the length of the long table in the white and gold paneled dining room. We ate in silence, as I covertly watched him in the light cast by the huge candelabra that stood in the middle of the table. We had been living together for almost four years, and I did not feel like I knew him any better now than I had done on that July day in 1789 when he had come to the Hôtel de Saint-Valèry to claim me as his bride.

I watched as he idly sipped his champagne and played with the fricasseed chicken on his plate. I had tried my best to love him, believing at first that he was the embodiment of all that my adolescent fantasies, however it just hadn't worked and now here we were sitting opposite each other in our beautiful dining room, eating in silence and ignoring all the multitudes of things that we needed to say to each other.

Unable to bear the silence any more, I stood up, shoving my chair roughly back and flinging my fine linen napkin onto the table. 'I have a headache,' I said before turning to leave the room.

'Wait.' I turned to look at my husband, who had put down his glass and was standing up as well. 'I need to talk to you, Lucrèce.'

I stared at him, my heart suddenly racing. 'What about?' I gestured to the footmen and watched as they walked regretfully from the room, no doubt to eavesdrop on the other side of the door.

'You know what about,' Armand said as the door closed behind them. 'Come now, Lucrèce, you must take me for a fool.'

I felt faint and held onto the back of my chair, struggling to compose myself. 'I don't know what you mean,' I whispered as my husband stood up and came to stand beside me, placing his hand on my white silk sleeve. 'Armand, please...'

He shook his head. 'I have known for a long time about you and Sébastien,' he murmured, bringing his lips close to my ears. 'Of all the men in all the world, why did it have to be that one?'

I shook my head, fighting the urge to run from the room. 'I don't know what you mean, Armand,' I tried again. 'There is nothing between Sébastien and I.'

'Don't lie to me, Lucrèce,' he said, taking hold of my arm. 'I know all about it. I've been having you followed when you go to meet him.'

'Nothing has ever happened between us,' I whispered, beginning to cry as his grip on my arm increased. 'Please, Armand, let go of me.'

He smiled then. 'Oh, I am going to let go of you,' he said. 'They warned me when we got married that you would probably be just the same as your mother, but you seemed so sweet, so innocent and perfect that I didn't listen to them.' He released my arm and pushed me away. 'If you had chosen any other lover then I might have borne it better, but my own cousin and closest friend, madame?'

I began sobbing, unable to bear the disdain and hatred in his gaze as he looked at me. 'I'm sorry, Armand,' I said. 'I swear that I didn't intend to hurt you, I really didn't.'

'So it was an accident then?' he sneered. 'You tripped over and fell into bed with each other?'

'No,' I whispered. 'No, we didn't.' I looked at him and took a deep breath. 'We love each other, Armand.'

'Love?' he almost spat the word back at me. 'And what would you know about love, madame?' He marched up to me, took my arms and shook me. 'You don't know the first thing about it! How could you? Love isn't creeping like a whore into bed with your husband's cousin when his back is turned!'

'Stop it! It wasn't like that!' I pushed him away and ran to the other side of the table, terrified now that he might actually strike me as he watched me from slitted eyes, breathing heavily and furiously. 'Armand, we are in love! We didn't want to hurt you or go behind your back, but in the end we just couldn't fight our feelings any more!' I pushed back my hair, which had fallen over my face when he'd pushed me over. 'I am sorry, Armand.'

'Sorry? Not as sorry as me, for taking a slut as a wife,' he said, pulling off his powdered wig and throwing it onto the table then running his fingers through his dark close cropped hair. 'I don't know what sort of future I imagined for us both, Lucrèce, but it wasn't anything like this.'

I shook my head. 'And what about Honorine?' I said, all the anger and hurt from all those years ago, welling up in my breast. 'What about her?'

'Honorine? That was a long time ago, Lucrèce...'

'I saw you both, remember?' I retorted. 'In the arbour on our wedding day. Do you remember that?'

He stared at me in horror. 'You are still upset about that?' he whispered. 'My God. Is that why?'

I shrugged my shoulders. 'I tried to love you, Armand but it was always there between us,' I said softly. 'I knew almost from the very first moment of our marriage that you were not to be trusted, that you had other loves that were not me.'

'I never loved Honorine,' he said, shaking his head sadly. 'She was a diversion, nothing more.'

I stared at him. 'You needed a diversion on our wedding

185

day?'

Armand looked away then, all his anger gone. 'I always assumed that you understood how it was between Honorine and I.'

I shook my head. 'How could I?'

A silence fell between us until he reached into his blue silk jacket and produced a sheaf of papers. 'Xavier has given me these identity papers and a travel permit so that we can leave Paris in the next few days,' he said, throwing them on the table between us. 'I would like it if you came with me, but as always the choice is yours, Lucrèce.'

I looked at the papers, which had spilled across the white linen tablecloth then raised my eyes to his face. 'No, Armand,' I said, reaching out and pushing them back towards him. 'I can't go with you.'

My husband picked them up and put them back in his jacket. 'I would like it if you reconsidered,' he said. 'Paris is no longer safe and I would feel better if you were at my side. At least think about it.

I shook my head. 'I want to be here should Cassandre ever return.' I gave a small shrug. 'I am sorry, Armand.'

My husband sighed. 'Let me know if you change your mind.' He went to the door and paused for a moment with his hand on the handle, waiting for me to say something before he gave a shrug of resignation and left the room.

CASSANDRE

Paris, October 1793

The gates swung open and the cart rumbled over the cobbles into the dank prison courtyard, where a group of filthy looking sans culottes loitering around the door. They spat on the ground and then shuffled slowly forward to pull the back from the cart and unwillingly help the small group of women inside down. I preferred to ignore the grimy hand that was proffered to me and instead jump down by myself, my thin leather shoes sinking unpleasantly into the mud as I did so.

'Welcome to Sainte-Pélagie, ladies!' one of them said with a grin and an appreciative look at the prettier prisoners, who shuddered and pulled their shawls closer as if to protect themselves. 'I trust that your stay here will be a pleasant one!' He stood aside as we filed past, clutching our few meagre possessions in our arms and looking about us in appalled horror. 'Hurry up, ladies! We haven't got all day!'

In a small, dark, shabby room that stank of cooking fat, wet dogs and stale breath and sweat we stopped to give our names to the guard behind the desk who barely glanced at us as he took our details and assigned cells. He looked up briefly however when I stopped in front of him and proudly gave my name, my voice ringing clearly in the gloomy chamber. 'Cassandre -Laure-Gabrielle-Violette-Célestine de Vautière, Vicomtesse de Barthèlmy.'

'Ci devant Vicomtesse,' he growled, waving me through without another glance. 'Put her next to Du Barry. I assume she can afford it.'

I followed the dirty jailor up the stairs and along a narrow filthy corridor. 'In here,' he muttered, opening a door and jerking his head to indicate that I should enter.

I looked down and saw that he had his hand open, waiting for money. 'Ah, yes.' I brought out my purse. 'I would like to write a letter and will need paper, a pen and ink.'

When the guard had gone, leaving my door unlocked and brusquely informing me that I should be back in my cell, ready to be locked in by nightfall, I allowed myself to look around the meagre, blue little room and then sank down upon the narrow bed with a shiver of distaste. Like the rest of the building, the room smelt of damp and decay and I pulled my heavy black cloak, which had once belonged to my Alexandre, closer about my shoulders as an outside gale made the thin window panes rattle.

There was a tap on the door, which was then pushed open to admit a pale woman with red rimmed eyes, dressed in an outmoded gown of stained, rusty black. 'You are new here aren't you?' she asked without preamble, her thin hands twisting nervously in front of her. 'What is the news? What is happening outside?'

I shrugged and gave a rueful smile. 'I don't know,' I replied regretfully. 'I have come from the Vendée and spent last night at La Force, so am as much in the dark as you are.'

'The Vendée?' The woman's eyes lit up. 'Were you at Nantes? I have a brother there.'

I sighed, remembering the horrors of Nantes, the savagery and the death. 'Yes, I was there.'

When the woman had gone, I wrapped my cloak around myself and lay down on the bed. Sleep was impossible so I allowed my thoughts to drift aimlessly. It seemed like such a long time since I had last been in Paris, since I had thrown everything that I knew and loved away in order to follow Alexandre to Brittany.

Alexandre. We were married in the tiny white walled chapel attached to his family's château, gazing deeply into each others eyes as we said our vows, the air filled with the soft summery scents of the roses and honeysuckle that adorned his mother's garden outside. I had proudly borne his name ever since, riding at his side into battle, sleeping beside him in the makeshift army camps and sharing his victories and defeats. I cried now and whispered his name: 'Alexandre, Alexandre...'

He fell at Cholet on the seventeenth of October. We had faced the Republican troops outside the town, massively outnumbered and beleaguered but willing to do battle nonetheless. The first barrage from the Republican muskets had felled thousands and the line had broken down, whilst Alexandre and his fellow leaders desperately tried to get their troops to pull together. Despite his pleas that I leave immediately and seek refuge outside the town, I had refused to leave his side and had stood up in my stirrups shouting encouragement to our men and waving my pistols in the air.

'Go now!' Alexandre had implored, grasping my reins. 'Please, Cassandre! I order you to leave!' He pushed his long dark hair out of his face. 'Go! Go now, before it is too late! They are bringing cannons forward!'

'I won't leave you!' I cried, snatching my reins back. ' I didn't leave Paris just to hide in a ditch while you face danger alone! If you die then I want to die at your side!' The ground shook as the cannon fire began. 'Alexandre, for God's sake, don't make me leave you!' Smoke was everywhere and we were surrounded by the groans and screams of the injured as the grapeshot slammed into our columns.

'It's hopeless!' someone shouted close at hand from the thick smoke that covered the field. 'We must return to Cholet and fight them there!'

Alexandre turned his horse and we rode back towards

Cholet. I was just starting to feel light hearted and giddy with relief when there was the sound of a shot and suddenly Alexandre had vanished from view, slipping silently from his saddle without a murmur.

'Alexandre?' I had instantly pulled up my horse and jumped down from the saddle. My husband lay completely motionless a little way off and I lifted my heavy grey woolen skirts and ran to him, ignoring the gun fire that peppered the ground. 'Alexandre?' I knelt beside him and gently lifted his head into my lap, gasping at the crimson stain that was quickly spreading across his chest. 'Please, my love, look at me.' There was no response. 'Oh God, no.' I covered my mouth with my hands as my entire world reeled. 'No.'

I was still kneeling there, cradling his head in my lap, when they came for me. Most of the survivors had been massacred, trying to get to safety in Cholet but the Vicomtesse de Barthèlmy was a prize worth capturing and so I was left alive.

'Shoot me now,' I whispered to the Republican officer who took my arm and pulled me roughly to my feet. 'I have nothing left to live for.'

They kept me overnight in a dirty cell in Cholet, while they decided what to do with me. I could not sleep, my every thought was of Alexandre and all I wanted was to be with him again. When my door was opened in the morning I fully expected to be dragged out and executed on the spot but was disappointed to hear that they had decided to send me under guard to Paris to be properly and publicly tried for treason. I begged them to kill me but they laughed in my face and refused.

The journey took several days and I leaned my head against the seat and stared out at the grey, misty countryside as it rolled past. Villages, trees, fields, children playing by the road, I gazed sightlessly at them all until finally sleep had arrived and taken me away to dreams of Alexandre and happier times.

Returning to Paris had been bitter sweet. As we drove through the filthy streets, I stared out of the carriage like a stranger, barely recognising the city where I had been born and that I had loved so much. It seemed smaller and uglier than I remembered, especially in comparison to the wide fields and endless skies of Brittany.

'Glad to be back, Citizeness?' Rouget, the young official escorting me had asked politely.

I smiled at him, appreciating his gentleness. 'I don't know yet.'

I was taken to La Force and could not help shuddering as I recalled the last time that I had been there, when I had gone with Adélaïde to find Eugène on that dreadful day. This time I was taken into the women's prison, which had once housed the unfortunate Princesse de Lamballe, but the memories lingered on and for the first time I felt a twinge of fear as I surveyed my grim surroundings and followed the silent turnkey to my freezing, stinking cell, which still had dark bloodstains from the massacres on the walls.

One night in La Force, shivering with damp and listening to the screams and groans of the other prisoners was enough to break anyone's spirit and I was profoundly grateful when the next day I was informed that I was to be transferred, along with a small group of other women prisoners to the far more salubrious Sainte-Pélagie, a former home for prostitutes which had become a political prison a few years earlier and currently housed Madame Roland, the celebrated Salon hostess and leader of the Girondins along with Madame la Comtesse du Barry, Louis XV's former mistress, fifteen actresses from the Théâtre Français who had been arrested for singing royalist songs on stage and, to my delight, my old friend Lauzun.

It was as I left La Force that I learned of the execution of Marie Antoinette on the sixteenth of October, the day before the doomed battle at Cholet. Even though there had been no love lost between myself and the unfortunate former Queen, I still felt saddened and shocked by the news and took a moment to wonder what had happened to the rest of the royal family. I remembered Marie Antoinette at Versailles, glittering with jewels and laughing with sheer joy as she opened a palace ball. She had seemed untouchable then and it was inconceivable that she should have come to a ghastly end on a blood splattered scaffold.

'Who cares about her? We have to save ourselves now!' A well dressed woman muttered when we were told the news. 'She did nothing for us and doesn't deserve our tears.'

Another one nodded in agreement. 'Yes, we are more to be pitied than her.'

'Indeed we are,' I murmured, pulling Alexandre's cloak closer and closing my eyes as the cart moved slowly forward.

As soon as there was enough light in my cell the next morning, I knelt down on the cold, dusty floor beside my bed and began to write a letter to my sister, using the cheap paper and spluttering pen that the jailor had, at tremendous cost, brought to me.

> *'A la Citoyenne Saliex, l'Hôtel de Saliex,*
> *Rue de Grenelle.*
> *Paris, ce 24 octobre 1793*

> *Ma chère soeur,*

>> *You will be no doubt surprised to hear from me after such a long time and I am truly sorry for that. It is all over for me, my husband is dead and I am currently being held in Sainte-Pélagie. I do not ask for help but desire only to see you again.*

>> *I am truly sorry.*

> *Cassandre de Vautière, veuve Barthèlmy.'*

I did not have to wait long for a response and was sitting reminiscing sadly about times gone by and people now departed with Lauzun, who was just as flamboyant and amusing as ever when the guards came to get me.

I was taken along white washed corridors, crowded with

staring prisoners to a small, shabbily furnished room which was used for official interrogations, where my sister, holding an enormous linen wrapped parcel and Xavier de Saint-Benoît were waiting for me. I paused for a moment in the doorway, shaking slightly as I saw my sister again, looking beautiful as ever in a gown of plain white muslin with a red silk sash around her waist. We looked at each other for a moment, and I smiled ruefully as I wondered how I looked to her with my hair cut to my shoulders, tanned by the Brittany sunshine and dressed in a plain grey dress. 'Cassandre?' Lucrèce sounded uncertain as she took a step towards me.

'You came,' I said, my eyes filling with tears as I stumbled to her. 'You really came.'

I saw Xavier nod to the turnkeys and then gently touch Lucrèce's shoulder. 'We will leave you now,' he murmured to us both. 'You have half an hour.' He did not wait for a reply but immediately left the room, locking the door behind him.

'Let me look at you!' I said, laughing and crying at the same time, and holding Lucrèce at arm's length so that I could see her lovely face. 'You look more beautiful than ever!'

Lucrèce sobbed. 'And you look so brown and thin!'

'No one would ever think that we are twins now.' I grinned and shrugged my shoulders, feeling more lighthearted than I had done in many days. 'I have been spending a lot of time outdoors. Who would have thought it possible?' I hugged my sister close. 'I do not think that I have ever before felt so alive as I did when I was in Brittany.'

'I was sorry to hear about Alexandre...' Lucrèce murmured. 'It must have been horrible.'

I shivered. 'It was. I have never loved anyone as much as I loved him,' I said gently. 'It was a revelation to me. I had no idea that it was possible to love so much.'

Lucrèce began to cry again. 'This is all so unfair.'

'I have no regrets,' I replied, smiling at her as we sat down at the table I reached across and took Lucrèce's hands in mine. 'Promise that you won't cry too much for me?' I asked with a rueful smile. 'I don't think that I can bear to be pitied.'

'I can't promise that,' Lucrèce replied.' You know that I can't. I'm going to do everything that I can to get you released.'

I shook my head. 'No, don't.' I reached across the table and took her hand. 'I don't want to be saved.'

'You could always say that you are pregnant when they come for you,' Lucrèce said hopefully. 'It would buy you some more time.'

'Time for what?' I could not help but look amused. 'No, I thank you, but I would rather not be exposed as a liar in front of all the world!' I took Lucrèce's hand again. 'Come now, do not look so gloomy! Tell me some gossip!'

Lucrèce smiled ruefully. 'I am afraid that I have none,' she said. 'Most of our friends have gone away now and those that remain live very quietly these days.' She blushed and looked away. 'Armand has gone,' she said diffidently.

I wasn't surprised. 'You did not choose to go with him?' I asked gently.

She shook her head and I decided to change the subject. 'And Adélaïde? Is she still happy with Xavier?'

'I believe so,' Lucrèce said. 'They are expecting a child. We see a great deal of each other these days although she is very busy entertaining Xavier's friends and attending the Assembly meetings with him.'

I laughed. 'Ah yes, Adélaïde was born to involve herself in politics! I can imagine her now in her red cap, sitting astride a cannon and storming Versailles.'

'I don't think that she is quite so bad as that,' Lucrèce said with a smile. 'Not yet, anyway.'

There was the sound of a key scratching in the lock before the door swung open and Xavier and two turnkeys entered the room.

'Was that half an hour?' I sighed and stood up, stretching my aching limbs. 'Time usually passes far too slowly in this place.'

Lucrèce and I embraced, trying not to cry in front of the men. 'I will try to come and see you again,' she whispered. 'Let me know if you need anything?' She pointed to the parcel that she had brought with her and which now lay on the floor. 'I brought you some clothes and a book.'

I kissed her cheek and squeezed her tightly. 'Thank you.' I smiled. 'I knew that I could trust you to take care of such matters.'

'What about food?' Lucrèce asked anxiously, clearly imagining some hideous prison diet of thin gruel and hard bread washed down with brackish water.

'I have arranged to pay for my meals to be brought in from outside and do not do so badly. I even got some wine last night, which was unexpected but nice.' I laughed. 'It was surprisingly drinkable.'

Lucrèce brought out a purse and slipped it into my hand. 'This is all that I had about me today,' she murmured. 'Let me know if you need anything more.'

I smiled and kissed her again then turned to Xavier and offered him my hand. 'Citizen Saint-Benoît, thank you for bringing my sister to me.'

He took my hand and awkwardly bowed. 'I'm glad to be of service, Citizeness.'

They came for me a week later while I was reading in my cell. As soon as I saw the two gendarmes standing on the threshold of the room, I knew why they were there and calmly placed a scrap of paper between the pages to mark my place. 'I am quite ready for you, gentlemen,' I said cordially with a smile. 'I shall come quietly.' I swiftly wrapped as many of my belongings as I could into a shawl. 'Will you be so kind as to send everything that remains to Citizeness Saliex?'

We made our way down the crowded corridor and I was amused to see my fellow prisoners avert their eyes and pretend not to see – I bore them no ill will for this as I knew, only too well, that it was motivated by a sort of fastidious politeness – we all had so little privacy now. Lauzun bowed to me gravely, a flirtatious smile on his lips as I went past and only blonde, vapid Madame du Barry broke down, as usual so that we were pursued down the winding stone stairs by her terrible shrieks. I sighed and rolled my eyes. That woman had never had any class.

At the foot of the stairs they took my bundle from me and then tied my hands in front of me with rope before leading me out to the cart that waited outside the gates. A dozen other prisoners from other prisons around Paris were already on board and stared at me curiously as I was helped in and my bundle thrown in after me. Another pair of gendarmes appeared a second later accompanying Manon Roland, who looked very pale but as haughty and full of self importance as ever. There was a ripple of interest in the cart as everyone craned to catch a glimpse of this genuine celebrity in our midst.

'Madame la Vicomtesse?' a tall, not unhandsome man who looked vaguely familiar asked me. 'I am sorry indeed to see you here.'

I smiled. 'Do I know you, monsieur?'

He staggered a bit as the cart began to move. 'I am the Comte de Vielle.' He smiled and looked a little embarrassed. 'We danced together at Versailles once upon a time.'

'Once upon a time,' I repeated, thinking of the fairy stories that Lucrèce, Adélaïde and I had read as children. Versailles was like a fairy story now, only there would be no happy ending and no handsome prince to wake me from this nightmare.

It did not take long for us to reach the Conciergerie on the Quai d'Horloge of the Île de la Cité. I must have passed the huge, pale turreted building a thousand times without truly seeing it and now I stared up at it in horror, imprinting each detail on my mind before I vanished within its walls.

Uniformed gendarmes surrounded the cart as soon as it passed through the gates of the Cour de Mai, seizing Madame Roland first and then before I had time to realise what was happening they had taken hold of me too and pulled me to the ground. My hands were untied and finally I was able to pick my belongings up and clutch them to my chest for protection. I looked in vain for the Comte de Vielle but he had already disappeared from view.

'This way, Citizeness!' A swarthy gendarme took my arm and led me towards a wicket gate beyond which lay the busy records office, where each prisoner's name was entered into the register by a pale, exhausted looking clerk. Everything about this dank, miserable room seemed calculated to provoke gloom from the dark walls to the filth and rubbish that littered the floor. While I waited in line, I stared about myself in horror at the confusion that surrounded us. Clerks and gendarmes ran in all directions whilst in their midst miserable looking creatures lay on the floor or huddled on the row of benches that had been placed against one of the walls. I soon learned that there was more confusion than usual because twenty one of the Girondin leaders, including the once influential Vergniaud, Gensonné and Brissot had that day gone to the guillotine and the prison was in uproar as a result.

I gave my name to the clerk and was then led immediately away. 'I can afford to pay,' I said to the gendarme, having been forewarned that the common cells at the Conciergerie were little better than airless, windowless pits into which they crammed as many prisoners as possible.

'Pistole?' he replied, using the prison cant for a private room.

I nodded and placed a coin in his grubby hand. 'Please.'

The room that he took me to was on the first floor and was small and simply furnished with a trestle bed and a table. There were thick patches of damp on the walls but there was at least a window and as soon as he had gone I went to it and leaned my face against the bars, straining to see the outside world but seeing only grey skies. With a sigh I turned away and began to unpack my meagre belongings, thankful that I had had the presence of mind to bring my book, paper and ink and a spare pair of red high heeled shoes. I sat down at the table and dashed off a hurried note to Lucrèce informing her that I had been moved to the Conciergerie and then went in search of a gendarme who would be willing to send it on for me.

After this there was nothing to do but take a walk about the gloomy, crowded corridors and then out into the cobbled women's yard where the female prisoners walked, did their laundry in a large stone fountain beneath a tree and flirted with the male prisoners who were separated from them by a metal grille at the other end of the yard. I was greeted with smiles and every sign of pleasure as I walked through the yard. Everywhere I looked there were familiar faces and it seemed as though the very best of Versailles society had been uprooted to this insalubrious little spot.

'Cassandre!' I heard myself being hailed from the grille which separated the male and female prisoners and made my way towards it, only to come to a sudden halt when I recognised Philippe d'Echevalier, a lover from my early days at Versailles when I had been young and desperate to score points against Eugène. He looked grimy and desperate.

'No,' I said, walking away again. 'I don't want to speak to you.'

He grinned and held out his hand, thrusting it through the metal bars. 'Come now, Cassandre, don't be foolish. Who else are you going to talk to? Your lover isn't here is he?'

'Leave me alone, monsieur.' I turned away, aware that we were being watched with some amusement by the other prisoners.

Life in the Conciergerie was every bit as tedious as that at Versailles. In the morning the female prisoners would take a walk in the yard en negligé in simple white muslin and linen dresses and with our hair hanging loose down our backs, whilst the men walked on the other side of the all too annoying grille and watched us. There was always an atmosphere of gaiety, thanks to another night survived and another new day beginning, and the air was usually filled with good natured conversation, jokes and shouted endearments and compliments from both sides. After an hour's promenade we would return to our own part of the prison before changing into our day clothes, putting our hair up and going out again into the yard for more conversation with the male prisoners. The more fashionable women such as myself then changed again for the evening and appeared en déshabillé again in plain white muslin gowns and as night fell on the prison, the yard and corridors filled with murmurs, sighs and hushed laughter.

Meal times were social occasions and all of the prisoners sat together on the trestle tables, men and women separated by bars but pulling our tables as close together as possible, exchanging food and wine and swapping gossip and anecdotes. Despite myself, I began to look forward to these times and sometimes even managed to forget the heavy stare of Philippe d'Echevalier, who still did his best to attract my attention, but without any success.

'You really should give him a chance!' one of the other women said to me at dinner one night, whilst everyone else was discussing that day's dramatic and unlamented departure of the hated Duc d'Orléans, Xavier's godfather for the guillotine. 'After all, what else is there to do in here?'

'Monsieur le Comte d'Echevalier is not an experience that I would like to repeat, Lucie,' I retorted with a lift of her eyebrow, shuddering as I remembered his rough hands and wet mouth. 'I wish that he would leave me alone.'

'He's quite handsome.' Lucie pouted and cast Philippe a speculative look. 'It seems a shame to let him go to waste!'

I sighed and took a sip of my wine. 'Please, be my guest.'

After dinner there was the usual roll call of the prisoners when the prison porters, with their dog curled up on the ground in front of them, read out a list of all those who were be called before the tribunal the following day. We all dreaded this ordeal but tried to hide our fear by appearing as light hearted and carefree as possible. It was all made so much worse by the fact that the porters were usually blind drunk and illiterate so that they could barely make out the names on the bedraggled piece of paper and, it was suspected, made wildly inaccurate guesses.

I barely allowed myself to breathe as the names were called out.

'Maillot, Tarante, Gericourt, Barthèlmy...'

I gasped and staggered a little. The moment had come. I wanted to run up to them and tear the paper from their hands and

199

see for myself but did not dare. After all my protestations that I wanted only to die and be with my Alexandre again, now that the moment was close at hand, I found that actually I wanted to live, just as I had promised him that I would do.

Lucie was beside me, shivering slightly in the chill autumn air. 'They asked for me as well, so we shall be going together.'

I looked down at the other woman and smiled. 'Then you can show me how to be brave.'

'Cassandre,' Philippe was waving to me from his side of the grille. 'Please, I must speak to you!' He looked pale and his habitual sneer had quite gone. 'Please.'

I straightened my shoulders and went to him. 'What is it, Philippe?' I said wearily. 'I don't want your pity.'

I saw that he had stubble on his chin and dark shadows beneath his eyes. 'I am sorry, Cassandre.' He reached out and grasped my wrist. 'Truly sorry. I just wanted to say that.'

I stared at him without saying anything.

His grasp tightened. 'I have never forgotten you, Cassandre.' He pulled me closer so that our lips were almost touching. 'Will you let me come to you tonight? I can bribe the turnkey.'

My first instinct was to slap him and pull away but then I looked into his tired, battered face and found that I could not leave. There was the memory of Alexandre between us but he wasn't there whereas Philippe, for all his faults, most definitely was. It was probably my last night on earth so why not spend it in the arms of someone familiar?

'I know about your husband,' he was saying now, echoing my thoughts and I wished that he would just shut up. 'I know that I can't replace him, Cassandre, but he isn't here for you now and I am.' He leaned in closer and I caught a whiff of his familiar lavender eau de cologne. 'I can bribe the guards to let me come to you.'

I closed my eyes, swallowed and nodded, hating myself as I did so but not knowing what else to do. The idea of spending this last night alone was too dreary to be contemplated.

However, when night fell and the prisoners were locked into their cells, I began to regret my decision and even hope that he would be unable to come to me. It might be better after all to be alone with my thoughts and prayers instead of cheapening Alexandre's precious memory. I lay on my bed and stared up at the little window, straining my eyes to make out stars in the darkness. There was the sound of footsteps outside my cell and my entire body tensed as I heard the familiar jangling sound of the gaoler's keys.

'Cassandre?' His hand was heavy on my shoulder. 'Cassandre, are you awake?'

I rolled over and looked up at him as he placed a lit candle down on the floor beside my bed. 'Philippe, I am not sure that I can do this after all,' I said.

He sat down on the bed and I shrank away, uncertain as to how he would react. 'I know,' he whispered after a moment. 'I didn't really think that you would.'

I sat up and cautiously put my hand on his back, which was still turned to me. 'You didn't?' I shook my head, confused. 'Then why did you come here?'

'I didn't want to be alone.' He looked at me then and I saw that his dark eyes were full of tears. 'Cassandre, you are not the only one to have loved someone and then lost them,' he said. 'My wife, Alexandrine was taken from me two months ago and I have been on my own ever since.' I nodded and patted his arm, not knowing what to say as he continued talking. 'I begged to be allowed to share her fate, to die at her side but they refused and now here I am, alone and waiting to be put out of my misery.' He looked at me then and put his hand over mine. 'I could see at once that you felt the same way, Cassandre, and I thought that you, of all people, would understand.'

'I do,' I whispered. 'Oh, Philippe.' I reached out my arms and he came to me, resting his face against my neck and sobbing. 'It hurts to be alone.'

If after a while we kissed through our tears and then lay

together beneath the thin blanket covering my bed, then who would blame us? We were two lost souls, desperately in love with people that we would never set eyes upon again in this life, clinging together in the darkness. When he gently pulled my chemise off and entered me, I wept as I clung to his hips, pulling him further and further inside, losing myself in the honest simplicity of the moment.

'Cassandre,' he murmured wonderingly as I pushed him over and straddled him, riding him with my eyes closed, thinking about nothing as the desperate feeling deep within me grew and grew. He reached up to touch my breasts and I threw my head back with abandon, trying not to think about the fact that this was the last time that anyone would ever touch my body, would enjoy me.

The next day, I thought about Philippe and our strange night together as I held my head erect and did my best to ignore the howls and shouts of the crowd on the other side of the barrier. We had been led into the formerly sumptuous but now sadly denuded Liberté Hall in the Palais du Justice, which lay alongside the Conciergerie, that morning and one by one had been called forward to face the often arbitrary charges against us. It proceeded much as any other trial with a judge, jury, witnesses and lawyers but everyone present knew that the dice was heavily loaded against the prisoners and that in most cases the outcome was a foregone conclusion. I faced charges of treason and five witnesses, including an inn keeper from Nantes, the officer that had arrested me at Cholet and a former maid servant dismissed for theft came forward to denounce my anti Republican sentiment and 'revolting aristocracy'. I barely glanced at them, feeling both contempt and disgust as they spun their lies and worked the watching crowd into a frenzy of boos and catcalls.

The fearsome, dark browed Fouquier-Tinville in his black silk robes and huge black feathered hat then proceeded to sum up the charges and I had to force myself not to tremble as I listened to myself being described as 'scandalous, disgusting and unwomanly, a denizen of the licentious court of the traitors Louis and Antoinette, cousin of the gold guzzling Polignac whore, former mistress to the ci-devant traitors Artois and Lauzun and with her crimes a disgrace to all of her sex'. I was taken away to the cells below while the jury came to their decision and scanned the faces in the crowd as I went past, looking for a familiar face. I quickly saw Lucrèce and Adélaïde, both pale and dressed all in black and standing near the front but, aware that spies were everywhere, I gave no sign that I had recognised them and they tried their best not to show any emotion.

Only half an hour passed before I was called back into the hall and I felt sick and faint as I followed the gendarmes, knowing that I would almost certainly not be allowed to walk free. Again I tried not to look at my sisters but I was constantly aware of their presence as I stood before the Fouquier-Tinville once more. I met his gaze fearlessly and gripped the ledge in front of me as he declared me guilty, amidst the cheers and shouts of the crowd and then asked if I had anything further to say in my defence.

I shook my head, staring at the gold medal saying 'La Loi' which swung at his chest. 'No.' An expectant hush then fell on the hall as he read out the sentence. 'Cassandre-Laure-Gabrielle-Violette-Célestine de Saint-Valèry, formerly known as Marquise de Vautière, ci devant Vicomtesse de Barthèlmy, you have been found guilty by this court and are sentenced to death, and to have your property confiscated for the State's treasury. Said sentence to be executed within twenty four hours on the Place de la Révolution in Paris and to be published in print throughout the whole Republic.'

There was a cry of agony and despair from the crowd and I knew without looking that it was Lucrèce. It took all of my self control not to break down myself at that moment but I forced myself to look straight ahead and show no emotion whatsoever. I'd be damned if the mob and Fouquier-Tinville saw so much as a tremble from me. The gendarmes took my elbows and led me away and I turned for a moment before the door closed, looking in vain for my sisters, for any friendly face but they had vanished from sight.

I was taken to a new cell and left there alone with my thoughts. On the table there lay a Bible, a piece of paper and a pen and ink. I stared at them for a moment and then shrugged and sat down on the rickety chair and, ignoring the Bible, pulled the paper towards me. I sincerely doubted that the letter would ever reach its destination but decided to take the risk anyway.

'A la Citoyenne Saliex et Citoyen Vautière,
l'Hôtel de Saliex, Rue de l'Université.

Paris, ce 7 novembre 1793

Ma chère soeur,

I hardly know where to begin. They have taken me to the condemned cell. I am sorry that I did not look at you in the court today but I did not wish to draw attention to you. I do not know what to say other than that I wish that I were with you now and able to embrace you both for the last time.

I do not know of any debts that I may be leaving behind but I know that I can count on you to discharge anything that needs to be done. They tell me that the Hôtel de Chainier has already been seized by the government – if any of the former servants come to you for help then please do your best for them.

Please do not wish that I had stayed in Paris instead of following Alexandre to Brittany. I have no regrets, ma chère soeur and nor should you. I had the honour to love and be loved by one of the most truly wonderful and heroic men of his generation and would not have exchanged this for a thousand lifetimes. I gladly go to him now and we will sleep together forever in the arms of posterity.

A thousand kisses for you both, my brother and sister and for our poor parents as well. Lucrèce, kiss those that you love most tenderly tonight. I wish that I was amongst them.

I die without regret and with a tranquillity that is born of innocence. Remember me as I was in happier times not as I am now.

Cassandre de Vautière, veuve Barthèlmy.'

After this there was nothing to do but sit staring at the bare, damp speckled walls until the gendarmes arrived to take me away to the small, whitewashed so called salle de la toilette on the ground floor where Lucie alone was already waiting for me, the other prisoners brought to trial that day having been acquitted or sentenced to imprisonment.

'I am glad that I will not be alone,' Lucie said with a sad smile. I watched as one of the executioner's assistants forced her on to a rickety wooden stool before producing a pair of scissors and roughly hacking at her long corn coloured hair, clipping it short at the back. He then tied her hands behind her back and turned his attention to myself, as I swallowed convulsively and stepped forward.

'Please see that this letter makes it to its destination,' I said, putting my last remaining coin into his dirty fist and then looking away as he crammed it into his pocket. For a moment I wondered where it would end up and wished that I had had the foresight to say something uncomplimentary about Fouquier-Tinville.

I sat on the stool and stared straight ahead, flinching only when the cold steel of the scissors touched my neck, which made the gendarmes laugh coarsely and make remarks about the 'national razor'. I looked down at the ground, where some of my auburn hair lay in thick, long strands around my red shoes and then had to quickly look away before tears overcame me.

'I feel like a complete fright,' I remarked to Lucie with a rueful smile, as they roughly pulled me to my feet and tied my hands behind my back. 'I do not think that short hair suits me. What do you think?'

We were taken out to the Cour de Mai, which actually seemed quite beautiful now in a stark contrast to the medieval grimness of the Conciergerie. Here, an open wooden tumbrel awaited us and without much ceremony we were both bundled roughly on to it. I turned my head to look at the beautiful Sainte Chapelle as the tumbrel lurched forward and then slowly passed through the gates.

The journey to the Place de de la Révolution took over an hour and we almost fell several times as the tumbrel passed over the busy Pont au Change, turned on to the Quai de Mégisserie and then bounced alarmingly over the streets. I looked high above the heads of the curious, staring crowd that lined the route to watch us pass and instead gazed about me at the city that had been my home for most of my life and which I would never see again. There was a brisk hint of the coming winter in the air and I wished that I was wearing something warmer than the black silk dress tied at the waist with a wide red sash, which I had donned that morning. I looked to the side and saw that Lucie, who was wearing a rather grubby gown of pale blue muslin, was shivering so hard that her teeth were chattering.

'I hope that no one thinks that I am afraid,' she whispered. 'I don't want the canaille to see me shiver and call me a coward.'
The tumbrel rumbled down the long Rue Saint-Honoré, past Rose Bertin's shop Au Grand Mogol where myself and Lucrèce had spent so many happy hours and the Palais Royal which was still as thronged and buzzing with life as ever.

We turned down the Rue Royale, at the end of which was the Place de la Révolution. We both staggered and turned pale as we caught our first glimpse of the guillotine, which rose, eerie and macabre in the distance and the crowd howled and jeered as we pressed together and stared in horror at our fate. 'My God,' I whispered, my stomach lurching in fright. 'I had no idea.'

The tumbrel rolled inexorably onwards and I did my best to steady my nerves by looking up at the beautiful buildings that lined the route. Lucie began to chatter nervously as though trying to make up for lost time and I forced myself to smile and nod as though I had not a care in the world. I guessed that my sisters were somewhere nearby but had no idea where to look for them in the large mob that surrounded the wooden scaffold.

The tumbrel came to a halt and gendarmes came forward to pull us both down to the ground. 'This is it,' Lucie said, shivering and trying not to look up at the guillotine looming above us both. 'The end.' She gave a nervous laugh which was abruptly silenced as the executioner Sanson's assistants took her by the arms and led her to the scaffold steps. I watched her go and then turned away as the other woman was strapped to the board and then swung into position. I closed my eyes tight as only a few seconds later I heard the sound of the fatal blade falling and the instantaneous roar of approval from the crowd.

They came for me next and impatiently I shrugged off the hands that seized me. 'I can make my own way up,' I murmured. 'I do not require your assistance, Messieurs.' I ran lightly up the blood splattered steps, turning at the top to look across to the Champs Elysées and then to the Tuileries.

There was an invigorating, autumnal freshness in the air and I savoured every breath as they roughly took hold of me and led me to the guillotine while all the while the crowd shouted and screamed and there was the relentless beat of drums.

'Goodbye life.' I thought of Lucrèce as I had last seen her and of Lucien and Adélaïde and then finally of Alexandre, holding me in his arms as we stood on a cliff top near to his home in the Vendée and telling me above the roar of the sea below us that he would love me always. 'Goodbye.'

ADÉLAÏDE

Paris, November 1793

Lucrèce and I stayed for a long time in the square after the guillotine's blade had fallen upon our sister and her body had been flung onto the cart that stood alongside the scaffold. We watched in silence as it rumbled away, leaving crimson droplets of blood in its wake, its terrible cargo bouncing slightly as it went over the cobbles.

'I can't believe it,' Lucrèce whispered beside me, wiping her tears away and pulling her plain brown knitted shawl closer. 'We should have done more to save her.'

I put my arm around her, as we turned and started to walk back to our carriage. 'We did everything that we could.' Ever since Cassandre's arrest, Lucrèce and I had worked tirelessly, writing letters and personally imploring for her release, but to no avail. Xavier had done his best as well, asking his friends Danton and Desmoulins to intercede on her behalf, but without success. Cassandre's position as an aristocrat and a well known traitor, had put her beyond the reach of any assistance.

'I'm sorry, Adélaïde,' he said to me several times. 'More than sorry.' He took my head in his hands and gazed deeply into my eyes, while his own reflected my sheer despair and powerlessness. 'You do believe me don't you?'

I leaned forward and kissed his hands, his cheeks and then his lips, which became salty with my tears. 'Of course, of course, Xavier.' I rested my head against his shoulder and sobbed helplessly, thinking of a Cassandre that I had never really known, the fond and loving elder sister that she had never been but I had always wanted.

After her execution, a sort of gloom fell over us all, as we struggled to come to terms with her loss. Lucrèce, left alone in Paris now that her husband had left for England, spent more and more time with me although I pretended not to notice that she avoided coming to my house when Xavier was there as she associated him with the revolution that had killed her twin, taken her husband away and, as she saw it, ruined all of our lives.

'How can he be friends with Danton and those other murderers?' she asked me once as we walked together by the Seine, averting our eyes from the Conciergerie towers, which loomed overhead and trying not to hear the distant cheers that floated across the river from the Place de la Nation.

I shook my head, brushing away my loose hair, which the wind blew into my face. 'They have been friends for a long time, Lucrèce,' I said. 'Xavier has known Georges since long before the revolution.'

'I see,' she said with a despairing shrug, then turned away as I watched her go, feeling heavy hearted that it had come to this for all of us and forseeing a time when I would lose Lucrèce too. Papa was the hardest hit by Cassandre's death; I visited him just once a few days after her execution to find the Hôtel de Saint-Valèry shrouded in darkness and with her portrait by Danloux, which hung in the grand salon, covered with a shimmering black taffeta cloth while Papa sat before it and wept into a black edged handkerchief. Grandmère was nowhere to be seen and indeed had apparently not left her house for several weeks.

I sat beside him for an hour, not really knowing what to say and occasionally patting his desiccated, cold hand as he wept before going away, never to return. I felt like I owed him some small, grudging amount of respect as he had raised me after all, however now that I knew for sure that he was not my true father, I revelled in the fact that I was free to walk away from him whenever I liked and with Xavier's love and encouragement, that is what I proceeded to do.

'You were so different when I first met you,' he whispered to me in the darkness of our bed. 'A quiet little mouse of a girl, with a nervous laugh. I remember thinking how unhappy you seemed.'

I kissed him, enjoying the feel of him against me as we snuggled together beneath the heavy crimson counterpane. 'You were right,' I murmured, with a sad pang as I remembered the poor little Adélaïde of 1789, who had been so afraid of life and at the same time so desperate to spread her wings and fly away. 'I only wish that you could have rescued me sooner.'

He laughed then softly and sat up in the bed, his auburn hair gleaming in the glow emitted by the dying fire that warmed our bedchamber. 'I would have done so, if I thought that I had had any chance with you,' he said with a wry, sidelong smile. 'It was when I escorted you to Bertrand's house on the Rue du Bac that I realised that my pretty little timid mouse was actually a very determined and courageous young woman.'

I smiled then and put my arms around him. 'I love you,' I murmured against his back, kissing his freckled shoulders.

He turned his head and smiled down at me in the way that I prayed would never cease to make my heart miss a beat. 'I love you too, Mademoiselle Adélaïde.'

Despite everything, despite the horror that was being enacted every single day in our city, and the devastation that it wreaked throughout the country that we both loved so much, despite all of this, we still managed to be happy in each other and when, at the start of 1794, I discovered that I was to have Xavier's child, it seemed as though our happiness was complete and perfect.

I went to visit Lucrèce at the now half empty Hôtel de Grenelle, to give her the news, tiptoeing carefully through the echoing salons, where the best furniture had already been covered in white cloths and dark patches covered the walls, where some of the paintings had been removed to safety in the cavernous cellars that lay underneath the house. I stared from the tall windows across the deserted gardens, now strewn with a thick carpet of pale pink and white blossoms which fell from the trees that bordered the lawns.

I found my sister dressed most becomingly in flounced black muslin and reclining on a pink silk upholstered sofa in her private boudoir, pretending to read one of Miss Burney's English novels but in reality daydreaming about Sébastien, who had all but moved into the Hôtel in Armand's absence. There was no sign of him in the exquisite, enormous rooms but I caught a whiff of his lemon and lavender cologne as I stepped into her boudoir and guessed that he had not long left.

Lucrèce greeted me with a genuine smile as I entered the room, and looked thrilled when I told her my news, even though I knew that it would be a blow to her as she had longed for so long to have a child. 'You and Xavier must be so happy,' she murmured, kissing me on both cheeks and drawing me down to sit beside her on the sofa. 'When is the baby due?'

I smiled. 'My physician says that he is due to arrive in July,' I said, unable to prevent myself from gently touching my stomach, where I knew the baby lay. 'I do not think that I can wait!'

'Oh, is it a "he" then?' Lucrèce said with a laugh.
I blushed. 'Xavier is convinced that we are having a boy.' I took her hand in mine. 'I hope that you are not angry with me?' I asked, not knowing what else to say.

Lucrèce gave a nervous laugh and looked quickly away. 'Why would I be angry?' she asked. 'I am delighted for you!' She gave a sigh and shrugged her thin shoulders. 'I must admit that I once had hopes that Armand and I would become parents but although that was not to be, I honestly do not resent anyone else having that happiness.'

I leaned forward and kissed her rose scented cheek.

'Thank you, Lucrèce.'

I felt sad when I left her all alone in her decaying mansion, surrounded by a dwindling number of servants and with only Sébastien to console her for her losses. My sister was still a young woman, with all of her life before her, but the air that surrounded her seemed tainted with disappointment and sadness.

'God be with you,' she whispered to me, holding me close as I took my leave of her. 'I pray that this horror will end soon.'

Xavier was waiting for me at our house on the Place de l'Opéra and I guessed from just one quick look at his face that something bad had happened. I quickly pulled off my hat and black velvet cloak, casting them aside onto a chair. 'What has happened, Xavier?' I demanded.

He sighed and held out a white slip of paper. 'Adélaïde, Bertrand has sent you this note,' he said. 'It was improperly sealed, I am sorry.'

I stared at him, taking the paper from his fingers. 'I don't care about that, Xavier,' I said, forcing a smile. 'You are my husband; we shouldn't have secrets from each other.'

'Not even this one?' he asked with a quizzical smile as I opened the note and began to read Bertrand's florid and extravagant handwriting.

'She is here.'

I stared at the paper, at first struggling to decipher what the cryptic message meant and then shaking with excitement as soon as the realisation that there could only ever be one 'she' dawned on me. I turned to my husband, tears welling in my eyes as I staggered towards him. 'Is it really true?' I said, as he caught me and led me to the chair, pushing my cloak and hat onto the marble floor. 'Has she truly come back?'

He smiled and kissed my forehead. 'I don't know, Adélaïde, but I think that you should waste no more time in going to her.'

I stared at him. 'Really? Right now?' I was breathless with excitement.

Xavier laughed. 'Yes, really.' He kissed me again. 'Were

you proposing to wait until tomorrow?'

I shook my head, then burst into tears again. 'No, of course not! Xavier, it is my mother! She has come back!' I stood up a little uncertainly then bent over to reclaim my cloak and hat from the floor. 'I must leave at once!'

My husband helped me into my cloak and then gravely placed my hat onto my head. 'I will take you there myself,' he said. 'I can wait in the carriage if you would rather not have me there with you.'

I took his hands and kissed them both, showering them with my tears. 'I want you there beside me, Xavier,' I said, smiling at him. 'You have taken such good care of me, my love and I want her to meet you.' I stopped then, remembering Lucrèce. 'I should let my sister know,' I said, looking about me stupidly for some paper and a pen, while Xavier regarded me with amusement.

'There is plenty of time for that later on,' he said, taking my hand and gently leading me from the room. 'You can write to her when we get home.'

I felt sick with nerves as the carriage bowled through the busy, noisy streets. Xavier tried at first to make conversation but after a while, when I failed to respond his voice trailed away and he left me alone to gaze out of the window, trying in vain to calm the frantic beat of my heart and the feeling of nausea that coiled and bubbled in the pit of my stomach.

It did not take us long to arrive at the Rue du Bac and I could barely wait for our carriage to come to a halt before I pushed the door open and jumped down onto the street. Xavier followed close behind me, his hand protectively at my elbow as I pushed open the gate then hurried across the courtyard to the bright red front door that I had come to know so well.

'Madame de Saint-Benoît,' Bertrand's footman had opened the door before I even had a chance to ring the bell. 'The master has been expecting you.' He smiled at me then stood aside to allow Xavier and I to enter.

'I'm so afraid,' I whispered to my husband, slipping my hand into his. 'What if she doesn't know me? What if she is like the others?' This last thought frightened me more than any other. I had pinned all of my hopes on my mother being different to the rest of my family; what if she turned out to be just the same?

'She won't be like them,' Xavier whispered back with a reassuring smile. 'She loved you, remember?'

I stepped into the room, holding tightly to Xavier's hand and hardly able to speak as I shyly looked at the woman who sat beside Bertrand on the pale pink silk covered sofa in front of the window, dressed in a simple white muslin gown, drawn in at the waist with a pale blue ribbon. I had expected many things but not the still radiant, blonde beauty who smiled nervously at me then stood up, her arms outstretched to welcome me.

'Adélaïde,' she whispered as I ran forward and her arms closed around me. 'My baby, my little girl.'

'Mother.' I closed my eyes, enjoying the comforting rose and carnation scent that clung to her fair hair. We moved apart and smiled shyly at each other, our fingers entwined. 'I can't believe that you are here at last.'

'I would have been here sooner,' she said with a smile and a shy backwards look at Bertrand, who was watching us both fondly. 'Only, I had no money and then I was too afraid to return in case the Comte sent me away again.' We walked to the sofa, where Bertrand obligingly moved up so that we could sit next to each other. 'In the end, I stayed with friends in Lyon and sent a letter to Bertrand, telling him where I was and within days he turned up on the doorstep.'

He laughed and kissed her on the forehead, clearly delighted to have her beside him again. 'I have never stopped searching for you, Sidonie,' he said. 'Nothing on earth would have kept me away once I had found out where you were.' They smiled at each other, truly in love as I enjoyed the novel sensation of having both of my parents beside me. I smiled across at Xavier, feeling oddly happy and complete.

The next few hours were spent together, drinking coffee and laughing and crying about the years that we had been apart. Sidonie told us about the night that she was sent away and her tedious life in a convent far away in the south of France, where the nuns had long since given up trying to attract her to their order and she had been sustained by the resolution that one day she would return to us all. In return, I told her about the years with Papa and Grandmère, about Penthémont and Xavier and the baby and then, with many tears, about the execution of Cassandre.

'I wish that I had been here,' our mother whispered, tears rolling down her cheeks as both Bertrand and I held her hands. 'I can't bear to think of it. My little Cassandre...'

The next few weeks were among the happiest of my life as while Xavier spent long hours with his political friends or at the debates at the National Assembly, I spent a lot of time with my mother, both at Bertrand's house on the Rue du Bac and also out and about in Paris. At first she was afraid of seeing my father, the Comte, who had been sent a letter by Bertrand's lawyers, informing him of Sidonie's return and intention to divorce him as quickly as possible, but after a while these fears began to shrink and she gradually became every bit as light hearted as she had been as a young woman.

'I've missed out on so much,' she said to me once, as we walked arm in arm through the gardens of the Palais du Luxembourg. 'There were times when I thought that my life in the convent would send me mad from boredom and I would never be able to come back to Paris and enjoy myself again.' She sighed and leaned her head against mine. 'I'm so delighted to be back. You can't imagine how much I missed you.'

We spent time with Lucrèce as well, who was gradually coming out of the depression that had swamped her after Cassandre's death. At first she was shy and nervous around our mother, not knowing quite how to address her and afraid to be hurt again but after a while things began to be mended between them and we began to spend several evenings a week together, just the three of us, having supper then lounging drowsily on the overstuffed sofas in Bertrand's opulent salon, talking about nothing and everything while footmen brought us endless pots of hot chocolate and plates piled high with cakes and fruit.

However, outside our contented little bubble, life was becoming increasingly dangerous for my husband and his friends. We often dined with Camille and Lucile Desmoulins, who lived next door to us on the Place de l'Odéon and gentle, pretty Lucile and I would sit beside the fire after dinner. We would admire her beautiful baby boy, Horace and smile at each other sympathetically as Xavier, Camille and often Danton too, who liked to call in unannounced, sat at the table, cracking walnuts and talking about politics late into the night.

On one damp, cold evening in mid March, we met up with Danton and other friends at a popular café in the Palais Royal then went together in the rain to the theatre, giggling and making a great deal of noise as we took our seats. There was a shout of laughter from the men when they looked up and realised that Robespierre and handsome, austere Saint-Just were sitting above us in one of the private boxes, elevated loftily above the masses and looking down upon us all with great disdain.

'How Antoine stares at us in disgust!' Camille Desmoulins delightedly whispered to Xavier, pointing to Saint-Just. 'He would behead us all if he could.'

My husband grinned, squeezing my hand. 'I don't doubt it.' He looked back over his shoulder at the unsmiling Saint-Just, whose cold blue eyes swept across the audience. 'Isn't he some sort of cousin of yours, Camille?'

Camille pulled a face. 'A very distant one, yes. As is Fouquier-Tinville, would you believe?' He laughed. 'I am not very lucky when it comes to family am I?' He stood up and waved to Saint-Just, who stoically ignored him. 'What?' he shouted at Danton, who looked at him in dismayed amusement. 'I am performing my family obligations! Don't you have relatives that you would rather not acknowledge but out of a sense of misplaced duty feel like you must anyway?'

Lucile gave a little shriek of laughter. 'Oh Camille! You promised that you would not mention your disreputable relatives in public any more!' She fell back against her seat giggling. 'Isn't it simply awful for us to be related to such people?'

The play began and a hush fell upon the audience. It was a tedious, moralising play with a simplistic message about the 'good' patriots and 'bad' aristocrats and I, bored as ever, by such performances began to slump in my seat and doze off only to be jerked awake by an eruption of shouts and mayhem as one of the actors spoke the line, innocuous in itself, of: 'Death to the tyrant!'

The theatre filled with wild applause and suddenly several of the men seated around them along with a few of Danton's friends jumped to their feet and turned to wave their fists at Robespierre and Saint-Just, while I looked up at them in bewilderment and Xavier tried in vain to calm everyone down.

'My friends, my friends,' Danton cried, smiling and gesturing that they all be seated again. 'Sit down and let the play continue.' He tried his best look annoyed but did not really succeed. It was obvious to us all that he was delighted to see Robespierre publicly humiliated.

'Vive Danton!' I looked to see who had shouted and then, like everyone else, looked fearfully up at Robespierre's box. Saint-Just had jumped to his feet and was standing protectively over his hero, who had gone very pale and was waving his hands nervously as though trying to make us all disappear.

'This is very unwise, Georges!' Xavier hissed at his friend. 'You shouldn't allow your followers to make such displays.' He looked around. 'It can only lead to trouble for us all.'

Danton shrugged his wide shoulders as he sat down. 'You worry too much, Xavier,' he said with a grin. 'We will have that powdered eunuch Robespierre running scared in a matter of days.'

'Are you sure about that?' Xavier looked frankly disbelieving. 'Georges, I have known Maximilian for many years and I don't think he is as weak as you clearly believe him to be.' He lowered his voice. 'I do not think that forcing his hand is the right way to go about this. He is more ruthless than you realise.' He sat down beside me and took my hand again. 'Don't be fooled by his soft voice and retiring manners, Georges. He'll have our heads if he can.'

'Poppycock!' Danton said with a laugh. 'I'm not scared of him! I defy him to do his worst!'

The next few days passed without incident, although we all felt uneasy and did not sleep well at night – however, despite much bold talk, Xavier did not run away and nor did Desmoulins or Danton, despite several attempts to make him leave the country before Robespierre ordered his now inevitable arrest. He laughed scornfully at the concerns of his friends and refused to abscond. 'You don't wear patriotism on the soles of your shoes!' he bellowed once at Camille, when he had tried in vain to persuade him to flee to his friends in England. 'I will never leave! Robespierre hasn't got the balls to move against me!'

Swayed by Danton's enormous confidence and Robespierre's inaction, Xavier and I gradually began to forget our doubts and fears and even, to some extent, believe that we could all bring the Terror to an end, not realising that time was already running out for us all.

Xavier and I had just gone to bed in the early hours of the thirtieth of March when we heard the noise that we had always feared coming from the street below – the sound of armed men marching, their boots clattering on the pavements and their uniforms clinking as they moved. I lay in the darkness with my eyes squeezed shut, praying that they would keep on marching and pass by our front door but even as I prayed, the footsteps halted and there was an abrupt banging on the door below.

My husband sprang from the bed and went to the window, while I struggled after him – encumbered by my pregnant state. We stood together in the window with our arms around each other, hardly daring to breathe as we looked down onto the square, which was now full of armed men, flourishing rifles and torches.

'Have they come for you?' I asked, too frightened to cry and feeling sick and faint with dread. 'Xavier what shall we do?'

'Wait!' my husband whispered, lifting a finger. 'Listen!'

I strained to hear what was being said below but then relaxed against him when I realised that it was not our door that they had knocked on, but that of Camille Desmoulins next door.

'They have come for Camille,' I whispered. 'Oh, poor Lucile.'

We watched as the men marched into the Desmoulins' house then shortly afterwards came out again, with Camille, looking pale and downcast in their midst. There was a tense moment when they seemed to pause for a moment outside our door and look up at the window at which we stood, but it was quickly over and they soon passed on, leaving the Place de l'Odéon silent and dark in their wake.

'Oh thank God,' I cried, embracing my husband, who looked shocked and more anxious than I had ever before seen him. 'You are safe!'

He looked at me then pulled me into his arms, resting his lips against my forehead. 'Safe for now,' he murmured.

The next morning we went together to the Ménage, the old riding school where the National Assembly had their meetings and pushed through the crowds to my usual spot on the balcony. News of the arrests of Desmoulins and Danton had already spread through the city and the hall was crammed with spectators, all shouting and speculating about what had happened. The general mood was decidedly ugly and I wondered if Robespierre fully understood what he had set himself up for by arresting someone so popular and well loved. He and Danton both came from very similar upper middle class backgrounds but whereas Robespierre was neurotic, overly concerned with his dignity and blatantly repulsed by the ordinary Parisians, Danton had the 'common touch' and was universally adored.

The speeches began. Danton's friend Legendre, who we both knew well, took the floor and began to speak. 'Citoyens, last night four members of this house were arrested. I know that Danton was one of them but the names of the others I do not yet know.' There was a chorus of howls and boos and he struggled to be overheard. 'Citoyens, I consider Danton to be as pure and honest as myself and I do not think that I can be charged with any action capable of shocking even the tenderest Republican sensibilities!' He ended by demanding that Danton and the others be brought to the Convention to be judged by their own peers – a popular motion that was greeted with a wave of cheers and shouts.

Sitting high above the action, I began to feel hopeful as speaker after speaker professed their support for Danton and each was greeted with cheers. This soon came to an end however when Robespierre, alerted no doubt by one of his loyal followers in the Ménage and followed by the rest of the Committee of Public Safety appeared at the door and confidently strode to the rostrum. A silence fell upon the hall as he mounted the steps and began to speak in his reedy, quiet voice which one had to strain to hear properly.

'Legendre has mentioned Danton, no doubt because he believes that a privilege attaches to his name. But we will have no more privileges and no more idols. We shall see today if whether the Convention has the power to break an idol long rotten or whether the idol is to stand until it falls and in its fall crush the Convention and the French nation...' And so he went on, until to my disgust he was surrounded by cheers and seemed to have the entire Ménage on his side. He stepped down and Saint-Just took his place, pristine as ever in funereal black with his long hair hanging loose and gold earrings swaying with each movement. It seemed incredible that someone so self possessed, so supremely focused and confident could be only twenty six years of age.

'I can't stay to hear this,' a woman muttered close to us. 'Saint-Just gives me the creeps. He is too clever by half.'

I longed to leave as well but I forced myself to remain until the end, curling my fingers through Xavier's as we sat through Saint-Just's denunciation of 'men who have long been betraying the popular cause, who have waged war against you in alliance with all the conspirators, Orléans, Brissot, Hébert, Hérault and their accomplices, and who at this moment are conspiring against the Republic with the allied kings.' Xavier closed his eyes in despair as he called the prisoners 'those last adherents of royalism who have been stalking liberty for five years as a tiger stalks his prey.' It seemed incredible that he was speaking of Danton and of his own cousin, Camille. I waited for someone, anyone to protest at this but there was not a sound in the Ménage as he spoke and gradually all hope began to fade away as both Xavier and I realised that no one would now dare to defend them.

The trial began a few days later on the third of April, the thirteenth of Germinal according to the new revolutionary calendar. The prisoners were taken to the Conciergerie in the morning and then led straight to the Tribunal. Lucile Desmoulins, Xavier and I waited patiently and in silence all morning at the front of the courtroom, determined to be there for our friends, but when the prisoners appeared, I had to hold Lucile upright as she almost fainted away at the sight of her beloved Camille, who looked tired and bedraggled after almost a week in prison. Cassandre's handsome former paramour from the old days at Versailles, Hérault de Séchelles who had been arrested a few months earlier for harbouring an émigré was also there, looking as polished and debonair as ever. Danton was the last to enter and I felt tears pricking my eyes as I gazed at him – he looked as exhausted as the others and there was something hopeless about the way that he walked, even though he tried his best to hide it beneath his usual brash veneer, joking with his guards and blowing kisses to Lucile and I.

The trial ran for three days and I was there with Xavier and Lucile every day to watch and will them on. Danton seemed to barely pause for breath as he fought for his life and those of his friends. 'When I think of the grave and unjust accusation brought against me, I cannot control my indignation towards my calumniators. I am a revolutionary heart and soul; how can I answer calmly?' he roared as the judges rang their little bells to silence him. He would stop at nothing in his determination to turn the tables on Robespierre and Saint-Just. 'Bring them to me and I will fling them back into the oblivion from which they ought never to have emerged! Miserable traitors, show yourselves and I will tear off the mask which preserves you from the common verdict!' There was riotous, ecstatic applause as the judges shouted and rang bells in an attempt to restore order.

And so it went on until he turned to the crowd and addressed us directly. 'For two days the court has known Danton! Tomorrow he hopes to fall asleep in glory. He has never whined for mercy, and you will see him going to the scaffold with that serenity of mind which comes from a good conscience.'

Again, instant uproar as the crowd cheered and demanded his release and that of the other prisoners. It really looked as though Danton would win and Xavier and I hugged each other, really believing that maybe, somehow and against all odds, everything would be alright.

Fouquier sighed, looking defeated by the chaos and shouting and noise. He tried a different tactic.

'You are tired, Danton, you need a rest. Tomorrow you can continue.'

The next day we were there early again at our usual place at the very front of the crowd. The prisoners were led in, looking exhausted but more defiant than ever. Danton began by demanding to know where their witnesses were and was told that Fouquier was waiting for the Committee of Public Safety's decision about this. This resulted in more ranting from Danton and Delacroix. 'What? Are my bitterest enemies to decide on a step which is mine by right of law?' At that moment no one could forget that Danton himself had been instrumental in the setting up of both the Committee and the Tribunal, before which he now stood. His enemies discovered a delicious irony in this but we, his friends could only bow their heads and look sorrowful.

'It is time to put an end to an altercation which is equally scandalous to the court and to the public. I shall write to the Convention for their decision, which will be scrupulously obeyed!' Fouquier shouted, finally goaded by Danton's insults. A letter was despatched immediately and the trial proceeded in much the same vein as ever with the same mixture of lies, propaganda and calumny directed at the prisoners and with Danton's voice roaring above it all.

There was a pause as an usher appeared and went to

whisper in Fouquier's ear, a difficult task considering the enormous plumed hat that he wore in his capacity as head of the tribunal. Xavier and I held our breath as he looked pleased, nodded and then jumped up to follow the man from the room, returning soon afterwards with a piece of paper in his hands. A hush fell on the hall as he began to read: 'The National Convention hereby empower the president to use all legal means to enforce his own authority and that of the Revolutionary Tribunal and to suppress any attempt of the accused to disturb the public order or to interfere with the course of justice. Anyone of the accused resisting or affronting the justice of the nation is to be immediately removed from the court.' The silence became ever more strained, ever more disbelieving as the meaning of the words became clear. Danton was to be effectively silenced on pain of being removed from the court.

'Tyranny!' The spectators began to shout and wave their fists at Fouquier, who took his seat with a very smug, self satisfied smile on his face. He had won. Xavier and I stared at each other in horror in the midst of the chaos, unable to believe what we had just heard and desperately frightened for our friends. 'What do they mean? What does it mean?' Lucile asked over and over again, holding onto my arm and beginning to cry. 'I don't understand.'

Danton went purple with rage and then with Delacroix, Camille, Xavier and Hérault leapt to his feet and began to bellow. 'You can't do this! You will never silence me! Never!' Camille began to tear up the pages and pages of notes that he had prepared for his defence and then threw the shredded paper into the crowd, screaming hysterically as he did so. It was the end and we all knew it.

'How did they do it?' I asked my husband, who stood shellshocked and silent at my side. 'The Convention would never have agreed to such a thing! They must be lying!'

Xavier shook his head. 'Someone is lying that is for sure.'

Later that day we would discover that Saint-Just had put the fear of God into the Convention by claiming that Lucile Desmoulins and 'her royalist friends' were planning to overthrow the republic. I ran immediately to the Desmoulins' house and hammered on the door, praying that Lucile had already taken little Horace and fled the capital. There was no immediate reply but then a surly maidservant opened the door a crack and told her that Citizeness Desmoulins had taken the baby to her mother's house and was not expected to return that night.

We saw her the next day at the trial, pale and defiant in a simple white silk gown and with Camille's baby, Horace wriggling and protesting in her arms. 'Wave to papa,' she whispered into his soft, sweet smelling hair. 'Wave, Horace!'

The decree of the previous day had effectively silenced the prisoners and the trial moved swiftly and inexorably towards its conclusion, with mere minutes passing before Fouquier turned to the jury and asked if they had been sufficiently instructed and were ready to come to a decision.

Danton leapt to his feet and rushed at Fouquier's desk, slamming his fist against the hard wood and yelling into the chief prosecutor's stern face. 'Tyranny! This is judicial murder! The trial has just begun and already you are silencing us, you infamous murderers! Don't trouble to deliberate, just take us to the scaffold straight away!'

Fouquier had won and he knew it. He ignored Danton as he would do a very troublesome gnat and stood up, beckoning to the gendarmes as he did so. 'In obedience with the decree issued by the Convention yesterday, the fourteenth of Germinal, I demand that the accused Danton is removed for contempt of court.'

Lucile screamed and went limp against me, as I desperately tried to hold her up. 'They can't do this!' She clutched Horace close and pushed to the front as Xavier held the spectators away from her. 'Camille! Camille!'

Danton was dragged away and one by one each of his friends followed him with Camille in particular struggling and fighting the gendarme who had seized hold of him, his cries drowned by the immense roar of disapproval and stamping of feet that spread through the court room.

The jury returned, shuffling and shame faced as they faced the now empty dock. 'Do you find Delacroix, Danton, Desmoulins, Philippeaux, Hérault de Séchelles and Westermann guilty of taking part in a conspiracy for the restoration of the monarchy?' I closed my eyes – they had not even been properly charged with this so how could the jury possibly have deliberated over it? It was all so preposterous.

'Guilty.'

Beside me, Lucile began to cry.

'Under the law of the 25th Ventôse as applied to Part II, Chapter 1, Section 5, Article 7 of the Penal Code, Fabre d'Eglantine, Delacroix, Danton, Desmoulins, Hérault de Séchelles, Philippeaux, Jullien, Basire, Chabot, Delauney, Frey, Espagnac, Westermann, Diederichsen, Guzman are condemned to death, and their property is to be confiscated for the state's treasury.' There was a dreadful pause filled only by Lucile's terrible sobs. 'Said sentence to be executed within twenty four hours on the Place de la Révolution in Paris and to be published in print throughout the whole Republic.'

I put my arm around Lucile, who was still sobbing and together the three of us stumbled from the hall, bound together by our shared sorrow and disbelief. 'I was so sure that Danton would save them all,' Lucile whispered. 'How could it have gone so badly wrong?'

'I do not know,' I said, looking at my friend with concern as Xavier rubbed her back and tried his best to calm her. 'What will you do now, Lucile?' I asked. 'If Saint-Just mentioned you to the Convention then perhaps it would be better if you tried to leave Paris?' I looked to my husband who, reading my thoughts, nodded. 'Xavier has papers...'

Lucile shrugged. 'I no longer care what becomes of me,' she said in a low voice. 'My life has no meaning or purpose without Camille beside me.'

I was shocked. 'But what about Horace?' I reached out to gently touch the baby's rosy cheek. 'He still needs you.'

Lucile shook her pretty head. 'No, he doesn't. Not really.'

She sighed. 'I love him dearly but simply cannot endure an existence without Camille. Do you understand, Adélaïde?'

I took a deep breath and looked at my husband, who looked shattered and pale with stress and lack of sleep. 'Yes, of course,' I lied, touching my stomach where my own baby slumbered. 'I do not think that I would be brave enough to sacrifice myself though.'

We took Lucile back to the Place de l'Odéon, where her mother was waiting for her and then walked in silence to our own house next door. I was aware of a very subdued atmosphere in the familiar streets – Danton was a local hero and everywhere I looked I saw sad faces and shaking heads as the people of the district tried to come to terms with the dreadful news.

'What shall we do?' Xavier asked me as soon as I had closed the door behind us and thrown my coat and hat onto a chair. 'I don't know whether to stay and fight or take you to safety.' He strode into our sitting room and I nervously followed him. 'I could never forgive myself if anything happened to you or to our child.'

I smiled and took hold of his arm, gazing up earnestly into his face, which I loved so much. 'Xavier, nothing is going to happen to us,' I said. 'Why would it?'

He stared at me. 'Why would it?' he repeated incredulously. 'Were you there beside me today or not, Adélaïde? My closest political allies have been condemned to death and the wife of one of my closest friends is about to be arrested,' he took my shoulders. 'That might well be us in just a few days once Robespierre and Saint Just decide that we have slipped the net.' He released me and turned away. 'I try to downplay who we are, but they never really forget, Adélaïde,' he said. 'They are happy enough to accept us now, but how long before they remember that I was the godson of the Duc d'Orléans and as for you...' He shook his head.

I sat down heavily on a chair and stared blankly into the distance, struggling to organise my confused thoughts. 'I see.' Only, I didn't. Not really. I raised my head and looked at him.

'What are we going to do?'

He sighed, began to turn away then thought better of it and instead knelt before me and took my hands in his. 'We are going to try to leave Paris,' he said. 'Perhaps even France, if we can.'

I stared at him. 'Are you serious?' I could hardly believe my ears – was my husband really suggesting that we run away rather than stay and fight.

He leaned forward and kissed my lips then rested his forehead against mine. 'Adélaïde, I have never been more serious in my life.' He stood up and went to the bookcase, where he pulled a heavy tome from a shelf, opened it and extracted a sheaf of papers. 'I have the papers ready,' he said, showing them to me. 'We can leave tonight if you are willing.'

I stared at him, thoroughly aghast. 'Tonight?' I clambered awkwardly to my feet, getting my heel stuck in my skirt and almost toppling over. 'Are you sure? Why so soon?'

He shrugged and placed the papers carefully on the table in between us. 'It's only a matter of time before Robespierre and Saint Just turn their attention to us and I just can't take that risk. I can't bear the thought of being taken away and leaving you and our child undefended.'

I went to him and took his hand. 'Can we take Lucile and Horace with us?' I asked, thinking of the doomed girl next door.

Xavier shook his head sadly. 'I asked her to come with us but she won't leave,' he sighed. 'Her only wish is to die with Camille.'

I shook my head. 'I don't understand,' I said.

My husband smiled, the first time that I had seen him do so for days, and clasped my hand. 'And I don't want you to,' he said, hugging me to him. 'Adélaïde, you have to promise me that whatever happens, you will continue to live and do your best to survive.'

I reached up and kissed his cheek, tears filling my eyes. 'I promise.'

It did not take us long to prepare to leave - I dismissed

my maids for the day and packed my trunks myself, piling in dresses, chemises and shoes along with the baby shirts and caps that I had lovingly stitched next to the fire while Xavier was busy with his political friends.

'We leave at nightfall,' my husband said as he threw shirts and breeches into a bag. 'My family have a house in Metz, in Switzerland. We will be safe there until it is time to return.'

'I've never been to Switzerland,' I said, carefully folding up a baby shirt and placing it on top of my clothes. 'I hear it is very beautiful though.'

Xavier smiled at me. 'It's extremely beautiful,' he said. 'You will be able to paint and sketch to your hearts content and go for long walks around the countryside. I used to love it there when I was a boy.'

As soon as it was dark, we attached our trunks to the coach and went through our silent, dimly lit house, checking to make sure that nothing had been forgotten and no clue of our destination remained. 'I have written letters to my mother and Lucrèce,' I said to Xavier, pointing to where they rested on the table. 'I hope that they will receive them.' I had wanted to say goodbye in person but Xavier had decided that it was far too risky. At that moment there was the clatter of horses hooves and wheels outside, followed by a knock on the front door. I stared at Xavier in terror, convinced that Robespierre himself had come to arrest us but he only smiled and went to open the door. 'Who is it?' I whispered, hardly daring to breathe.

After what seemed like an eternity, the sitting room door opened and to my immense and wholehearted relief, my mother and Bertrand appeared in the doorway. 'Maman!' I ran to her and hugged her close. 'I wrote a letter for you but this is much better!' I pulled away, tears rolling down my cheeks. 'I hate that we are going away, so soon after finding each other again but hopefully we will see each other again soon!' I looked to Xavier, who stood beside Bertrand. 'It won't be forever, will it?'

He shook his head. 'Not forever.' He looked to my father, Bertrand who nodded, a serious expression on his handsome face.

'In fact, Adélaïde...'

'We are coming with you!' my mother exclaimed. 'Did you really think that I would let you go without me?'

I stared at her in amazement. 'You are coming with us to Switzerland? Oh, really, truly?' I looked at Bertrand, who moved forward and took my mother's hand. 'And you too?' I asked him as he smiled upon us both.

'Of course,' he replied in his rich, beautiful voice. 'There is no force on earth that can keep me from the side of your mother now that I have found her again and as she chooses to go with you, there must I go too.' He lifted her hand to his lips and I noticed for the first time that an emerald ring gleamed on her finger.

'Are you betrothed?' I asked, thoroughly delighted and all of our current woes forgotten as I hugged them both.

My mother blushed and smiled. 'Bertrand asked me as soon as my divorce from the Comte became official. We will marry as soon as we reach Switzerland,' she said, looking adoringly up at her lover. 'I can't wait to be Madame Bertrand instead of Madame la Comtesse.'

Xavier smiled and opened the door. 'There will be plenty of time to discuss this once we leave Paris,' he said, chivvying us all out of the room. 'We need to make haste though.' He pulled some papers out of his coat and handed them to Bertrand. 'These are for you and Sidonie. You are too well known to travel under an assumed name without attracting suspicion so they are made out in the names of Monsieur and Madame Bertrand. I will act as your coachman, while Adélaïde will be your dresser, Mademoiselle St-Humbert.'

Clearly my mother and Bertrand had decided not to bother travelling light so the carriage became a tight squeeze once all of our baggage had been attached to the outside and piled up on the seats, but we managed to fit inside fairly comfortably and after one last sad look up from the windows at the house that had been my first home after my marriage, Xavier, his face hidden by a woollen scarf and a hat pulled low over his brow climbed up onto the perch and we were off.

I stared out of the window as we drove through the dark, deserted streets of the city that had been my home as long as I could remember, taking in every single detail of the beautiful houses and wishing that I could hug it all to me. Seeing my sad expression, my mother leaned forward and squeezed my hand. 'We will be back soon,' she whispered. 'Don't worry.'

I nodded. 'I know. The current horror can't go on forever. The French people won't tolerate it.' I rested my head against the window, wondering when I would be back again and how long it would take for those who were left behind to decide that enough was enough.

The carriage suddenly came to a halt and I realised that we had realised that we had reached the barrier at the edge of the city, where our papers would be checked. It was imperative that we all acted out our parts perfectly in order to be allowed to carry on towards safety and freedom.

'Halt!' We all held our breath as the carriage was surrounded by members of the National Guard in their white, blue and red uniforms. Two of them held the horses reins while another pulled open the door and peered in at us. 'Citizen Bertrand?' he asked, peering at my father. 'Are you leaving Paris, Citizen?'

Bertrand nodded, confident and urbane as ever and not betraying the slightest ounce of fear. 'I am indeed, Citizen,' he replied with his charming smile. 'I have decided it is time to tour the provinces and raise morale amongst our fellow Citizens. Robespierre himself has approved the act that I have written for this purpose.'

The guardsman looked impressed and slightly abashed. 'Nonetheless Citizen, I regret that I must ask to see your papers,' he said. 'You understand, of course, that this is absolutely necessary?'

Again that charming smile as Bertrand immediately handed over our papers. 'But of course, Citizen,' he said. 'The safety of the republic is the priority of us all.'

I stared out of the window, feeling sick with fear as the guardsman went through our papers, raising his eyes a couple of times to look at myself and my mother. Finally, he folded them up again and handed them back to Bertrand. 'It is all in order, Citizen,' he said with the glimmer of a smile. 'I hope that you have a pleasant journey and return soon to Paris.'

Bertrand smiled and nodded in an affable manner. 'I hope so too, Citizen.'

The door was slammed shut again and after what seemed like forever, the carriage began to move again, the wheels rolling noisily over the cobbles as we slowly went past the group of guardsmen, who all peered curiously into our coach now that news had presumably spread about who travelled within.

Inside, we all held our breath and held hands until we were past the barrier. 'I can't believe how easy it was,' my mother said with a sigh of relief. 'I can't believe that they let us go.'

I wiped away the tears that rolled down my cheeks and wondered how Xavier, perched alone at the front of the carriage was feeling. 'I can't believe it either,' I said as we picked up speed and left Paris far behind us.

1794

Lucrèce

Paris, June 1794

They came for me while I was still asleep. I always knew that one day my luck would run out, but I had hoped that it would be while I was wide awake, fully dressed and the very picture of innocence in my prettiest white silk gown and armed with a rehearsed spiel of clever little lies and excuses which would fall artlessly from my petal pink rouged lips. Instead I was dressed only in a thin cotton chemise and was momentarily bewildered when I heard the banging on the street door and then the shouts and cries of my few remaining servants as they let them in and the men swarmed all over the house in search of me.

'Madame,' my maid ran into my room. 'There are guardsmen downstairs! They have come to take you away!' She ran to pick up my pink gauzey dressing gown, which had been thrown carelessly over a chair and handed it to me as I stared at her in stupid confusion from the depths of my elaborately swagged and gilded bed. 'Quick, madame! They will be here for you soon! You can't let them see you like this!'

I nodded and began to pull on the dressing gown. 'Get me a plain dress,' I ordered, finding my voice at last as I stumbled from the bed, 'and pack me some things.' I picked up the miniature of Sébastien, which lay on the table beside my bed and held it tightly in my hand, drawing strength from him and wishing that he was there beside me now. 'Don't worry, Rosalie,' I said, briefly touching the girl's cheek. 'They won't harm you.'

'It isn't me that I'm worrying about, madame' she said with a sad look.

Gathering all of my courage, I left my room and stepped out onto the landing, where a crowd of men waited for me. Most were in the uniforms of National Guardsmen but a few other ragged hangers on lurked around the edges, staring at me and whispering to each other. 'Citizeness Saliex?' one of the guardsmen asked, reading from a sheaf of grubby papers that he held in his hand. 'We have orders here for your immediate arrest.'

My legs shook beneath my light nightdress, but I managed to control myself enough to smile and ask: 'May I get dressed first?'

'Of course, Jacquinot will go with you,' the guardsman said with a dismissive wave of his hand as one of his companions, clearly Jacquinot stepped forward. 'You have ten minutes.'

I nodded. 'Thank you.'

The guard stood by the door as I stepped behind a screen in the corner of my room and allowed Rosalie to help me get dressed. Her hands fumbled with the laces and buttons as she put me into a plain pale blue silk dress and fastened a muslin fichu around my shoulders, tying it behind my back.

'I have put three dresses, some linen and two pairs of shoes in your bag, madame,' she whispered. 'Let me know if you need more and I will try to send it to you.'

When I was ready, I picked up my bag, kissed Rosalie on the forehead then followed the guardsman from the room and down the stairs to the huge hallway, where the other men waited for me. They were staring around themselves in mingled envy and anger, taking in the luxury and beauty of my home, which still looked lovely even though so many things had been hidden away.

'Come now,' the leader said, stepping forward to take my arm. 'We have no time to lose, Citizeness.'

I resisted the urge to shake off his hand. 'Do you know which prison I am being taken to?' I asked.

He laughed and after a pause the others joined in as well. 'Well that depends on which one will have you, Citizeness,' he said. 'The prisons in Paris are full these days and it is almost impossible to find space for all of the prisoners.'

I shuddered, unable to imagine what sort of conditions I was about to be exposed to.

He grinned at me. 'If the sainte guillotine did its work a bit quicker then we wouldn't have this problem.' He crashed one of his hands against the palm of the other, as if in imitation of the guillotine's blade as I hastily averted my eyes.

They took me first to the Plessis prison on the Rue Fromontel and then the feared Bicêtre, but both were bursting at the seams with prisoners and were unable to take me. They had better luck at the Porte-Libre prison on the Rue Saint-Jacques, near to the Jacobins club frequented by Robespierre and his followers. One of the officials jumped down from the carriage and after a muttered conversation with the gendarmes outside the gates, disappeared inside briefly before coming out with yet more gendarmes, who pulled the door open and intimated that I get out of the carriage. I grabbed my bag and hastened to obey, looking at each one fearfully and pulling my cloak closer.

'Come along, Citizeness,' one of them said impatiently. 'We haven't got all day!' He went to take my arm but something about the way that I looked at him made him stay his hand and then move aside to let me pass.

I walked through the gate and the lichen covered entranceway beyond and then found myself in darkness. I looked about myself nervously until a dry cough alerted me to the small clerk sitting behind a desk in the corner.

'It is very late,' he grumbled, as I approached him. 'Get a move on.'

'I'm sorry,' I faltered, dropping my bag to the floor.

He sighed. 'Your name please, Citizeness?' He picked up his pen.

'Lucrèce-Angèlique-Athénaïs-Honorine-Lucie-Yolande de Saint-Valèry,' I said before pausing, uncertain about how to present my married name. 'Saliex.'

The clerk glanced up at me. 'The ci-devant Duchesse de Saliex?' His tone was unfriendly.

I followed two of the gendarmes and a turnkey along a stone flagged corridor and up some stairs to another corridor, which was lined with doors. 'In here,' the turnkey said with a jerk of his head towards one of the doors.

I smiled and went into the room, still clutching my bag to my bosom. It was not so bad after all – blue and stark, it reminded me of my old dormitory at Penthemont. When the men had gone I sat down on the edge of the narrow, hard little bed and allowed myself to cry a little.

'Madame la Duchesse?' There was a discreet cough outside the door and I looked up to see a woman looking in at me. 'My dear, I thought that I recognised you when you went past.' She stepped into my cell and looked about herself with fastidious distaste. She looked immaculate in sea green muslin embroidered with gold and tied high under her bosom with a spangled sash and I cast an ashamed look down at my stained and crumpled blue cotton dress. 'I'm Fanny de Beauharnais,' she said with a smile as I stared at her. The name sounded familiar but I couldn't immediately place it.

'All the best people are languishing in Paris' prisons at the moment!' Fanny said airily as she led me down a crowded corridor. I stared around myself in astonishment at the gorgeously dressed people who clustered in little groups to watch us go past. 'This is a prison like no other!' she said confidingly behind a painted fan that she had whipped out of her sleeve. 'We have so much fun! You have no idea!'

I continued to stare at her. 'But the... the guillotine.' I did not understand. 'Don't you care?'

Fanny pouted. 'We try not to think about that,' she said with a dismissive shrug. 'We are not immune of course and occasionally one of our number will... leave us but why dwell on such unpleasantness when there is fun to be had and pleasant summer evenings to be enjoyed in the company of handsome poets?' She put a hand on my arm and smiled. 'You'll soon see what I mean.'

I eyed Fanny's sumptuous dress and powdered hair. 'Should I go back and get changed?' I gave a smile. 'I did not know that I would need an evening dress when I was arrested.'

'You are fine as you are,' Fanny said. 'It is your first night here and you look so charming anyway!' She led me down a flight of stairs at the other end of the corridor, chattering all the while about our distinguished fellow 'guests' ('prisoners' I silently amended) and the treats in store for me. 'We have even managed to put together a string quartet!' she cried brightly as we came to the bottom of the stairs. 'So we have music every night.'

We walked down a paved corridor and through a small arched cloister until we came to a door, over which was written: 'Man cherishes liberty even when he is in prison.'

'Droll isn't it?' Fanny said with a laugh as she pushed the door open. 'Now, welcome to our little company!' She led me into a candlelit room, which had once clearly been used as a chapel.

'Everyone, may I present Madame la Duchesse de Saliex!' She turned and whispered to me: 'No one bothers with that hideous ci-devant nonsense here.'

Feeling rather overawed, I forced a smile and swept a low curtsey to the people assembled in the room. There must have been fifty or sixty of them, all dressed in their best and seated quite at their ease playing cards, playing instruments, embroidering in front of the fire or standing chattering in small groups. It could have been any salon in the years before the revolution and I felt myself blinking back the tears as I was hailed with smiles and great pleasure. It was a long time since I had encountered such courteous friendliness.

'Welcome to Port-Libre, Madame la Duchesse,' one finely dressed gentleman said with a flourishing bow. I vaguely recognised him from Versailles and smiled in response. 'You are very kind, monsieur.'

It was a very strange evening but not an unpleasant one. Fanny had clearly not lied when she said that all the best people were currently languishing in Paris' prisons and I wondered at a regime that could willingly and knowingly keep its finest minds imprisoned in such a way.

Life at Port-Libre, if not entirely pleasant, was at least bearable. There were no bars on the windows or locks on the doors and an atmosphere of cheerful acceptance and even gaiety prevailed, which kept everyone's spirits up and made us all feel much braver than we would have done elsewhere.

In the morning there was the usual roll call, dreaded by every prisoner in Paris, after which anyone who had been named by the Tribunal or who was to be transferred would be taken away to wait for the tumbrel that would take them to the Conciergerie or elsewhere. After the round of farewells and embraces had ended, everyone left behind composed themselves and went about their day as though nothing had happened.

We were all allowed a surprising amount of freedom and everywhere I wandered there seemed to be something happening – an impromptu concert or a poetry reading or even dancing. Everyone spent their time either in each other's cells, walking outside in the pleasant cloister, sitting under the trees in the gardens or gathered in the former chapel which served as a salon, a general meeting room and also a refectory. There was chatter, music, song and also romance everywhere.

We all ate together in the chapel and there was a pleasant, convivial atmosphere at meal times. Everyone helped to lay the tables and then all of the prisoners sat together and did their best to forget their grim surroundings by talking as much as possible and extravagantly praising the food, which was admittedly much better than could be expected. Everyone was expected to bring their own plate and spoon to the table and Fanny generously lent some to me, whispering: 'We are not to be trusted with knives and forks apparently' with a hurt look.

After dinner we washed our hands in the elegant

fountain in the cloister and then took a turn about the gardens. As the sun began to set over the roof of the former convent, some prisoners read each other poetry and flirted, laughing softly, beneath the acacia tree in the corner. Being naturally shy by nature I spent a great deal of time reading books lent to me by Fanny and in a strange way it began to remind me of the peace that I had found at Penthemont, all those years ago.

It was not to last though and after about six weeks my name was called out in the yard and I was told that I was to be transferred to the former Carmelite convent on the Rue Vaugirard, known as 'Les Carmes'. I was hugely relieved not to be taken to the Conciergerie and even managed to look cheerful as the other prisoners came forward to say their farewells and kiss my cheeks.

Les Carmes was a huge contrast to the relatively salubrious surroundings of Port-Libre. After giving my name to the wizened clerk in the filthy records office, I was taken down a long, dank corridor to the dormitories which had once housed the Carmelite sisters but now provided shelter for seven hundred prisoners. I looked around myself in horror and disgust at the lichen covered, mouldy walls and the dirty floors which were covered in all manner of refuse and filth.

'In here, Citizeness.' The turnkey shoved open a door and jerked his head to signify that I should enter. 'You won't be here for long so don't bother making yourself too comfortable,' he said with a nasty laugh.

I stared at him and then turned away and went into the room. It was simply furnished with grubby white washed walls and eighteen small, narrow beds pushed up against the walls – nine on each side of the room. There were two women, both of whom looked vaguely familiar, sitting together on one of the beds at the far end and I hesitated on the threshold, uncertain as to what to do. I had become used to the solitude of my little cell in Port Libre and had not expected to share a room with anyone.

'Madame de Saliex!' one of the women smiled and waved, calling out in an English accent. 'Are you in here with us? Well, how fun!' She languidly stood up and came to kiss my cheeks, surrounding me with her heavy rose perfume. 'You don't remember me do you?' she said with a laugh. 'My name is Grace Elliot. I used to be friends with your sister, Cassandre.'

I smiled. 'Of course! I remember now!' Scottish Grace had once been mistress to the Duc d'Orléans and she and Cassandre had caused a scandal by driving about Paris with tricolor feathers in their hats and earrings made from the stones of the Bastille swinging from their ears. 'Cassandre was very fond of you.'

Grace smiled sadly. 'I was so very sorry to hear about what happened,' she said simply before leading me to the group of women. 'Let me introduce you to our little company! Madame la Duchesse d'Aiguillon   you probably already know,' she gestured to a smiling, pretty young woman with long dark hair.

'Yes, we have met several times at Versailles,' Madame d'Aiguillon said, jumping up to kiss my cheeks. 'I am sorry indeed to see you here in this place. Have you only just been arrested? It is all such a terrible bore is it not?' She yawned behind her hand, her blue eyes dancing merrily all the while.

I opened my mouth to reply but was interrupted by the arrival of another woman, this one thin with pretty dark eyes and curling chestnut brown hair. 'And this is Madame de Beauharnais.' I was momentarily confused but then recalled Fanny talking about a much loved niece, who was also in prison. This must be she.

'Rose to you,' she said with a smile that revealed delightful dimples in her pale cheeks before sitting down on the bed next to me. 'No need to introduce yourself - you've been pointed out to me many times at the Opéra. Tell us everything! Have you only just been arrested? Where did they take you first of all?'

'I have just been transferred from Port-Royal,' I said. 'I must tell you, your aunt Fanny was there as well.'

Rose looked sad. 'Yes, I know, it must be dreadful for her.'

'It isn't too bad there,' I said, trying to cheer her up. 'The prisoners there do their best to enjoy themselves.' I looked around the damp, dirty walls of our cell and shivered. 'I don't suppose there is much fun to be had here though.'

Rose shrugged. 'Not much but we manage.' She languidly stretched her arms above her head but then stopped suddenly and stared at me. 'Wait! I have something to tell you as well!'

I raised an eyebrow. 'Oh?'

'It's your husband.' She paused dramatically. 'He is in here as well. They brought him in yesterday evening.'

I went at once to the courtyard below, where I found him standing with a group of other men in the corner. Armand looked as immaculate and soignée as ever in dove grey silk, with his dark hair tied neatly back with a black ribbon but I had never before seen his face more careworn and anxious.

'Ma beauté,' he whispered, immediately coming forward and taking my hands as he looked deep into my eyes. 'I had no idea what had become of you.' He kissed my hands and then my lips. 'I hoped that they would not be able to find you.'

I shook my head. 'I was arrested at the start of June,' I said, wiping away my tears. 'They took me to Port-Royal and then transferred me here.'

'Then they must have taken you at the same time as me,' he said, smoothing my hair away from my temples. 'Did they not tell you that I had been also been arrested? I came back to France in March but didn't get far before they caught up with me.'

'I asked everyone if they had seen you but they claimed not to know,' I replied furiously.

He sighed. 'The intolerable cruelty of it all.' We walked a bit further along. It was a bright day and the yard was full of people taking full advantage of the sunshine.

'Armand, what do you think is going to happen to us?' I asked at last, twisting my hands together. 'I don't even know what I am accused of.'

'I have seen so many people taken away,,never to return and I don't think that many of them knew what they were accused of either,' he said sadly.

We had to separate soon afterwards as it was time for dinner and at this prison male and female prisoners ate at different sittings rather than all together as they did at Porte-Libre.

Upon entering the cold dark refectory I was hailed by Rose, who was sitting at a wooden table near the door.

'Come and sit with us!' she cried, making space beside her. 'The food here isn't nearly so bad as one might think, despite the hideous décor.' She handed me a earthenware bowl.

I smiled my thanks and sat down, nodding politely at Madame d'Aiguillon and Grace Elliot and the other women on our table. The atmosphere was not quite so gay and jolly as at Port Royal but every one did their best to make the meal times as pleasant and sociable as possible.

I was introduced to another cell mate, the exquisitely beautiful, blonde Delphine de Custine, who was in mourning for her husband who had recently perished on the guillotine. As it was forbidden to wear black or make any display of grief in memory of executed persons she looked extremely conspicuous amongst the pale, faded colours worn by the other women. 'But what can they do?' she said with a gentle smile and a not so gentle flash of her mesmerising pale blue eyes. 'They have already put me in prison anyway.'

'So how did my poor aunt Fanny look?' Rose asked me with a smile. 'Has she surrounded herself with lovers as usual?'

I blushed. 'She is very... popular,' I said after a careful pause, not wishing to gossip about the absent Madame de Beauharnais.

The other women looked at each other and burst out laughing. 'Popular!' Rose cried, kissing me. 'Oh my dear, how your modesty shames us all.'

I did not immediately understand but later that night, Rose and I stayed up talking in the draughty dormitory, long after the others had gone to sleep, tossing and turning on their cold, hard little beds and pulling their blankets up above their heads in order to ignore the ceaseless scratchings of the rats and other vermin that plagued the prison. Their room was much tidier than most of the others because Rose, Grace and the other women did their best to keep it and themselves as clean as possible.

'Why didn't you emigrate when you had the chance,'

Rose whispered. 'I would have gone if I could.'

I shrugged. 'Because we had done nothing wrong, we stupidly believed that we had nothing to fear.'

'It doesn't work like any more does it?' Rose said with a low laugh. 'I don't think that anyone here has really done anything wrong. It seems like, all it takes is for someone to take a dislike to you and poof here you are, in this miserable hole.' She leaned forward confidingly. 'My husband, Alexandre, is here as well,' she whispered. 'We separated many years ago when our son was a baby and hadn't seen each other for months until we ended up in here together. It is very strange to be reunited after all this time apart.'

'It's peculiar how things turn out,' I said, thinking of myself and Armand.

Rose leaned forward so that her lips were beside my ear. 'He is in love with Delphine,' she whispered. 'Which hurts me much less than it should. They've both done their best to be considerate towards me so what could I do but give them my blessing and be happy for them?'

I looked over at Delphine, who was asleep on the bed opposite with her long blonde tresses hanging almost to the floor. 'I could not give them my blessing,' I whispered. 'I think that I would have scratched her eyes out.' I remembered the long ago days of Armand's infatuation with Honorine and my fingers curled into claws.

Rose laughed. 'I have often thought about it,' she confided. 'I think that he must really love her though. She is so very beautiful so how could he not? He calls her his reine des roses. No one has ever called me anything like that.' She dashed away a tear. 'It doesn't really matter does it? Not in the end.'

I shook my head then moved forward and hugged her. 'No, not really.' We cried together for a little while then Rose gave an embarrassed laugh and wiped both of our faces with the edge of her pink embroidered shawl.

'Besides, I am not exactly lonely,' she whispered, drawing a mirror from beneath her pillow and checking her hair. 'I am not without consolation.'

'Oh?' I raised an eyebrow. 'Is it another prisoner here?'

Rose nodded, blushing a little in the sparse moonlight that filtered past the heavily barred windows. 'His name is Lazare Hoche. Have you heard of him?' I nodded, who had not heard of the brave and gallant General Hoche of the Army of the Rhine? He was a national hero thanks to his exploits against the Prussians - although not so much of a hero as to be able to escape the long arm of the Committee of Public Safety and escape arrest himself.

'Is he your lover?' I asked now, amazed that my friend could have caught such a man. Not that Rose was without charm, quite the reverse in fact, but it just seemed so bizarre that anything the slightest bit romantic could happen in such a terrible place. That a pretty little woman could ensnare a national hero. That a nobleman could fall in love with a beautiful widow and call her his 'reine des roses'.

Rose nodded and smiled. 'We do not get to meet in private every night,' she whispered, 'but he often bribes the turnkeys and they take me to his cell on the men's side of the prison.' She laughed. 'It is well worth the risk for he has his own cell and lives in a very different style to the rest of us poor wretches.'

'I am glad for you,' I said with absolute sincerity, kissing Rose's cheek. 'Is it very easy to bribe the turnkeys?' I asked.

Rose giggled. 'Oh, extremely easy! They all drink and are not at all adverse to the extra bit of income. The doors between the two parts of the prison are kept locked but it is easy enough to get them to unlock the door and let us through. I think that everyone in here has taken advantage of this at some time or another and really, it is a good idea, Lucrèce to spend as much time as possible with your husband because if you can declare yourself enceinte they cannot execute you.' She shrugged. 'That is what I intend to do when they come for me.' She patted her hair again before slipping the mirror back under her pillow. 'Just one more day might be enough.'

Life in Les Carmes was exceedingly tedious and along with all of the other prisoners, I whiled away the long hours reading, talking about absolutely nothing at all, playing endless games of backgammon or having my tarot cards read over and over again by Rose, who never went anywhere without a battered deck that she claimed had been given to her by a witch on Martinique.

As she had advised, I did my best to see as much as possible of my husband and every few nights we would drop some precious coins into the hands of the turnkeys and meet in his cold, stinking cell for a few precious hours more whilst pretending not to see the other whispering shadows that floated about the prison at night. I felt some small shame as I gave myself to him, remembering Sébastien who no doubt waited patiently for me on the outside, if he had not already been arrested himself, but then I would remember that Armand was my husband and right now, my only chance of survival.

'If you were to become pregnant then you would be saved,' Armand whispered to me once in the darkness, his arms tightening around me as he spoke.

I laughed softly and kissed him. 'I do not think that I could bear to conceive a child in such a place as this.'

'Who cares so long as you both live,' he replied, suddenly serious. 'There is no hope for me, Lucrèce, but you have a chance at least.'

The days and weeks merged into each other so that I no longer had any idea what day it was or even how long I had been incarcerated there. Only the ever increasing and appalling heat made it clear that Spring was swiftly becoming Summer and when the prisoners took our daily walk in the walled cloister at the heart of the prison we lifted our faces to the sun and basked beneath its soft, warm rays. It was not all pleasant though as the badly ventilated cells became so overheated that we were forced to wring our clothes out at several points during the day and morale became ever more dangerously low as people became too indolent to care much about their appearance or surroundings any more.

Rose, Grace and the other ladies of our cell did our best to keep up appearances and be as elegant as possible at all times but we were fighting a losing battle as most of the other prisoners seemed to prefer to laze about in filthy, damp clothes and with undressed hair and unshaven faces.

'It really is too dreadful,' Delphine remarked with a disdainful sniff as she complacently smoothed down her pristine black silk skirts. 'I do wish that people would have a bit more pride in themselves.'

Three weeks had passed since the last group of prisoners had had their names called and been led away to the Conciergerie to face trial and probable execution. It seemed like an eternity and with each passing day we all became increasingly more tense as the dreaded roll call was expected and then failed to occur. Every day we all rejoiced that we had escaped the guillotine once again but the prolonged suspense and complete lack of news about the outside world was slowly driving us all to despair. Rose's spirits in particular became quite shattered after Lazare Hoche was transferred to the Conciergerie and she took to spending hours on end lying on her bed and softly sobbing into the threadbare blanket, much to the horror of the other ladies, who rather deplored such an extravagant show of emotion.

'Come now, Rose,' Delphine murmured one day, whilst seated beside her friend's bed and idly patting her hand. 'Please do pull yourself together! Really, my dear, you must not give the canaille the satisfaction of seeing that they are distressing you.' She sighed. 'You must at least try to give the appearance of being brave.'

Rose lifted her head. 'I do not feel very brave at all,' she admitted between her sobs, 'and why should I? They want to kill us, Delphine! How can you sit there and behave as though it really doesn't matter?'

Delphine shrugged her shoulders indifferently. 'Because I would honestly rather die than let them know that they have caused me to feel the slightest bit of fear.'

'Ah, you French ladies,' Rose groaned, sitting up and

wiping her wet face with the back of her hand. 'You are nothing like me.'

Delphine smiled, not entirely kindly. 'I can see that.'

Afterwards we all went out for our usual walk in the cloisters with the other prisoners and I was watching Rose and Delphine standing in the shade of a tree talking to Alexandre de Beauharnais with a cheerfulness that to a casual onlooker would have given no clue that he was husband of one and lover of the other when the door at the top of the stone steps opened and the prison clerk appeared, flanked by a pair of turnkeys holding dogs on leashes. All conversation came to a halt and we all turned and stood motionless, staring up at him in mute horror. Armand and I moved very close together and he held my hand tightly, entwining his fingers through mine.

The clerk opened the paper and began to read out the list of names. As each person heard their name, they raised their arm to signify that they were present and had heard correctly, then in as composed a manner as possible said farewell to their friends and loved ones before being led away.

There was no crying, no begging for mercy and no fuss.

'Champcenetz, Charost, Harrop, Ward, Salm, Beauvoir, Beauharnais, Saliex...' Forty five names, all male, were read out.

I suppressed a cry and looked up at my husband in despair as he raised his arm above his head. 'Armand, no.' I clung to his other hand. 'It is too soon. We have only just found each other again.'

He smiled down at me and gently touched my cheek. 'I must go, Lucrèce,' he said, bending down to kiss me on the lips. 'I love you. I am only sorry that I did not say that often enough.' He pulled his plain gold wedding band and a ring bearing the Saliex crest from his fingers and pressed them into my hand. ' Stay alive and remember me to our child, if there is to be one.' And then with a final kiss and press of the fingers he was gone, led away by the turnkeys and straightening his broad shoulders as he prepared to follow them up the stone steps and out of sight.

I heard a wail of sheer despair behind me and turned to

see that Rose had collapsed and was lying on the ground in a dead faint. 'They took her husband,' I could hear people murmuring, tutting and shaking their heads. 'It is all very sad but really...' Ignoring them I went to kneel beside my friend and tried to raise her head.

'She has taken it very badly,' Delphine whispered, needlessly. 'It is all very embarrassing.'

Two of the turnkeys carried Rose to our room and placed her on her bed and there she remained, unable to eat or sleep and in a state of morbid despair and misery. The other women were embarrassed by this highly inappropriate display of emotion ('You can see why she was never received at Versailles,' Madame d'Aiguillon whispered to Delphine) but kindly Scottish Grace and I did not care and did our best to cheer our friend up and make her comfortable, although for me this was to be an ordeal as I was also beset with fear and dread about my husband's fate.

After a few days a few letters arrived from the Conciergerie – amongst them was one for Rose from her husband, which made her collapse again in tears. I also received one from Saliex, inside which I found some locks of hair – a dark brown that I recognised as his and also a few auburn tresses that belonged to myself. I raised his lock of hair to my lips and inhaled its faint lingering scent of lavender and rosemary before turning to the letter. It was the second time that I had unfolded a last letter from a loved one and for a moment it really felt as though my fingers lacked the strength for the task.

22 July 1794

My dearest wife, how I long to see you and take you in my arms. My only regret in dying is that I will never see you or any child that we may have had. Remember me always, do not forget me and if there is to be a child, teach them to be everything that I was not. I wish that I had taken more opportunities to tell you how much and how sincerely and ardently I love you.

I still do not know why we have been brought here but we have all been interrogated on several occasions and it seems that we are the victims of informers. It is the opinion of Beauharnais that we are done for and I am inclined to agree with him, much though it pains me. I do not think that we have very long left and by the time you receive this poor missive it will most probably all be over for me.

Farewell, my darling Lucrèce, I kiss you a million times. When the fatal moment comes to claim me, I will be thinking of you.

Saliex.

Rose and I sat for a long time in a stunned silence, unable to believe the terrible blow that fate had just dealt to both of us and after a while, Delphine joined us holding a necklace that Alexandre had sent to her, which she wordlessly fastened around Rose's neck.

The already dismal atmosphere at Les Carmes took a decided turn for the worse after this and the prisoners found it more difficult than ever to keep their spirits up. However, I woke up on the morning after I received Saliex's final letter with a renewed sense of energy and purpose. I could very easily have remained in bed and cried and bewailed my fate but I knew that Armand would have wanted me to carry on. I was absolutely certain that he had faced his death with courage and pride, not allowing his enemies to see the slightest ounce of fear, and I resolved that I would follow his example. To my surprise Rose also got up the next morning in a more buoyant and philosophical frame of mind and was even quite cheerful at times.

'I was extremely fond of my husband,' she whispered to me by way of explanation, 'even though he treated me very badly.' Unlike me, her eyes were not fixed on posterity but on escape and the world that lay beyond the prison's thick stone walls. Rose was desperate to survive this at any cost. 'I have to live,' she said with

251

a wild laugh. 'A fortune teller on Martinique once told me that I will be a queen one day!' Everyone laughed with her before shaking their heads pityingly as she danced away.

Almost a week after Saliex and the other men had been taken away we all heard the sound of distant gunfire and shouting and running feet outside the prison walls. We all stared at each other in confusion and the dawning horror as we assumed that yet another prison massacre was about to take place. Rose almost fainted with fear and had to be carried back to our room, where she cried for several hours and jumped up in a panic every time anyone walked in. 'Do you think that they will come to kill us all?' she asked Grace and I a dozen times. 'Should we try to barricade ourselves in tonight?'

No one was able to sleep that night and we all lay awake on our hard, uncomfortable beds, straining to hear the slightest noises and silently praying that we would be spared. It was a boiling hot night and I had stripped down to a thin cotton chemise before lying down on top of my itchy blanket where I lay awake for several hours, gazing unseeingly into the darkness until finally dawn began to break and the gloom slowly lifted from the room.

Slowly the prison began to shake off sleep and everyone congratulated themselves on having survived the night without being murdered. Clearly it was a false alarm after all. Rose, Grace and I went for breakfast in the courtyard and then took our customary turn about the cloisters before returning to our room to change into our simple, plain cotton day dresses. I was just tying Rose's wide pink sash around her narrow waist when we heard a hoarse shout and a muffled scream from one of the other rooms. We all stared at each other in dread then lifted our skirts above our ankles and, like everyone else, rushed to see what had happened.

The commotion was coming from a room further down the corridor, which had less bars than the others and a view over the street below. 'What is it? What has happened?' Rose demanded breathlessly, crossing herself. 'Are they coming to kill us?'

The women standing at the window turned and I saw

with immense relief that they were grinning. 'No one is coming to kill us.' They pointed down into the street, where I saw a woman pointing to her dress and then waving a stone in the air before drawing her finger across her throat in a time honoured and gruesome gesture. 'Robe and pierre,' they all chorused, laughing with relief and mounting joy. 'It must mean that Robespierre is dead.' We all looked at each other in astonishment and disbelief. Could it be true?

It was indeed true and the news spread through Les Carmes and all of the other prisons like wildfire. Robespierre, Saint-Just and their followers had been overthrown by the Convention and executed the next day on the Place de la Révolution. The executions were at an end. The Terror was over. Rose and I jumped up and down hugging and crying when the news was confirmed, wild with joy at the prospect of seeing our loved ones again and bitterly, desperately sad that the end had come too late for our husbands and so many other dear friends and loved ones. 'If only this had happened a week ago,' Rose whispered.

It had originally been expected that all of the prisoners would be released immediately but as the days passed it became clear that matters were not quite so straightforward and indeed so many people were imprisoned that it was quite impractical to release all of them at once. No one really minded though, so long as the dreaded roll calls and departures of the tumbrels had come to an end.

Over a week passed before the turnkeys came with orders to release Rose, whose passage out of Les Carmes had doubtless been paid for by one of her many admirers. I was both sorry and pleased to see her go and we hugged for a long time before she picked up her bag and left the room, without a single backward glance. Grace was next to leave, blowing kisses and smiling gaily as though leaving a particularly thrilling party and then after her it was Delphine, looking as exquisite as ever and looking forward to being reunited with her young son.

When the turnkeys finally came for me I was lying on my

narrow bed, staring up at the cracked and damp speckled ceiling and thinking about Armand. 'Citizeness Saliex?' I turned my head on the pillow and looked at them. 'We have orders here for your immediate release.' I did not move. 'Citizeness, you are free to go.'

I was in a complete daze as I packed my bag for the last time and then followed the men from the room, pausing only once on the threshold to look back and commit it to memory. Rose had clearly wanted to forget all about it as swiftly as possible but I wanted to always remember where I was when Fabrice's last letter was brought to me and I learned that he was dead.

Back down the damp and malodorous corridor, through the gloomy records office and then out into the bright July sunshine. I stood for a moment blinking wildly, blinded by the glare of the sun but then gradually my vision cleared and I realised that I was outside and standing in the street. It was the same as always and also completely different. The streets looked much as they had always done but there was a new vibrancy in the air that I did not recognise but which I found intensely exhilarating.

'Lucrèce.' I turned my head and there was Sébastien, standing with his hands outstretched just as I had always known he would be.

Acknowledgements

With many thanks to Dave, Felix and Oscar, without whose sterling assistance this book would have been finished in half the time. Much love and many thanks also to the all the readers of my Madame Guillotine blog who have been excellent cheerleaders through the hideously solitary writing process.

Many many thanks also to Susan Higginbotham and Catherine Delors for providing blurbs and advice. Special thanks also go to editor extraordinaire Jane Holland for her work on this book and all her help and encouragement.

Blood Sisters is the culmination of many years of work, reading, hanging about Paris in a starry eyed manner and obsessing about the French Revolution. I hope you enjoyed it.